# THE GREEN TOWER

BOOK THREE OF THE FIVE TOWERS

# THE GREEN TOWER

a novel by

## J.B. SIMMONS

ISBN 978-1-949785-06-7

Published in the United States by Three Cord Press


www.jbsimmons.com

*Our thirst for more could not be quenched.*
*The more we grasped, the tighter we clenched.*
*We scampered and gathered and gathered to hoard.*
*Possessions became our master and lord.*

*And when we're old with our treasures all heaped,*
*a sad example of what greed has reaped.*
*Our fists still clenched in a grasping motion,*
*till at our death, when our hands are opened.*

Irwin Mercer

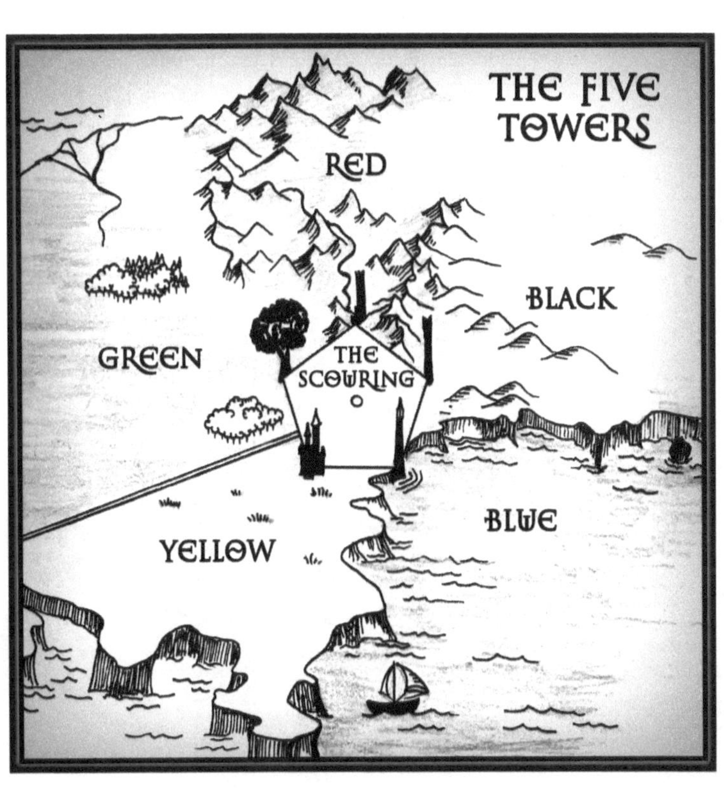

THE FIVE TOWERS
RED
BLACK
GREEN
THE SCOURING
BLUE
YELLOW

# 1

VINES CRADLE MY body like a net. They are brown and as thick as my thumb. They should be breakable. I've tried, but the organic ropes do not weaken. Not even gnawing works. It only leaves a bitter and dirty taste in my mouth. The cords might as well be chains. At least they leave gaps wide enough for my arms and legs to stick through.

A warm breeze makes me spin, like a bug dangling from a spider's web. Everything around me is wood. Wooden floor, wooden walls, wooden ceiling. The room has a dozen odd angles and grooves. Thick tree branches jab up through the floor and out the roof.

With each spin I see the girl again. She dangles in a net like mine, like another caterpillar in a cocoon. We're just out of reach from each other.

"Hey, you awake?" I ask softly.

She doesn't bother sitting up. Her golden hair spills out through the bottom of her net as she twists and stretches and spins slowly. Her blue eyes blink sleepily.

"I am now."

"Sorry, I was…" *Feeling bored.* But that's a bad excuse

for waking her up. "Any luck with the vines?"

"No." She yawns widely. "I'm going back to sleep."

I yawn back. "I'll let you know if anything interesting happens."

She closes her eyes and turns her head to the side, resting it on her hands. The motion is enough to make her dangling net spin again, with her body curled into a sleeping ball at the bottom.

She sleeps a lot. I can't hold it against her. Sleeping makes the time pass. My eyes feel heavy, too, but this time I resist it. Someone has been bringing food, and I'm going to find out who they are. Get some answers.

It always happens the same way. We drift to sleep. We wake with new food resting on two small tables beneath us, one under each net. Each table holds a wooden cup of water and a wooden bowl of food. The food is usually a few mushrooms and strips of salted meat. Once or twice it's a bowl of strange, nutty paste—with mushrooms, of course. Always mushrooms. They taste like dirt. But we lick the bowls clean every time, starved by the time the meager food has arrived. We use the empty bowls for our necessities. We don't talk about that. We don't talk about much. We've tried guessing about who we are, where we are, and why we're here. Neither of us knows, so there's not much to say. Despair brings quiet, and quiet brings sleep. We wake up to the old bowls gone and another fresh batch of food below us, but no sign of how it got there.

Not this time. I will stay awake.

My eyes blink heavily. I *will* stay awake. I hum and

shake my head. I yawn.

*I will stay…*

When I wake up, water and food have been brought. The girl is already eating. Her slender arm reaches down through the net for another handful. My bowl has four mushrooms and two strips of the dried, salty meat. One more strip than last time. I start with the water. Then the meat. It tastes wild.

"You going to eat your mushrooms?" the girl asks.

She's managed to sit up, with each of her legs sticking through gaps in the bottom of the net and resting on the table beneath her. She bends her toes back and forth, making her cocoon sway.

I tell her she can have them. We've come to a little arrangement. She offers me her meat. I offer her my mushrooms. The problem is: we haven't managed to make the exchange yet. We've tried three, maybe four times now. The food always ends up on the floor.

I scoop up the handful of mushrooms from my bowl and maneuver around to sit as she does, legs hanging out and balancing on the table. We face each other, both rocking our cocoons.

With my toes pressed against the table, I kick off as hard as I can. The table falls over, knocking the empty bowl and cup clattering to the floor. Now the momentum is going. I shift my weight inside the net, going with the motion, picking up the pace.

It takes some time before I match her rhythm. But when I do, our nets move in tandem, forward and back, forward and back, until—at the height of the swing—we can extend our arms to within an inch of each other.

"Okay, ready?" I hold out the mushrooms.

"On three." She holds out the meat. Her net swings toward mine, higher and higher. "One," she says, coming close.

We swing back and forward again.

"Two," we say together.

As we make the third swing, our arms extend and our eyes lock onto each other, concentrating.

"Three!"

*Perfect.* My right hand delivers the mushrooms the same moment that my left hand grabs the meat. I clutch the treasure inside my net as the swinging slows. It seems silly, but it feels good to have pulled it off. Maybe because I'm bored, tied up, and otherwise useless in this net. Or I'm just hungry for more meat.

The girl smiles at me. "Nice work. Next time we'll do even better."

"What do you mean?" I ask.

She glances down. There's a dark object on the wooden floor—a mushroom.

"One casualty," she says in an amused voice. "But you got all you bargained for. You owe me."

I can't help but smile. "Okay, room for improvement."

"And plenty of time to practice," she says.

Our swaying nets gradually fall still again. We eat our bartered food in quiet. We can hear things outside the room. Birds sing. Squirrels chatter. Occasionally there are other voices talking. They're too distant to make out words, but it's somehow comforting to know that we're not the only people in existence.

When I ask the girl who she thinks they are, she tells me she'd like to figure out who she is first. "But whoever they are," she says, "they must not be too bad. They feed us, right?"

I'm not so sure. I may not remember anything, but my gut tells me it's not right to tie someone up in a net. I also know that the girl and I are young—too young to have done much to deserve this. We seem innocent. My only blemish is a pair of matching scars on the backs of my hands.

The girl soon falls back to sleep. I try to stay awake again. I yawn but manage to fight off the sleep, determined to see who brings the food. I want answers, and I want out of this net.

A long time later, there's a sound below. A plank of wood lifts on the floor beneath me.

*Stay quiet, stay calm,* I tell myself as my heart pounds. I peek through almost-shut eyes, enough to see but not be seen. A head emerges through the hole in the floor. It's a girl with straight brown hair and brown doe eyes. She doesn't look at me.

*Breathe deeply,* I remind myself, *like you're sleeping.*

The girl moves very quietly, very deliberately. She would not have woken me up. She sets a tray down on the floor beside the fallen tables. She picks them up, then places a fresh wooden cup and bowl on each one. She reaches into a bag hanging from her shoulder and retrieves mushrooms. After she fills the bowls, she pulls a large piece of dried meat and a knife out of the bag. She uses the sharp blade to slice off two pieces of meat for each bowl. Just as she begins to put the meat and knife away, she pauses, staring at the floor.

A dark spot holds her attention. It's the mushroom that had fallen on the floor—the casualty of my exchange with my companion in the net. The girl bends down slowly and picks up the mushroom, studying it. Her head turns to the nets for the first time, as if she previously had no concern for us. I know I should close my eyes, but I'm too curious. And then it's too late.

As her eyes connect with mine, she jumps in surprise. "You should be asleep!" she gasps in a whisper.

"Who are you?" I ask.

She glances down at the mushroom in her hand, then at me again. "You didn't eat…" She stops herself, bringing her hand over her mouth.

"What do you mean?" I say. "Please, tell me where I am."

"Oh dear." Her hand falls to her side, limp as a dead fish. "Daniel was going to show you everything, but…"

"But what? Who's—"

"Oh!" she interrupts me in a pained voice. "Now you won't be ready! We'll have to start all over!"

"Slow down," I say. "Can't you just—"

She cuts me off again. "I'm sorry. I have to…" She springs into motion, grabbing the tray and dashing through the opening in the floor.

"Wait, wait!" I'm shouting as she flees, but she's already pulling the plank back into place and disappearing from sight. As I'm trying to make sense of all this, a glint of metal catches my eye.

She left her knife on the table beneath me.

# 2

THE GIRL STILL sleeps in the net beside me, her body cradled in the vines, her hair spilling through the gaps like liquid gold. Not even my shouting woke her up. Nor did it stop the other girl, the one who brought the food, from dashing out as soon as she knew I'd seen her.

*You didn't eat…* she said.

I didn't eat the mushrooms. They must put us to sleep.

But why does she care if I saw her? She said I wouldn't be ready…ready for what? Why won't I be ready? And who is Daniel?

I shake off the questions and focus on the knife.

The hilt hangs off the corner of the table, just beyond my fingertips. My breath steadies as I concentrate, my body still swaying slightly in the net. One wrong move and I might knock the knife off the table. It's my only hope of getting out of this hanging prison.

Focus. Get the knife.

My arm stretches and two fingers pinch the tip of the blade, dragging it carefully away from the table's edge and pulling it up. I clasp it with both hands, staring at it in fascination. The hilt feels smooth in my hand. It looks made of bone. The sharp metal blade has intricate carvings of a forest. The lines are so delicate I can see the individual leaves of trees and the eyes of a stag with huge antlers in the center. Who carves meat with a blade this nice?

"Stop thinking," I whisper aloud to myself. "Get out."

Still mumbling *get out* under my breath, I grip the knife tightly and press the blade against one of the vines forming the net. It does not slice like butter, or even meat. Not surprising since I couldn't even chew through the vines. It's also hard to get leverage while hanging in the net, but I position myself to press down with all my weight, sawing back and forth.

The knife starts to cut through the tough fibrous rope. Once the first slice is made, the rest of the vine gives way more easily. I keep at it until I've sliced through ten vines in a straight line at the bottom of the net.

It's enough to slip out. I try to catch my fall by grabbing at the net, but only lose my balance and fall to the floor, also knocking the table and the food down in a loud clatter. Hurrying to my feet, I stretch and breathe deeper, tasting freedom.

The girl, amazingly, is still sleeping.

"Hey, you!" Standing on my tip-toes, I reach up and tap her back. I give a little shove, making the net swing. "Come on, wake up!"

It takes a few more taps and shouts before she finally stirs. Her eyes slowly open, seeing me, then seeing the knife. She gulps. She looks surprised or terrified, maybe both.

I lower the knife. "A girl came while you were sleeping. I stayed awake. When she saw me, she ran out and forgot her knife."

"How did you…?"

"It's the mushrooms. Listen, we have to hurry. Want out?"

She gazes down at the knife uncertainly. "But…surely someone will come back. She will realize she left the knife. They might…well, I doubt we are supposed to get out."

"*Supposed to?* Who cares? Come on, scoot over and I'll cut your net."

She still looks doubtful, but she does as I say. I manage to climb onto the little table beneath her net. Working from my knees, I have more leverage and make quicker work of the vines. When the gap is almost large enough for her to fit through, I tell her to grab hold of the net and let herself down slowly.

I slice through one more vine. The hole breaks open.

She comes falling out, collapsing onto me, and knocking us and the table all down in a crashing heap.

"You didn't hold on!" I say, scrambling to my feet and holding out a hand to help her up.

"I tried." She takes my hand and stands, stretching her arms high over her head. We've been hanging for who knows how long beside each other, but this is the first time we've been so close. Her blue eyes, golden hair, and elegant features look out of place. She wears light brown shorts, cut off at the knee, and a brown shirt cut off at the shoulders. My clothes are similar. They are soft and look like deerskin. We're both barefoot.

"Ahhh, this feels much better." She cranes her neck back, looking up at the net. "Thank you for cushioning my fall. It broke open so quickly."

"That's gravity…"

Curious blue eyes meet mine. "What is gravity?"

"You have to be kidding," I say, but it's clear she's not. I don't know how I know what gravity is, but it seems like such an obvious thing that I can't believe she doesn't know. "Gravity is a force of nature that…" The muffled sound of footsteps overhead makes me stop. "I'll explain later. Let's get out of here."

"But we do not know where we are. Where will we go?"

"We'll figure it out."

I kneel beside the plank that the other girl entered through. The knife wedges into a crack and lifts the wood just enough for me to grab the plank and slide it away. A steep, narrow staircase leads down.

Holding the knife ready, I go first. The wood creaks beneath my feet. My head drops out of the room, and I freeze.

We're in a tree. It's larger than I could have imagined, with a trunk at least fifty feet wide. Branches twist and weave around us, with dozens of rope bridges connecting them. Small wooden buildings are scattered among the branches. The foliage is so dense that I can't see where the tree ends, around or above us. But far, far below the thick trunk meets the ground, where there's a dense forest of much smaller trees.

"What are you waiting for?" the girl calls out above.

"Sorry, you have to see this."

I back away from the staircase. She descends and looks around in wonder. But then she glances past me and her eyes widen.

"Welcome," says an old man's voice.

# 3

THE OLD MAN leans on a gnarled staff, studying us with dark, beady eyes. I'm not sure if his long beard is hair or moss as it hangs over a velvet green robe. I'm not even sure if he's human. He looks like a larger, living version of the mushrooms that were putting us to sleep.

"Who are you?" the girl asks, coming to my side.

"My name is Daniel." The old man's voice creaks like a tree bending in the wind. "I lead this tower."

"What tower?" I ask, gripping the knife firmly. Surely I can outrun him if it comes to it. But then what? Swing down the branches? Yes, whatever it takes to get free.

"The Green Tower," Daniel says. "Would you like to know how you got here?"

"Yes." The girl bows as she speaks, as if we stood before a king. "I would very much like to know."

"I will show you." Slowly, deliberately, the old man raises his staff and points it at the wooden building above us—the room where we'd been tied in nets. "We cleanse your system before we restore the memories that you've already seen. It makes for a…fresher start."

I take a step back. *Cleanse our system?* Is that what he calls the mushrooms, the nets?

"It's no use running." Daniel stares at me, as if reading my thoughts. "You must be cleansed, Cipher."

"You don't know me." I feel defiant, but I'm shaken inside. *Cipher? Is that my name?*

"We have met," he says. "This, too, I will show you. But you must let the cleansing complete. It should not be much longer, even with your escape… Most unusual, that was. But no surprise, I suppose. You obey your instincts, and Abram always said you were special."

I'm speechless, wanting nothing to do with this odd man. He let me be tied up in a net. Questions race through my mind but not as fast as my heart pumps blood to every muscle in my body, swelling, building, desperate for freedom. I glance over my shoulder. A rope bridge leads to a small wooden building, and a hanging ladder descends as far as I can see. Maybe it goes to the ground.

"So you will show us our pasts?" the girl asks.

"Yes, precisely." The old man sounds pleased.

But I turn to her in disbelief. "We can't trust them."

She shrugs. "I would like to learn more."

My voice rises almost to a shout. "They tied us up!"

"Please, calm down," she says. "I told you we were not supposed to leave the nets."

"What do you know?" I ask her, eyes narrowing.

She shakes her head, but doesn't answer. Her blue eyes are unnervingly blank, tranquil.

"She's quite right," the man says. "Trust the Provider."

I back away, still clutching the knife with one hand, and my other hand grabs the vine railing at the start of the rope bridge.

"If you go, you may find a taste of freedom." Daniel sounds unconcerned with whether I run or not. "But freedom in the wild will bring pain. You cannot be satisfied there. You will come to the Green Tower again."

*More like the Green Prison.* I don't need to hear more. I'm not going back to the hanging net. With a final glance at the girl, I turn and sprint along the bridge away from her and the old man.

"Wait, no!" the girl calls out.

"Scouring tribe!" The old man's voice booms. "Stop him!"

I don't look back. The bridge swings and bounces as I race along it. I'm halfway across when a boy appears in the doorway of the small building ahead. He raises a bow and draws an arrow.

An archer. Aiming at me.

Instinct takes over. Survival, the cruel master, makes my arm pull back, knife gripped at the ready. Before I've even thought about it, the blade is spinning forward, end over end at the archer. He has notched an arrow. He pulls the string taut.

My vision focuses on the knife flying through the air. It's a foot off, to the left. It's going to miss. Panic and fury swell in me and my mind grabs hold of something unseen.

*The air. Moving.*

Suddenly I see it. Strands of energy flow together as if

channeled by my mind. It creates a small current of wind that nudges the spinning blade to the right. *Turning, turning, there!*

The knife stabs straight into the archer's shoulder. The bow and the arrow drop. I look down at my still legs and realize I've stopped moving. But the rope bridge is still bouncing. Footsteps pound behind me. I turn and see others charging.

I take off again. I pause for a moment to kneel down beside the archer. He looks at me through wet, pained eyes.

"Sorry," I say, before yanking the knife out.

He screams in agony. No time to care, no time to look back. I dash into the building where he appeared. There's a hole in the center of the floor. A ladder made of vines and wood dangles below. I bite the knife blade between my teeth, then grab hold of the ladder with both hands.

I climb down the rungs as fast as I can. Taking two at a time, I drop twenty feet, then more. But it's too slow. Above, the others have reached the building with the ladder. They are going to come after me. Or worse…one of them has a knife out, sawing at the ladder.

I glance down and swallow in fear. The canopy of the forest looks like a hundred-foot drop.

My hands grab tighter onto the vines. I step off the wooden rungs and press the insides of my ankles firmly against the ladder's sides. I take a deep breath and start to slide.

Faster then faster, gravity does its work—*how did she not know about gravity?*—and air rushes up at me. The canopy is closer. I'm almost close enough to jump. But I don't get a chance to try.

The ladder suddenly jerks, then drops.

Again I see the air. It rushes past me in blue ribbons. In desperation I grab for the threads and weave them as I did to move the knife. I pull up, trying to lift myself. I slow slightly, but it's not enough.

The trees reach up like greedy fingers. My body plummets into their leaves, twigs, and branches. Hard blows hit and twist me as I bounce down. The knife between my teeth gets knocked loose, cutting my lip as it falls. My right ankle catches between two branches, twists, and pops. I fall head over heels, flailing my arms, trying to grab onto anything, clenching instinctively but uselessly to the ladder. I glimpse a thick branch just as my head bashes into it.

The ladder suddenly catches and comes to a halt. I barely keep my grip, gazing desperately up into the tree, wondering how long I can hold. My head throbs as I glance down. But then a shallow laugh slips out of my lips. The ground is only five feet below me. I drop onto a carpet of soft moss, hurting everywhere.

# 4

THEY'LL COME FOR ME. Daniel, the old man, trapped me in the net. He commanded the guards who tried to shoot me with arrows, who cut the ladder. He must be the harshest type there is.

I look up, neck aching. No one is coming yet. Maybe they think I died. I probably should have. And I'd feel dead if it didn't hurt so bad.

I force myself onto my knees, wincing and still breathing hard as I study the surroundings. Ahead there's forest as far as I can see. The underbrush is light—a few feathery ferns and moss. Behind me it looks like there's a dark, brown wall. It's the base of the enormous tree. There is a single, large opening, like a door, where it meets the ground. No one is going in or coming out, but it won't be long. Past the tree is a true wall, made of dull grey stone, stretching as far as I can see. I need to go the opposite way.

My first attempt to stand fails. Back on my knees, I prod around the worst spots. The right side of my head feels like a giant whacked me with a club. My hand comes away from my hair covered in blood. Every movement makes my pulse pound like a jackhammer in my head.

*A concussion*, I think, and the thought is new, yet vaguely familiar. I picture an image of a jackhammer, though I can't remember when I ever saw one, or learned about it.

*Stop thinking. Move.*

With a hand on the tree trunk—the same trunk that hit me, and saved me—I try again to stand and manage to rise unsteadily to my feet. The pain in my ankle is unbearable. It won't hold any weight. I need a crutch.

I spot a serviceable stick on the ground a few feet away. Probably knocked loose when I fell.

*Take that, tree.*

I crawl to the fallen branch, which is mostly straight and as thick as my wrist. I break off the side twigs and stand, leaning heavily on the makeshift staff. It'll have to work. After a few shuffling steps I spot something shiny under a fern: the knife. I tuck it into the waist of my shorts and limp quickly away from the giant tree, senses on high alert.

The only noises are birds singing, bugs chirping, and my shuffling steps. The forest floor grows denser. Bushes with glossy green leaves slow my unsteady march. Roots grab at my throbbing ankle. It becomes harder to know which way I'm going. The canopy allows only rare pinpricks of sky to peek through. The giant tree is no longer visible behind me.

Surely any of those guards who wanted to catch me could have by now. They must assume I'm dead. Or they just don't care. I keep moving forward anyway. The more distance between the giant tree and me, the better.

The sky begins to darken. The cool air grows colder in the shadows. My stomach churns in hunger. My eyes scan the undergrowth for something to eat. The knife is tucked into my pants, but there's no way I'm catching any animals with my hurt ankle. My best hope is berries or…more mushrooms. The thought sinks me into despair. Maybe the girl was right. Maybe the hanging nets weren't so bad. We had a roof over our heads and food came regularly. But the cost was too high: freedom.

There's a gap in the trees overhead. My feet come to a halt. The sky is midnight blue and dotted with stars. The bright spots draw my gaze up and up, taking in the light, unable to look away.

*Cipher, come back.*

The words come down as if carried by starlight. I see the threads of this light—this thought—but I don't hear it.

The words come again. I shiver as I *see* them entering my mind, clear but visible, like cold water pouring into a glass.

*It is me, Emma. Look at the stars. See me.*

My thoughts follow the light back up to the stars. It takes immense effort and concentration. But the stars take my thoughts and channel them across the sky, racing from star to star and following the voice down to a tree. The tree. I see it as if I'm floating before it.

*Yes, yes! Here!*

The words attract the starlight like a magnet, pulling my attention to a long branch at the edge of the tree's canopy, where a girl sits. The pale light gives her blonde hair the luster of silver, her face a gentle glow. She's the girl from the net.

She smiles. *Hi, Cipher.*

*It's you,* I think, and she hears it, or sees it, through the light. *How are you doing this?*

*Daniel told me we could, because we came so close to the White Tower together. And see, it is working. You can trust me. It is safe here. Please, come back.*

I hesitate. *They tied us up. They drugged us.*

She shakes her head. *You left too soon! Daniel showed me everything, Cipher. We were paired in the Red Tower. We were in the Blue Tower before that. Your name was Paul Fitzroy. You were a doctor. Come back and you will understand. It is not safe in the forest. The tribes will capture you. You must come back.*

The words don't make any sense. Towers? Tribes? Even as my mind resists, the girl's blue eyes capture the starlight and threaten to overwhelm me. It could be another trap.

*No.*

*Cipher, please, remember. It is me, Emma.*

Her voice, her eyes, they soften me. I want to remember. I want to know why we're here...

*Follow the starlight,* she says, *it will show you the way back.*

I step forward. Pain shoots from my ankle, sharpening my thoughts and blurring the vision. I steady myself, leaning on the staff.

*Keep on,* she urges, *this is the way.*

No...Daniel and his guards tried to kill me. She is on

their side now. I can't trust her. I force myself to look down, away from the stars and the blue-eyed girl.

*Wait, please!* the girl says, but her voice fades to nothing. The vision is gone. Her spell broken.

I limp and stagger ahead through the forest again, away from the gap in the trees and the starlight. The woods are dark and silent. No light reaches me on the forest floor. No more voices come. I try to keep my bearings, remembering the direction that my thoughts had traveled to the tree and the girl, and going the opposite way.

It is not long before I feel lost. Hobbling on my staff, going around trees and thickets, climbing over roots and under fallen trunks, I turn slightly, then slightly again. The darkness makes it hard to tell which way is straight. The trees ahead of me all look familiar, like I've already passed them.

I stumble over a bush and stay on my knees. It's no use going forward in the dark. I lay down my staff and knife beside each other on the ground, pointing the way I think I should go. I'll start again in daylight.

The bush I fell over has small, juicy berries. I nibble at one, though I can't even tell what color it is. Maybe red or purple. It tastes fine. It could be poisonous, but my stomach tells me it's worth the risk. Handful after handful are stuffed into my mouth.

With a belly full, I lay back, beside the bush, body aching. The ground smells like decaying leaves and pine needles. I curl up for warmth. Within moments the chanting bugs lull me to sleep.

I dream I'm in the net again. But this time I turn into an owl and fly away, the wind rushing under my wings as I glide over the forest. Another bird joins my side. It has golden brown feathers and bright blue eyes, like the girl from the net. *Cipher, come back*, she says. *You will remember. I am Emma. Daniel will show you. We will soar to the White Tower.* I try to tell her we can't trust the old man, but the only thing that comes out my mouth is the deep hoot of an owl. She flies back and I see smoke in the distance, rising from the dense forest. I fly toward it and descend toward the flames.

The smell of burning wood wakes me, and I instantly sense I'm not alone. I lay still and crack my eyes open.

A man kneels over a fire beside me. He tends to a skinned animal roasting on a stick. He wears a dark green cloak with fur along its edges and the hood pulled up, shadowing his bearded face. A knife hangs from a sheath at his belt. It looks like my knife, which is nowhere to be seen. A long bow and a quiver of arrows lay on the ground beside him. Whoever the man is, he could have easily killed me while I slept. He could easily kill me now.

The smell of roasted meat makes my stomach groan. There's no use pretending to sleep. I struggle up to a stiff sitting position. My head throbs. My ankle pushes angrily against a tight bandage, feeling like it would swell to the size of a melon if it weren't contained. This man must have wrapped it while I slept.

"Who are you?" I ask through parched lips.

"The Hunter." His voice comes out raspy but quiet,

like leaves rustling in the wind. He points to a leather pouch on the ground near me. "Have a drink."

I take the leather pouch. The contents slosh around inside. I try a sip. It's cold, fresh water, and it's delicious. I study the man as I take another sip. He looks as natural as a deer in this forest. *The* Hunter, he said, not *a* hunter.

"Why are you helping me?" I ask.

He rotates the roasting meat. "You're in no shape to be in this forest alone. How did you get here?"

"I fell out of a giant tree, then I lost my way."

"You *fell?*" He eyes me up and down, his gaze pausing for a moment on my scarred hands. "You're not from a tribe, are you?" He doesn't wait for an answer. "Where'd you come from? Red? Did Behemoth spit you out here?"

"What's Behemoth?"

"Bah, a Red creature. Better to fall out of the tree than face it." He removes the meat from the fire and steps to me. He holds out the stick. "Careful, it's hot."

I pull off a piece and blow on it before taking a bite. The meat tastes good, salty. "What is it?" I ask.

"Baby behemoth."

I freeze, mouth open, before taking the next bite.

The man lets out a quiet laugh. "It's squirrel. Eat up. We're leaving soon."

"Where are we going?"

"Deeper into the forest," he says with a slight smile. He starts whistling softly as he gathers up his things. "Can you walk?"

I stand slowly, using my walking stick as support. The

man is almost twice my height beside me. I take a feeble first step. My ankle folds like paper beneath me.

The Hunter helps me back to my feet. I try another step, and fall again. This time he catches me as I collapse. "Finish eating, then I'll carry you."

I don't have much choice. I'm hurt, lost, and he could easily overpower me. Maybe I should panic. Maybe I should feel fear. But I breathe a lot easier in the forest than I did in a net. Maybe he gets lonely out here, being *the* Hunter. Whatever his reasons, I'm glad for the help, and especially the food. There's no scrap but bones left when I finish with the meat. I top it off with a few berries from the bush that I'd slept under.

"I wouldn't eat those," the man says, after I've already stuffed a second handful into my mouth.

"Why?" I mumble as my chewing stops.

"They'll mess with your sight, your dreams," he says. "They twist the past."

I spit out the rest of them, and he nods as if satisfied. Maybe that explains my weird dream as an owl, with the girl named Emma and the old man named Daniel.

"What do you know about the past?" I ask.

"More than I'd like," the man says, rising to his feet. "You will, too, soon enough. Want a taste of it?" He holds out a hollow cup the size of a thimble, filled with a dark liquid. "Usually you get it only in the tree, at the Jubilee. But I keep a nip on hand, for rare cases like this. Drink up. I'll get you where you need to go."

"Where's that?"

"Drink up," he repeats.

I don't have much choice, and I'm curious…I take the tiny cup and bring it to my lips. The liquid pours thick as honey, but not as sweet. It's bitter, sliding down my throat and pulling my eyes shut.

# 5

WHEELS ROLL OVER the floor, rattling slightly. Water drips onto my head. Above, there's a leafy vegetable. It's moist, still dripping. The wheels keep rolling. Mom puts a bunch of carrots into the cart. They drip, too. It's like a rolling rainforest.

We leave the produce aisle. The next aisle has some cans. Then we reach the promised land: the cereal aisle. I can't stay on the cart for this. I climb out from below it and hold the edges, my feet on the bottom rails, leaning back until my arms are straight and I'm like a windsurfer riding a wave into sugary bliss that will fill my breakfast bowl. One of the boxes jumps out at me. There's a rainbow and a pot of gold and marshmallows.

"Lucky Charms!" I shout, pointing.

"Sorry, honey." Mom stops and bends down to the bottom shelf. She pulls out a boring looking bag and holds it up to me. "They're basically the same."

"Lucky Charms!" I shout again.

"Sorry, honey. This one's a dollar cheaper."

I don't want to cry, but I want the Lucky Charms more

than anything. My lower lip quivers. The craving rises and swells and bursts out like water from a dam, tears falling, arms thrashing.

Mom scoops me up. I'm screaming as loud as my little body can. She run-walks with me down the aisle to the back of the grocery store where there's a restroom. It's not the first time she's taken me there. I remember what happened last time. I don't want that. But I can't stop. The screaming goes and goes and goes.

She opens the door. She sits on the closed toilet. She pulls down my pants and lays me over her knees.

*Smack.*

I freeze at the first spank. I go quiet.

Then I wind up again, with a whole new sort of emotion.

By the time the second spank lands the battle is on. Punishment against wailing. I lose count after the fourth spank.

In the end we're both crying. Mom's hugging me tight, sobbing. I'm whimpering in pain and fear. She's so much bigger, so much stronger. And now she's so sad. Just because I wanted the Lucky Charms.

The significance of this settles over my fledgling brain like a net over a bird. We can't have Lucky Charms or anything like them. They cost a dollar more. We don't have a dollar more.

But why not?

Why can't Mom have a dollar more?

I decide then and there, in my youthful way, that if I

ever get the chance, I'll have the extra dollar.

We leave the restroom and buy the cheap bag of generic cereal and the next day it tastes just like Lucky Charms but that's not the kind of thing I could know. All I could know is that needing another dollar is no way to be. I'll be rich, and if I ever have a kid, I'll buy him all the Lucky Charms he could ever eat.

Something jostles me. I'm being carried. Up and down.

Dappled light falls on my closed eyelids. There's a sticky, bittersweet flavor in my mouth.

It goes dark again. Another vision forms.

The house in front of me belongs in a magazine. And, really, *house* is an understatement. It's an estate. These are the Hamptons, and this is prime oceanfront. Thaxton stands in the front doorway. He wears a pastel button-down, with the sleeves rolled up, pleated khaki shorts, and loafers on his tanned feet.

"Madison, Paul, so glad you're here!" Thaxton says. "Everyone else is out back. Come on in, grab a drink, and join us."

We follow Thaxton inside the house. Madison gave me a ride here in his convertible. I'd always wanted to see the Hamptons. It only took four years of schmoozing through college to get here.

The foyer has black and white parquet floors. A butler in a blazer holds a tray of tall drinks with ice and cucumber in them. "Pimms, sir," the butler says as I take one.

We pass through a few immaculate rooms before going to the back deck and walking out to a grassy lawn that leads straight to the sand. A dozen adirondack chairs face the sea. I sit in one and listen to the group talk about what they'll be doing this summer, about the travels they'll have before starting grad school or jobs on Wall Street. Two others are going straight to med school like me, but I'm the only one who needs loans.

I don't pay much attention to the conversation. I can't help looking back at the estate. It isn't fair that Thaxton has had this all his life, that he was born into a place where he has a butler serve him drinks and parents who lend him a house in the Hamptons. No wonder he has so many friends. No wonder everyone likes him, or at least pretends to, even though he has an annoying laugh and looks down on anyone who doesn't wear loafers.

I let my flip-flops slip off. I sip the ice cold Pimms. Lucky Charms are no longer enough. I want to have everything Thaxton has, and more.

# 6

WHEN I WAKE UP, a girl's face is inches from mine. I'm flat on my back, on the ground. She leans over me, smiling. Her short hair is so blonde it looks white, like freshly fallen snow on her head.

"Finally," she says. "Violet, he's awake!"

Another girl rushes over as I rise up on my elbows. My back is against the wall. The two girls have me cornered in a dim room. The walls and low ceiling are wooden, like bark. The ground is dirt but there's a worn fur rug with a small table on it.

"He looks surprised," says the blonde girl, giggling as she looks down at me. "And kind of cute."

"Oh stop, Lily, he's listening," says the girl who rushed over. She must be Violet. She has dark hair, almost purple. "Of course he's surprised. He was asleep when the Hunter brought him here."

*The Hunter.* He's the man who gave me the sticky liquid to drink. There was a grocery store…a mansion in the Hamptons. None of it makes sense, rattling around in my brain. I know where the Hamptons are, but not where I am. I don't like it.

"You know the Hunter?" I ask.

"Everyone knows the Hunter," says the blonde girl named Lily. "Daniel says he's an old friend and was once a powerful king. It's the Hunter's job to make sure everyone gets back to the tree, dead or alive."

"Dead...?"

"Oh, temporarily, you know what I mean!" Lily says, grinning. "Anyway, the Hunter's nicer than he looks."

It's true, the Hunter helped me, but that doesn't mean I can trust them. These girls don't seem right in the head. "What about you?" I ask.

"Oh we're not as nice as we look," Violet says.

"Speak for yourself," Lily says.

"Fine. Lily is as nice as she looks, but I guess that all depends on how nice you think she looks. So...what do you think?"

"Um, you both look nice?" I say.

"A charmer!" Lily laughs and playfully pokes me in the chest. "What's your name?"

*My name...* The old man in the giant tree called me Cipher. The rich boy Thaxton called me Paul. But maybe that was a dream. The Hunter's drink put me to sleep, like the mushrooms. Is it some kind of magic? Did I really move the air when I threw the dagger and when I fell from the tree? Maybe it's all a dream. Except...my head and my ankle still hurt, and the girl's poking felt real enough.

"Cipher," I say, "or maybe Paul?"

"I like Cipher," Lily says. "Pleasure to meet you. We

don't get many visitors. We're scouts for the Eagles. The Wolves are always prowling around here, but everyone knows the food has run out. Not much use raiding anymore. Might as well wait for the Jubilee. The Hunter said you fell out of the tree. I believe it with all your bruises and swollen spots. Tell us all about it."

"Lily, where are your manners?" Violet asks, turning to me. "You must be hungry. Would you like to eat?"

I tell them yes. It's true even though the Hunter fed me a full meal. Maybe he carried me farther than I would have guessed.

"How long have I been sleeping?" I ask.

"All day," Violet says.

"You needed it!" Lily adds.

They help me over to the small table, where there's water and a bowl of nutty paste, a lot like what was served in the giant tree. I sniff it and smell no mushrooms.

As I eat, the two girls begin to answer my questions. I learn that this home is built into a hollowed-out tree, by a fresh creek that runs into a larger river that falls over a cliff. Below the cliff the Green Tower's lands are wilder, a thick jungle, until they meet the sea. The girls say it would take several days to reach the coast from here.

They also tell me about the four tribes: Lions, Snakes, Wolves, and Eagles. The tribes battle for territory and food. Apparently food is scarce. The best way to survive is to stay with a strong tribe until the Jubilee. That's when everyone in the Green Tower gathers in the tree. It happens every fifty days. It's a complete reset. The tribes relinquish their land and start all over again, sometimes with new members.

"Where are the other Eagles?" I ask.

The girls exchange a look. "He can't be a spy," Lily says. "He really doesn't know anything. The Hunter would not have brought him here if he was from a tribe."

Violet studies me, as if brooding over something. "How did you get the scars on your hands?"

"I…don't know."

Lily holds up her hands to me, which have eagle eyes imprinted on them where my scars are. "Each tribe has a mark," she says. "So it's weird. You have scars instead."

"There's no use taking him anywhere," Violet says. "He could be an Eagle next time. It'll be up to Jade—our leader. It's better to wait. Safer. We've made it this long. I'm not getting caught by the Wolves or anyone else."

"Fine," Lily says. "Only two more days before the Jubilee!"

"What happens if you get caught before then?" I ask.

"You get a collar." Lily puts her hands to her neck. "Every tribe leader gets a bunch of silver links that force you to obey. It's like being a slave. It's the worst…other than being wiped, or sent to the Scouring."

"What's the Scouring?"

"You hit your head harder than I thought!" Lily says. "Didn't Daniel show you?"

I shake my head. "I ran away from him."

"Oh my." Violet's hand covers her mouth.

"This is very unusual," Lily says. "Daniel shows

everyone why they're here before they leave the tree. Why did you run away?"

"He had me tied up in a net," I say. "Can't you tell me why I'm here?"

"No," Violet says. "We have no idea why *you're* here."

Lily studies her friend. "We could tell him why *we're* here."

"We've only just met…" Violet says.

"And how long have we known each other? One Jubilee?" Lily says. "Why don't we make him an honorary Eagle?"

"Fine," Violet replies. "We have to pass the time somehow."

"Wonderful!" Lily claps. "We'll tell you our stories. It's the best thing we have to give, and you know what Daniel always says…"

"Giving sets you free," they say together.

"Okay…but, can you start at the beginning?" I ask.

The girls share a smile, then Lily starts to talk. She tells me that we're in a place called the Five Towers, which is where some people went after living on a planet called Earth. The giant tree is the Green Tower. The other towers are Yellow, Blue, Black, and Red. Each tower sends out a dozen fighters to try to capture each other in a battleground known as the Scouring. Among the towers, Green is in last place with the fewest people, but we've had a few captures lately, apparently including me. Daniel leads from the tree, and its sap shows memories.

This could be what the Hunter gave me. The visions

could have been real…*my* memories. But I am younger now than I was in the Hamptons. Which means, if the girls are right, I…*died?*

It seems impossible. I am breathing. My young body is full of life. Heart beating. Mind thinking. Ankle throbbing. And yet…the memories felt so real. Not like dreams. If they were real, *and* this is real, then why is this happening? I have to find out—without getting trapped in a net again.

The girls tell me that every fifty days, at the Jubilee, everyone gets to drink the sap. No one quite knows how it works, but it sounds like my best hope.

"Do they tie us up at the Jubilee?" I ask.

"Of course not!" Lily says, and both girls laugh. "It's a feast, a big celebration!"

"And it's how you learn your story," Violet says. "Go on, Lily, tell him."

Lily gives her story. She says that she lived in a city called Los Angeles, in a country called the United States. She married a man who sold cars. They had two kids, but the sap hasn't shown her much about them—not even their names. Her main memory is about a closet. Whenever Lily moved to a new house, the closet grew. It filled with nicer and nicer things. Jewels. Dresses. Shoes. All the best brands. Lily rattles off a dozen names—Gucci, Tiffany, Louis Vuitton—which mean nothing to me, except she makes it all sound very important. She seems sad to have left it behind on Earth. It's the only thing that dampens her otherwise bubbly spirit.

Violet speaks about her past more grimly. She lived in a

place called the Roman Empire and served the Emperor's mother, Helena Augusta Imperatrix. She accompanied Helena on many travels searching for holy relics. Helena was a decent master, herself having been born a commoner. But once Violet found a relic and thought no one noticed. It was a small, rusted nail that she believed to be priceless. She'd taken it and kept it in a pocket of her servant's robe. When this had been discovered, her mistress Helena carried out the sentence against those who took a relic for themselves: execution.

"They hammered nails—just like the one I'd taken—through my hands…" Violet shudders. "The last thing I remember is the Imperatrix, Helena, watching me hang."

# 7

LILY AND VIOLET treat me like a bird with a broken wing. They insist that I stay in bed, hidden within the hollowed-out tree. They take turns staying on watch outside. We finish eating the last of their meager supplies—a handful of nuts and berries.

It's the evening of the second day when Violet rushes into the tree, breathing heavily and eyes alert. "Wolves," she whispers urgently. "At least three, coming from downstream."

Lily moves immediately to the door. "Let's run."

"They'll catch us," Violet says. "You two go. I'll stay and distract them."

Lily shakes her head. "I'm not leaving without you."

"Then we'll all get caught."

"No, we go together," Lily says. "We hide. If they get close, we use the power."

Violet's face is intense as she studies Lily, then nods.

They tell me to stay close and to be as quiet as possible. The three of us slip out of the tree, with me hobbling on my stick as we move toward the creek. The forest is silent.

There's no sign of Wolves.

We step across a line of stones through the creek. Violet leads us through the shallows on the other side, walking upstream. The water is frigid around my feet. It feels good around my throbbing ankle. A shout behind us makes Violet freeze.

"They found it," she whispers. "Come."

She scrambles up the riverbank. Lily and I follow. Then they start to climb a dense pine tree. Violet and Lily breeze up the branches smoothly. It's much slower for me, climbing mostly on one foot, but I manage to reach them near the top. From there we can see downstream, to the hollowed-out tree that we abandoned.

"Oh no," Lily whispers.

Orange flames lick the sides of the tree's trunk, quickly blazing into the canopy above. The light reveals three silhouetted figures. They're walking away from the burning tree, toward us.

"Ready?" Lily asks Violet.

"Only when they look," Violet whispers.

"What—?" I start to ask, but Lily clasps a hand over my mouth.

She leans close to my ear and whispers, "Shhh, don't move." She lowers her hand from my mouth to my hand. Violet takes my other hand. They peer out of the tree, toward the three figures prowling upstream through the middle of the water.

"Hello out there!" shouts one of the boys. "Come out, come out, wherever you are!"

The two others laugh. "They're scared of you, Baron," says a girl's voice.

"Nothing to fear," says the boy, drawing closer to us. His voice is clear and strong. "We did not see any food in your little home. Join us and you may have a nice meal before the Jubilee. If you come out freely, we will not collar you. You will end as victors, with the Wolves."

"And what if they don't come out?" asks the other boy with a laugh. He is looking up, toward the trees. They're only a stone's throw away. They'll see us soon.

"Why, then they shall wear collars."

Violet and Lily, sitting to either side, grip my hands tightly. Energy suddenly courses through me, like electricity tickling my skin all over.

Below, the lead boy pauses in the middle of the creek, wielding a torch, scanning the woods. The flames show his dark hair, broad forehead, and cold, granite eyes.

He looks straight at us.

But then he moves on, looking away.

"Come out, come out, wherever you are!" he shouts.

He and the others walk upstream, right past us. Their banter continues loudly, growing more and more distant. The fire has spread. A half dozen trees now burn.

Lily and Violet gaze out at the blazing forest, their pained expressions glowing in the firelight.

"What happened?" I ask softly.

"We disappeared," Lily says, turning to me.

"How?"

"Ask Violet," Lily says. "She's the best at it."

"We were hidden," Violet says. "If you focus on what's around you—the colors and the textures—you can blend in. But you have to have memories to do it."

"That's amazing," I say.

Violet shrugs. "It doesn't last long. Only about as long as you can hold your breath."

Lily laughs softly. "Or as long as it takes for three Wolves to pass us."

"The threat's still here," Violet says. "They could circle back. We have to make it until dawn."

"You saw them," Lily says. "They're heading upstream, toward the tree. Baron will want to be there at the start of the Jubilee. He'll want to be declared the winner again."

"We can't count on that." Violet glances out at the forest. A soft, cold rain has started to fall. It patters softly on the leaves above us. "This will put out the fire. We'll stay here until morning."

# 8

THE RAIN HAS stopped when I hear the stick break. The sound is close, below the tree where Violet, Lily, and I are perched. It could be an animal, maybe a squirrel. It's too dark to see anything. The forest fire has died, but the air still smells of smoke.

There's another rustling sound. Closer now.

I glance to Violet and Lily. Violet sleeps, wedged between the trunk and a branch, but Lily is wide-eyed, looking down through the tree. She sees me, puts a finger to her lips for silence, and touches Violet's arm. Violet opens her eyes, confused.

The rustle comes again. A bough of pine needles bends below us.

Violet clenches my arm. We go invisible.

A moment later something grabs me, tight around my ankle, and yanks me off the branch. I try to grab hold but the wood is slick. One of the girls screams. A dark figure shoves me, and I crash down through the tree.

I land flat on my back, hurting and stunned. Flickering torchlight reveals a face above me. It's the boy from before, the one they called Baron. His eyes are even colder, more granite, up close.

"What do we have here?" he asks, kneeling and studying my hand. He glances at my other hand, then his eyes fix on mine again. "Which tribe?" he demands.

I yank my hand away. "I don't have one."

"Impossible." He stands and looks to a girl with a collar around her neck.

"I've never seen this," she says. "And what are those scars? They look like the one you have."

Baron doesn't answer. He turns away, but not before I notice his hand. It has a criss-cross scar like mine.

I scramble to my feet, wincing at the pain, just as two figures crash down beside me and struggle on the forest floor. One manages to pin down the other. It's Lily, on her back, with a boy pressing her to the ground.

I dash forward, but something snaps around my neck. I grab at it and feel cool metal.

*Be still, be silent. Don't think. Watch.*

Baron's words enter my mind like iron bands. I try to move, but can't. I try to think, but can't. I have only my senses. The smell of wet forest and smoke. The feel of the metal collar at my neck. The pain of my bruises, my ankle. The sight of Lily pinned down beside me.

"Where's the other?" Baron asks.

"She was with them," the other boy says, rising from Lily and brushing himself off. He is tall, with wild brown hair.

"*Was?*" Baron asks.

"She got past me." The boy stares at the ground, scratches his bare neck. "You didn't see her?"

Baron scowls and turns to Lily, who's rising unsteadily to her feet. "Eagle, who was with you?"

"A forest fairy," Lily says.

"You think this is a game?" Baron asks.

"I'm not afraid of you."

"And why should you be?" Baron holds his arms wide, as if greeting an old friend. The collared girl and the other boy stare at Baron with excitement. "I reward those who work with me," he says.

"You will never find her." Lily looks to me. I try to react, to form any expression, but the command is absolute—*be still, be silent.* Lily glances at my collar and grimaces.

"I see you do not understand," Baron says. "I do not need to capture her, or you, to win. Yet I am curious, where did you find this boy with the scars and no tribe's mark?"

"You are not my leader," Lily says, taking a step back.

Baron blinks slowly. "So you do not know?"

"If I did I wouldn't tell you."

"You have spirit. Maybe you can join my Wolves, but first…" Baron turns to the collared girl and reaches behind her neck. The girl gasps as the collar releases. Baron steps toward Lily with the open collar in his hand.

Lily turns and runs.

Baron commands the other boy: "Bring her."

The boy charges after Lily and, moments later, there's a

scream from the darkness of the forest. The boy drags Lily back to Baron with her wrists tied together. Lily twists and writhes as Baron kneels down and snaps the collar around her neck. Then she stands, her face pale and calm, her body perfectly still.

The torchlight flickers and dims. Behind us, the other girl is nowhere to be seen. Her torch lies on the ground.

"Go get her," Baron says to the boy, who immediately bounds off into the dark forest.

Baron picks up the fallen torch, then looks to Lily. "Tell me everything you know about this boy."

"He told us his name is Cipher and that he ran away from Daniel," Lily says. "He was hurt when the Hunter brought him to us. He remembers very little."

Baron rubs his chin. "I see. Who was the other Eagle with you?"

"Violet."

"Does she know more?"

"She usually does."

"I want to speak with her. Call for Violet. Do whatever it takes to get her to come to me. If you have not brought her by dawn, do what you must to forget all about this."

Lily walks off into the forest, yelling out: "Violet! Hey Violet! Everything is okay now. Cipher and I are safe. Where are you? Violet! Violet?"

*Stay close*, Baron commands me, then strolls away.

I follow him, hobbling as fast as I can on my busted ankle. Lily's shouting fades. All is quiet for a few moments. Then I hear a girl's scream.

I grit my teeth, still following Baron but the command to be still has lifted. I grab frantically at the collar, trying to rip it away, but the effort twists my insides. A sudden sickness makes me fall to my knees and vomit.

"You cannot take it off," Baron says. "Follow."

The forest becomes eerily quiet again. The only light is from Baron's torch. We track the creek upstream for a long time, until Baron finally stops. He orders me to be still. The wild-haired boy returns with the girl who ran away. Now she is motionless and draped over his shoulder.

"She was heading to the Eagles," the boy says.

Baron glances at her hand, which shows a wolf's head. "She is still with us. Build a fire, then keep an eye on her. The other Wolves are coming. Guard the perimeter until they arrive."

The boy nods, and soon a fire burns warmly. Baron orders me to sit on one side, and he sits on the other. He begins to eat dried meat. I watch him in silence. I cannot move or think. Feelings swirl uselessly inside me— exhaustion, pain, anger, and confusion. Baron's granite eyes study me, his expressionless face glowing in the firelight.

*Tell me everything you know*, he commands.

The whole story spills out in a jumble—how I was tied up in a net, how I escaped and the Hunter found me and gave me a liquid that showed me visions of a poor boy who wanted to be rich, how the two girls took care of me, how we hid, and how he caught us.

By the time I finish, the sky shows the first gray of dawn. There is a gentle breeze. Birds sing happily in the trees around us.

Baron studies me quietly, thinking, then he asks, "What do you know about John Davison Rockefeller?"

"Nothing," I say.

He nods. "Put out the fire, without touching it."

I don't understand, but I have to obey. As the breeze blows, I see the ribbons of air and I funnel them toward the fire. At first the coals burn brighter. Then I pull more of the air, lowering it over the fire like a blanket, suffocating it.

Baron stands and mutters something softly. It sounds like, "a worthy foe…"

He puts his fingers to his mouth and whistles loudly. The same boy from before comes quickly. This time he is not alone. A crowd emerges from the woods—twenty or more of them, almost all wearing collars like mine. Lily and Violet are not among them. The group looks rough. Gaunt, dirty faces. Torn, gashed clothes. Hard, weary eyes. Their hands show the marks of a wolf, and they look to Baron as if he's their savior.

"What are we?" Baron asks.

"We are Wolves!" they shout, and a few of them howl.

"Come, Wolves, it is time to celebrate."

He leads us through the woods. We soon come to an open expanse, where a grassy carpet stretches before us to the great tree. It rises many times higher than the other trees and extends over them. Through a few gaps in the leaves the sky is bright blue. Behind the tree there is a grey stone wall. It stretches as far as I can see in both directions.

Our group steps out of the forest and onto the soft grass. A few others have already gathered at the base of the great tree. Before the immense door is a tall, hooded man—twice as tall as everyone else.

The Hunter. He watches as we approach.

Baron goes straight to him and stops, hands on his hips. "What are you waiting for?"

The Hunter draws a knife and throws back the hood of his cloak. His bearded face holds a wild, ferocious energy as he looks past Baron to the rest of the crowd.

"The Jubilee begins!" the Hunter announces. "No more fighting. No more tribes. You enter the Green Tower as guests of the Provider."

He turns to the door and stabs his blade into it.

Things happen all at once. The door swings open. The collar around my neck falls loose and drops to the grass. Thoughts flood into my mind, bursting from the dam, as I eye Baron striding through the doorway into the tree.

He collared me, and Lily. He used us. He forced us to talk. And now I'm free to return the favor.

I grab the collar off the ground and lunge after Baron, summoning the wind. The threads fling forward like a grappling hook, to drag him back. A few more feet and—

The punch hits me right in the gut.

I double over in pain, losing control of the air, dropping the collar. Then I'm lifted by a fist clenching my shirt. The Hunter's wild face is inches from mine.

"No. More. Fighting."

"But Baron—"

He pulls me closer. "You want to go back in a net?"

I swallow, remembering where I began in this place. "Okay, sorry, but…when *can* we fight?""

The Hunter lowers me to the ground. A smile, or maybe a snarl, curls up under his beard. "Tomorrow, after the Jubilee. Enjoy the feast."

# 9

THE CROWD MOVES single-file through the door into the trunk, and I step into line. Inside, there are steep stairs carved into the dense wood. I follow after a flaxen-haired boy with a snake imprinted on his hand. He's as skinny as a twig, like he hasn't eaten in days. At places the stairs go completely vertical, with rope ladders to climb—not easy with only one good ankle. A faint light comes from a few glowing objects along the wooden walls. I can't make out what they are. It's very dark.

When I reach the top, I climb out onto a large wooden platform. It sits high in the tree, at the place where the huge trunk splits into a dozen or more thick branches that extend up into the thick canopy above. Scattered among the leaves are little wooden buildings, connected by countless rope bridges and ladders. The flat platform easily holds the dozens of boys and girls gathering around. It could fit twice as many. There are several long tables with an incredible feast laid out.

Violet rushes up to me. She has smudges of dirt on her cheeks, under her intense eyes, but she looks unharmed.

"Cipher!" she says. "You made it."

My voice breaks as I respond, "I haven't seen Lily..."

"What happened?"

"Baron caught us. I couldn't do anything. He put a collar on her and me. He sent her after you, to try to trick you into coming. He told her that if she did not bring you to him, she had to forget everything."

Violet's eyes go wide. "Oh no. I'm so sorry."

"Where were you?" I demand.

"I ran. Hey, don't look at me like that. Lily will be glad. Now I can help her remember."

"Didn't you hear me? Lily's lost!"

"No, she will wake up here again." Violet takes a deep breath. "Look, I know this is hard to understand. There's someone I want you to meet." She looks toward a small group gathered near us and calls out, "Hank!"

A tall, sandy-haired boy emerges from the group. He has broad shoulders and a lion mark on his hand. As he approaches, his face lights up. He wraps me in a huge hug before I can even react.

"Cipher!" he says. "I can't believe you're here!" He steps back, studying me. "So it's true...you don't remember me?"

I don't.

"I'm Hank." He clasps my shoulders and looks down at me. "Hank from America. Hank from Blue, and from Red. Your friend, Hank."

"Okay..."

He lets out a heavy sigh. "You must have been

captured from Red and wiped. Didn't Daniel give you the fruit?"

I shake my head. "I ran away."

Hank grins, then starts to laugh. "Same old Cipher, trying to do everything your way. I'm sorry, I know it shouldn't be funny, but… Well, listen, don't worry about it, when Daniel comes, I'll take you to him. He gives one fruit to each person captured in the Scouring. The fruit gives memories back—whatever you've learned already in the towers—and there should still be one for you."

This boy is friendly and nothing like Baron, but his words leave me only more confused. "What *is* this place?"

"I thought you told him," Hank says to Violet.

"I did," Violet says. "He fell out of the tower and got banged up pretty bad."

Hank turns to me. "You *fell* out? No wonder you look so rough…"

"I didn't exactly fall," I say. "I was climbing a ladder down when some guards cut it. They tried to kill me."

"Wow, didn't know that could happen," Hank says. "That must be why Daniel hasn't given you the fruit. Did you meet him?"

"Briefly. I don't trust him."

Hank smiles. "No change there. You didn't trust Abram, either, not at first. Daniel isn't so different from the other leaders. He will show you the past. Then you'll be back on track."

"On track for what?" I ask.

"To lead this tower, of course. You've already led two

towers. You were the most powerful boy in both Red and Blue. Green has the lowest numbers of all five. We need your help to start winning in the Scouring."

"I knew you were different," Violet says, with her arms crossed. "But so is Green."

"Just wait 'till you see his power," Hank says.

"My power?" I think of how I shifted the dagger through the air and put out the fire under Baron's command.

"You control the air," Hank says. "You have more power than anyone. You told me that the more you remember from before, the stronger you are."

He sounds so confident of this. "What do you know about my past?" I ask.

"Ah, right. Well, see…" Hank looks down. "You were a doctor in America. Some fancy, smart kind. Listen, it's better if you see all this for yourself. Daniel will give you the fruit, then some sap. You'll get that wind back, and you'll be drawing on others' powers again, like you did with…"

"With who?"

"There was a girl, Emma," Hank says. "You captured her from Yellow. She and I followed you to Red. The two of you are very powerful together."

*Emma.* The one who spoke to me through the stars, the one who hung beside me in the nets. I didn't trust her…

"Emma is in the tree," I say.

"What!" Hank gasps. "In Green? How do you know?"

"We were together, hanging in nets, before I escaped."

"Amazing," Hank says, rubbing his hands together. "We're all set then. You and Emma are even stronger together than the two of us. You draw on each others' powers. We're gonna be unstoppable again. We're gonna get past Baron."

"Sounds rosy…" Violet mumbles.

"Just you wait!" Hank says. "But hey, you two look starved. Let's eat."

We go to one of the tables. It is covered with heaping servings of roasted meat, vegetables, roots, mushrooms, and fruit. There are stacks of empty, wooden bowls. I follow the Hank's lead and take one and fill it with whatever food looks good, which is all of it. Except the mushrooms.

We sit on the wooden floor and eat. A group slowly gathers around us. Most of them have lion marks on their hands, like Hank's. Baron and the Wolves sit on the opposite side of the platform. Few people pass between the two groups.

As the day ends and the tree grows dark, hundreds of little lanterns appear in the air, drifting slowly down from the branches above. One of the lanterns floats to me and lands softly on my hand. It's a tiny person with effervescent wings that glow. Like a fairy. I smile as I watch its wings flutter and take off again.

"Nice light, don't you think?" Hank says. "In Red there was fire everywhere to light the way. The leader Rahab and all the girls could make fire. In Blue there was a bright blue orb on Abram's staff and lots of candles. Here there are silent, glowing fairies. I like this."

"I'm not sure…" I say.

"Trust me, there's a lot to like in the tree," Hank says. "Too bad we don't get to stay long. Just tonight for most of us, unless you get picked for the Scouring tribe. Look, he's coming."

A small, bent-over man has emerged from a building nestled high in the tree on the opposite side of the platform. I follow as Hank and everyone else hurry to their feet and move toward him. The man walks slowly down a set of wide stairs, which are carved into a thick branch that rises from the platform. The man leans heavily on his staff with each step. He stops above the wooden platform as the crowd gathers around him. The long beard and dark, green robe mark him as Daniel.

He suddenly disappears, just as the Hunter did. One second there, and then not.

The crowd cheers loudly.

Daniel suddenly reappears further down the stairs, only two steps above us, with his staff lifted high. "Welcome to the Jubilee!"

# 10

"COME, SCOURING TRIBE!" Daniel keeps his staff held high. A murmur spreads through the crowd as others begin to appear among the canopy behind Daniel. They descend down through the tree as he did, then come to a stop on the broad stair below him, which rings the thick branch rising out of the platform.

The group stands facing us. Eleven of them. Six boys, five girls. They wear the same kind of clothes as the rest of us, though much cleaner. One of them is Emma, the girl who hung with me in the net and spoke to me through the stars. Her long blonde hair hangs over her sleeveless shirt like golden thread. Her blue eyes search the crowd, then stop on me. She smiles.

"You have fought for Green, but you have only held our ground." Daniel's voice holds no anger, only regret. "Two captured from Red, yes, but two lost. Our numbers remain at ninety-two. This Scouring tribe is released."

Daniel holds his staff forward, and they move down the stairs and scatter among the crowd.

"Now," Daniel announces, "it is time to name the new

leaders."

Before he has finished saying this, Baron begins to climb the stairs to Daniel. He stands by his side, looking out over the crowd with his hands clasped behind his back and chin up.

"Baron has won…again," Daniel says. "He caught eight for the Wolves. However, seven of his tribe died. That's seven who will join us without a trace of memory. A tragic way to win…." As Daniel falls quiet, I think of Lily. I still haven't seen her. The old man continues, "Stephen, come and tell them what you've told me."

A skinny boy with red hair and freckles moves out of the crowd and climbs the stairs to Daniel's side, opposite Baron. The old man whispers something to him. Then the boy faces us. His shoulders are so scrawny that his vest hangs like it would from a stick.

"There was a trap," the boy says. "It was a false ground trap. One minute I'm walking through the forest, hunting a rabbit, the next I'm at the bottom of a ten-foot-deep pit. There was no way out. I had no food with me."

The boy's voice quivers. Daniel puts a steadying hand to his back. "Go on, Stephen, tell them."

"I yelled for help," the boy continues. "A day passed. Then another. My lips were parched. I was so weak. Still I shouted, hoping someone would hear. On the third day, when I could barely sit up any longer, I heard something above. A boy's face appeared above the pit, gazing down at me. A water flask hung down from his shoulders. I shouted up to him, *Help, please, I'm dying. Give me water, anything.* But the boy only smiled and said, *Good luck, Eagle*, before disappearing from view. I would have died—would have been wiped—if not for the Lions finding me the next day. They put me to work as a servant, but it was better than the alternative."

"Who left you in the pit?" Daniel asks.

Stephen lifts his stick-thin arm and points to Baron. "Him."

Baron's granite eyes do not blink. "I had only one collar left. It was better to save it than use it on…him."

The crowd near the front starts shoving and fighting. I hear someone shouting, "Wolf! Wolf!"

*Boom.*

A sudden shockwave pulses through the air, silencing the crowd. Daniel raises his staff, then slams it down.

*Boom.*

Another shockwave hits us.

"None may fight here," Daniel says calmly. "This is the Jubilee. There are no rules except for the Scouring, the Jubilee, and the Tribes. The process continues as it must, until you are scoured. Victory here is not final. Consider the cost of winning." He looks to Baron, then out over the crowd again. "What must we learn?"

"Giving sets you free," others mumble around me.

"Freedom!" Daniel shakes his head as if disappointed. "It's a promise, not a duty. You thirst for more. You hunt and hoard. But you will learn to trust the Provider, no matter how much it hurts. Thank you, Stephen, for sharing your story. Perhaps the next tribe leaders will share as you have. Jade, Hank, and Seneca, come forward."

A mix of cheers and boos stirs among the crowd. Hank gives me a surprised shrug, then moves toward Daniel. He steps up beside Baron and two girls who look like they could snap a tree with a stare. One of them is tall, with dark skin and feathers in her hair. The other is a shorter, copper-skinned girl with hawkish eyes and high cheekbones.

"Jade caught three for the Eagles, though they lost many," Daniel announces. "Hank caught two for the Lions, including his rescue of Stephen. Seneca also caught two for the Lions. Now these four leaders will choose their tribes, and Baron will select those for the Scouring. The rest of you come and drink deep of the Provider's bounty."

The crowd rushes forward, sweeping me up with it. I reach the bottom step below Daniel, where a line of kneeling boys and girls has formed on both sides of a trough of liquid. Each of them leans over it, scooping a sticky, amber liquid up to their mouths. Some of them slurp up the liquid straight from the trough. They look like a pack of hungry pigs.

"It's the sap," Hank says, coming to my side. "You will drink. We all will. But first, the fruit."

He leads me past the trough of sap and up the stairs, where Daniel observes the crowd. As we go someone clasps my arm, stopping me.

It's Emma. She takes my face in her slender hands. "I'm so glad you're back," she says.

I don't know what to say. Her tender touch overwhelms me. "I'm sorry, I still don't remember…"

"Everything will be okay," Emma says. "Daniel gave me the fruit. He will also give it to you."

"Yes," Daniel says with a raspy voice, stepping down to us. "You are most fortunate. Those who are not cleansed rarely get the fruit."

I take a step back from him. "I'm not going into a net."

Daniel peers deeply into my eyes, as if studying something through them. "You see, Cipher, not everyone has such a—how shall I put it—distilled essence. Most come here confused. You, however, seem bent only on forward motion, under your own control. Has it bothered you to know nothing of your past?"

"A little," I say. "The Hunter showed me something."

"Ah, but those seeds will wither and die on barren rock. You may have Genius and Passion under rein. Yet still you fear much. You obey your instinct rather than trust. You need the Provider's fertile soil to help you grow." Daniel looks to Emma and Hank. "This will take him some time. Please, excuse us."

"But I want to talk with him after he remembers," Emma says. Hank nods in agreement.

"This is not possible now," Daniel replies. "The fruit is as much as I can give."

Emma sighs, her head dropping to her chest. Hank turns to go, but Emma sweeps me up in a tight embrace. She whispers into my ear, "We will work together again, Cipher. We even have the starlight at our command now. You will see. Once you remember, find me, then help me find my son, Oliver, okay?"

*Her son?* She's too young to have a son. But I nod anyway. She leaves and joins the crowd around the sap. Many of them are no longer drinking. They are laid out on the ground, curled up as if asleep.

"Come," Daniel says, taking my arm again. He leads me up the stairs, away from Emma and Hank and the others.

We reach a small building where the door has an intricate carving of a tree in the center, shaped like the Green Tower. Daniel taps his staff against the wood and the door swings open. The space inside is tiny. It would not fit even five people. It is also empty except for a dozen glowing fairies overhead and a wooden bowl in the center of the floor, with a single bright red fruit inside it.

"Go on," Daniel says, "take and eat and know."

I pick up the red fruit from the bowl. It fits easily in my palm. The flesh is soft and smooth and enticing. Turning back to Daniel, I ask, "How does this work?"

"The Provider gives what you need. Not always what you want." His eyes look amused underneath his bushy gray eyebrows. "You may want to sit down."

"Who is this Provider?" I ask, as I sit cross-legged on the wooden floor.

"A facet of the same jewel. Now, eat."

I bite into the fruit. The juice, sweet on my tongue, goes down easily.

A flash suddenly sets my mind ablaze. Information blitzes into me like lightning, revealing whole parts of myself as plain as day. I was Paul Fitzroy. I was a neurosurgeon in Chicago, with a wife and a son. Some of the past lays still, like lifeless ashes leftover from a fire. Scattered in those ashes are memories of a conversation in an elevator, of a red-haired woman named Samantha.

Other parts of the past are gaping holes, entirely missing. Like how Dr. Fitzroy died and got to this place with five towers. Like how my son died. I try to push into these memories, but their darkness is impenetrable.

The brightest memories are more recent. I woke up as a young boy in the Blue Tower. I called myself Cipher. I was the first to bring the five towers to 720 and make equilibrium possible. Abram told me the towers must reach 144 each. I grew in power and learned of Genius. I led the Blue Tower to capture many in the Scouring. Then I went to the Red Tower and found my mother. I learned of Passion. I overcame Max to become the Alpha. I paired with Emma. My mother went up into the White Tower, and I…couldn't. Something caught me. Now I know: it was the Green Tower. They captured me. Now I am here. Now I must learn again.

Everything Emma and Hank have said to me suddenly makes sense. Emma said we must work together. I can help her find her son. I have to get back to her.

I surge to my feet, remembering where I am. The old man watches me from the doorway of the small wooden room.

"You're Daniel, the leader of the Green Tower!" I say.

"Same as always," he replies with a smile. "Took a while to realize that, eh?"

"I'm sorry I ran."

"No need to apologize," he says. "Some fear is natural. Some comes from the stains you have brought with you. The fear—like the cravings that spawn it—must be scoured. Shall we begin now?"

He leads me back the way we came, down toward the platform. The tree has become very dark. Only a few of the glowing fairies remain to light the way. It's as if hours passed while I ate the fruit and remembered. When we come to the sap, everyone is sprawled around, motionless.

"The sap brings deep sleep," Daniel says. "It shows you the past. As the Sieve does in Blue."

Daniel was there, at the Sieve, along with Abram. He looked into my past while I had a vision. It was the vision of my son's birthday party. I was late. I was never there for him, just like my own father wasn't for me.

But Daniel had hope then. He saw the scar on my hand and said, *The end is near.* But the end of what? And why did Baron have the same scar? I hold out my hands to Daniel, now with the two matching cross-cross scars imprinted deeply in the center, as if something had stabbed clean through my hands.

"You told me before that these mean the end is near," I say. "Did you mean the end of the five towers?"

Daniel stares down at my scars. "You got the second one from Red?"

"Sort of…my Mom and I were in the Scouring, and she was clutching my hand before she went up in the White Tower. When she let go, it left this. What does it mean?"

"Two scars, two towers." Daniel strokes his long beard.

"How many do you expect to receive?"

"I have only two hands."

"Ah, but you also have two feet, and a body. There are five towers, after all."

"Okay, five scars. But why?"

"So that you can know why you're here."

"And then what? I get to leave through the White Tower? Like my Mom?"

"Hm, no," Daniel says. "Do not compare yourself to others. Only *you* brought the towers to 720."

"But my Mom left. And before that, I saw a boy in the Black Tower leave. So aren't there 718 now?"

He shakes his head. "Two more came, the moment each of the others left. More may leave. More may come. Thousands. Millions. However many must churn until you find the way out. Or, rather, until the way has found you."

"That's not fair." I glance around at the sleeping boys and girls on the platform. "Why does it all have to rest on me? Shouldn't I be able to leave like everyone else?"

"Do not overestimate yourself," Daniel says gently. "Rahab told you the truth. Your capacity for power comes from the gap between what you could have done on Earth, and what you did. You have much to be scoured, even more than the others who bear the scars."

"*Others?*" But I suddenly remember. "Like Baron?"

"You received your scar first, but there are five towers and there will be five chosen ones with scars."

"Five, five, five. Why is it always five?"

Daniel smiles. "When you know this, you will know the

way. But stains from your past still obscure your vision. It is time for you to see more. It is time to drink the sap."

I start to protest, to ask more, but he points his staff and I know I have no choice. As I move to the liquid, it entices me as the fruit did. I kneel and dip my hand into the dark, sticky sap. The taste is sweet on my tongue but bitter as it goes down.

# 11

THE LEAVES OVERHEAD sweep past in a furious fiery blur. Green has turned to yellow, orange, and red. Scattered leaves drift down melodramatically, stark against the cloudless blue sky. But they can't catch us. We're driving too fast. The air smells fresh and crisp as it blasts my hair back. Above the sound of a motor and wind, a singer's voice rasps along with a twangy guitar.

*The answer, my friend, is blowin' in the wind.*

As the car crests a hilltop, my gaze turns down, leveling with the horizon where rows and rows of hazy blue mountains climb lazily on top of each other. We fly down the hill, no other cars in sight. Just the leaves and birds and Susan behind the wheel of the classic green convertible. A Jaguar, I'd noticed.

She's smiling the most innocent smile. Large sunglasses hide her eyes, but I know that they'd mirror her lips. She's the most genuine and good person I've ever met. She's cute, too, with her brown hair tied in a tight ponytail, a khaki blazer, and snug jeans.

I wish those were the only reasons I'd agreed to meet

66

her family. They're certainly reasons enough. But I know what will happen if Susan utters "I do." Those two words are awfully cheap for gaining a fortune.

*Yes, 'n' how many times can a man turn his head*
*And pretend that he just doesn't see?*
*The answer, my friend, is blowin' in the wind*

We turn off the mountain road. There's a stone entrance with a wrought iron gate and a sign that says "Private Drive." Susan leans toward a small box by the gate and says something so softly I can't hear the words. But apparently the box did, because it replies, "Welcome Susan. Your family is eager to see you."

As the gate opens, she looks at me and laughs. "Sorry, kind of cheesy, right? They just installed this thing last year. Daddy picked out everyone's secret passcode and greeting. You should hear my brother's!"

She accelerates along the private drive, lined with tall oaks shading perfectly manicured grass. After several climbing turns, the drive leads to the most magnificent mountain house I could imagine. It's not so big that it's ostentatious, like the Biltmore Estate a couple ridges away, but this castle makes my classmate's place in the Hamptons look like a guesthouse.

We stop in the round driveway beside a fountain where a marble faun spits water up into the sky. Or maybe it's a satyr. I could never tell the difference. Hopefully Susan's family won't quiz me.

The family comes out to greet us, security cameras no doubt having warned them of our approach. It's all hugs and smiles. They seem to truly like each other. Susan's father, Jonas Rockefeller, gives me a firm handshake and says he's glad to meet the young man who has been spending so much time with his daughter. Susan's mom wraps me up in a big hug and says she's heard so much about me.

Her brother hangs back, with a football in his hands. "Hey, wanna toss?"

Susan had warned me about this. Her little brother—who's a head taller than I am—plays wide receiver at Yale. He always wants to see how the guys dating his sister throw the ball, like it's some kind of test.

"Sure," I say.

He hands me a football and takes off around the fountain. "Hit me!" he shouts.

I throw the ball and manage to clear the fountain. He catches it easily. Then he tosses it back in a rifling spiral. It hits my hands and bounces to the ground. I pick it up to throw again, but he's already returning with a look of disappointment.

Whatever. I don't throw spirals. He wouldn't either if he'd never had a father, buried his mother during college, and survived three years of medical school. Besides, it's not her brother I need to convince. It's her parents.

Inside the estate, Susan and her mother give me a tour. It takes over an hour. My favorite part is the pool house out back. It's larger than any home I've ever lived in. The saltwater infinity pool beside it makes the water disappear into the mountain view on the horizon. Greenish blue to blueish green. After they escort me to my guest room, again larger than my apartment, I shower and put on the nicest clothes I own, minus the tie.

A few hours later we're sitting down at a twenty-foot-long table, with three giant roasted turkeys spread at regular intervals around an assortment of other gilded dishes. Susan's father sits at one end of the table, and his brother is at the other. There are thirty of us gathered. Cousins, nephews, uncles, and one grandmother—herself the granddaughter of the oil tycoon who turned this family into one of America's richest.

A prayer is said. The feast begins.

Halfway through the dinner, Susan's hand finds mine under the table. She's glad I've come. I held out for a long time. Everyone knows medical school allows few breaks, so the family will forgive me. But I know this is what she really wanted, to feel like I'm part of her family, accepting and being accepted. More than anything, I feel certain that she really loves me. It's flattering. I like her quite a lot. With my career prospects, she does not believe I would marry her for the money, not entirely. She knows about the student loans, but she thinks I'll land the right residency for surgery, join a top practice, save a bunch of lives. She doesn't know I swore to be more than a servant boy to the true upper class. She doesn't need to know that. Later that night when she sneaks into my bedroom, she believes it when I tell her that I love her.

We stay at the mountain estate two whole days. On the last day her father summons me to his study. It's just the two of us. He sits behind a desk that looks hewn from an entire redwood. He comes around and sits with me in front of a fireplace. The leather chair welcomes my body like we're old friends. An amber drink is poured. We toast to a good weekend.

"I'm glad you came," her father says. "Because I need to tell you something."

"What's that, Mr. Rockefeller?"

"I've seen the way my daughter looks at you," he says, daggers in his eyes. "If you ever hurt her, in any way, well, that would be a tragic mistake."

"I understand, sir." And I do understand. She's a modern princess, after all. "Actually, I wanted to talk to you, too."

"Oh, why's that?"

"Because I feel the same way about Susan. I love her. I'm planning to ask her to marry me, and I know she and I both would welcome your blessing."

He doesn't flinch. He sets down his glass and studies his hands. When he turns to me, all square-jawed and granite-eyed, I don't know whether to smile or brace myself for a punch. I settle on an awkward grin, while my fists clench the leather chair like a man in a crashing airplane.

"You're going to be a doctor," he says.

"Yes, sir."

"What kind?"

"Neurosurgery."

"Which do you think is more important: the brain, or

the heart?"

"We can't live without either one. Sir."

He nods gravely. "I'll give you my blessing to propose, but it will need to go through my lawyers. You understand?"

Yes, of course, a prenuptial agreement. No one marries into a family with this kind of wealth without agreeing in advance about where the money goes—that is, not to me—if things go wrong. I do not intend for that to be a problem.

"Yes, sir," I say, but I can't leave it at that. "I want to be clear, I'm here because I love your daughter, not because of money."

For the first time, he smiles, like he's caught me in some mistake. He stands and extends his hand. As we shake, he says, "Money and love are like the brain and the heart. You can't live without either one."

# 12

"COME ON, BOY. Get up!" Somebody is shaking me. Somebody pulls me to my feet.

People stir all around. The wooden floor creaks. Birds sing outside. It looks like morning, soft and warm and bright. I rub my eyes. Jonas Rockefeller and his mansion and his daughter are gone. This is the Green Tower. Someone must have moved me while I slept.

Twenty boys and girls are lined up behind a door. They, like me, are spotlessly clean, with new deerskin shorts and vests. I recognize only one of them—a girl near the front with faintly purple hair, Violet. She talks with a tall, dark-skinned girl who puts her hand to the door and pushes it open. Her hand has a blue eagle painted on it. I look down. An eagle looks up at me from my own hand, obscuring the scar underneath it.

"That's Jade, our leader," says the boy who woke me up. He has red hair, freckles, and the eagerness of a beagle. I realize he's the one who told the crowd about how Baron had left him to starve at the bottom of a pit.

"Stephen, right?"

He nods. "Jade told me to help you. Now come on!"

He races out after the others onto a rope bridge. I follow and stagger as the bridge sways and swings under the herd of trotting feet. The ground is far, far below, appearing between the leaves and branches. Gripping the rope railings, it's all I can do to keep up.

I can't blame an injury this time. My ankle feels brand new, like it had never sprained or broken or whatever it was. The side of my head does not even have a scab from the wound. There are no scratches or bruises to be seen on my body—only the marks on my hands.

We make our way down and out. More rope bridges and ladders lead away from the tree's center and toward the canopy's edge. We come to a small wooden hut. It's the same one I tried to climb down when I ran away. Below I see our group scrambling down the ladder.

Stephen is five rungs down when he looks up and sees me watching him.

"Come on!" he shouts.

I shake my head, dizzied by the height and remembering the last time, when they cut the ladder and sent me crashing into the trees. It's a miracle I survived.

"You can't stay! They'll wipe you. You want that, or to fly with the Eagles?" He doesn't wait for an answer before continuing down.

It's an easy choice. I hurry after him. The climb is just as harrowing as I remember. But it ends better, without anyone cutting me loose. When the ladder reaches the top of the trees, I scramble down through the branches to the forest floor, where the air is thick and the light is dim. There's howling in the distance, like the Wolves. Baron will be leading them. And now we can fight.

Stephen stands waiting. "You were slow," he says. "We have to catch up. If there's trouble, head that way."

He points into the forest, away from the giant tree, and takes off at a sprint. We leap over roots and dodge around trees. The underbrush grows thicker. The howls draw closer.

We come to a wall of tangled briars, as tall as I am.

"Time to split. Go that way." Stephen points around the thicket, then he plunges straight into it.

I find my way around and hear a shout nearby. When I come to the other side of the thicket, Stephen's nowhere in sight. I almost shout for him but the howls are so close. Better not to draw attention.

I keep going the same direction we were headed, without seeing any sign of him or anyone else. When I reach a familiar spot by a creek, I stop to catch my breath. Downstream stands the hollowed-out tree where Violet and Lily took care of me. There's no trace of the fire that burned the tree before we left. Maybe Violet will be there.

But when I reach the tree, it looks like no one has ever set foot inside. Moss and spider webs cover the entrance. I use a stick to clear the way. Inside there's no table, no fur rug, no food. Only darkness and a stale, earthy smell.

I sit on the dirt, resting, thinking. Just days ago this place was like a home. I remember it perfectly. I see the exact spot where I slept. Now my body has healed, so maybe the forest has, too. It's like everything reset while we slept in the giant tree. How long did we sleep? A night? A hundred years? The vision comes back, of me as a young doctor. Was that a hundred years ago? My name had been Paul Fitzroy. My intentions had been terrible. I was going to marry a girl for her money. I wonder if that's why I'm here in Green, if somehow these tribes and the scarcity and the Jubilee are supposed to teach me something like the pairing did in Red, like the classes did in Blue.

Howls cut off my thoughts, bring me to my feet.

I hurry outside, listening as the howls approach, readying to summon the wind. A sudden snap makes me turn. Violet stands there, bent over with her hands on her knees, breathing heavily.

"Figured you'd come here," she pants.

"The tree," I say, pointing to it, "it's like we were never there."

"Happens every Jubilee. We have to go. It's not safe. Baron knows about this place now."

"I'm not afraid of him."

She stands up straighter, still catching her breath, and looks at me like I'm crazy. "You don't stand a chance. He will have a whole tribe at his command. He will crush you. He will collar you again."

My fingers go instinctively to my neck. Baron could have many collared servants, maybe some with powers, maybe even Emma. I don't know what I'd do if she attacked me under Baron's command. I will be outnumbered. But…I meet Violet's gaze. I'm not alone.

"We could use your power to hide," I say. "I'll attack before they know what's hit them."

"How do you think they snuck up on us? They can go invisible, too."

"But I—"

"Look, I heard Hank," Violet says. "You may be strong, but you're not ready to face Baron. We must get to the Eagles. We will be stronger together."

My fists clench, but what I've learned tempers my anger toward Baron. This is the Five Towers. We cannot die. We can only be wiped and remember again until we get to the White Tower. That's how my Mom made it out. That has to be my focus—to get back to the Scouring. But if I must join a tribe and beat Baron's Wolves to get there, so be it. I can wait for that. Baron will not stand in my way.

"All right," I say. "Lead on."

Violet takes off like Stephen did before. She's even faster and more nimble than he was. She seems to know the forest like the back of her hand. I struggle to keep up.

"Hurry!" she shouts back to me.

As I chase after her, I weave the air into a steady wind at my back. It makes every step lighter. I weave more and begin to gain on Violet until I'm running at her pace. Then I propel both of us forward. It feels like we're flying through the forest. The howls gradually fade behind us.

Violet calls for me to stop when we approach the top of a cliff. Her hair is lavender in the sunlight, and there's a breathless smile on her face.

"That was fast, kind of fun," she says. "Your power?"

I nod. "I got it back."

"Good. It'll help with life as an Eagle." She points toward the cliff. "Our nest is just below."

The three suns are low on the horizon, above the dark blue sea in the distance. Between the cliff and the water there's a vast, uninterrupted jungle. But to get there it's a long, long way down. I back away.

"Don't worry, you'll get used to it," Violet says. "Follow my lead."

She steps to the edge and drops to the ground. Taking hold of vines that drape down over the cliff, she slides backwards on her stomach, inch by inch, until her feet hang in midair and then her body drops out of sight.

"Come on," Violet calls up. "The vines will hold."

I take a deep breath. This time there's no Scouring tribe coming after us, but if I fall and die, I'd still be wiped. I can't count on another magic red fruit waiting for me. Daniel said that was rare. Better to be careful, and keep the wind ready.

Kneeling down, I grip the vine firmly. It feels solid as a rope. Ahead it snakes along the ground until it reaches a cluster of other vines coiling up and around a tree. I test it with a firm yank. Very solid. I crawl backwards, belly on the ground just like Violet did, until my feet and legs extend over empty air. Holding fast, I slide the final inch that puts my center of gravity beyond the edge.

The vine holds. I summon the wind to steady myself and climb down slowly, keeping my eyes on the vine and not looking up or down. As I descend, the cliff face opens into a deep crevasse in the rock. My toes touch down on a ledge. It's about twenty feet below the top of the cliff. I take two steps forward before I'm confident enough to release the vine, and the wind.

Violet stands waiting. "We're almost there."

She leads me into the darkness of the crevasse, where I hear voices. It grows darker and darker, but then, around a sharp bend in the rock, the tunnel opens up into a large cave. The cave is entirely open on one side, revealing the jungle below and the sea in the distance. No vines dangle here.

A girl stands on a large rock at the center of the cave's opening, just where the stone floor meets the air. Her silhouette is framed by blue sky and the view beyond.

"Here," Violet says, sitting and patting the ground.

I sit with her. Others sit in a line beside us, forming a crescent around the girl in the front. One of them is Stephen. He wears a fresh, bloodied bandage on his arm. He catches my eyes and gives me a friendly wink, as if to say: *We made it.*

The girl standing before us is tall and strong, with short black hair, chocolate skin, and bright green eyes. She holds a spear made of sharpened stone, with a feather tied under the tip. Her vest does not conceal her sinewy muscles. A bag hangs over her shoulder. It looks full and heavy.

She taps the staff as if calling for order.

"Welcome, Eagles," she says. "I'm Jade. As long as we remember, I've been leading this tribe, so I'm going to tell you how it goes. I know some of you were wiped. We'll put you with others who have been here before. You'll learn fast. We survive by staying perched up here. No tribe has ever taken the nest from me. But we can't all stay here. There's water but no food. So we send out watchers and hunters to gather what we need. These groups sometimes lose a few, or capture a few. After fifty days, the Hunter will let us back into the tree for the Jubilee. Rinse and repeat. Simple as that. Now, whoever doesn't remember being an Eagle before, stand up."

Five of us stand.

Jade looks us up and down. "Strong additions," she says. "Now tell us who you are, if you know."

A girl near the front speaks up. "You called me Celeste. I woke up in the tree with all of you. No memory before that."

"Welcome, Celeste," Jade says. "I remember you. You were an Eagle last time. You disappeared on day sixteen. We'll talk more after this. Next?"

A boy goes next. "My name is Franz. Or, that's what Pete tells me."

"Yes," says another boy, presumably Pete. "I don't know which tribe he was in before, but we were…acquainted on Earth. I'll tell Franz what I know about him. It's not much. He was Austrian nobility, high above my rank."

The next two who introduce themselves are girls with no memories, and no one who remembers them. They look afraid. I wonder if Lily is in another tribe, feeling the same way. Daniel said Baron did this to seven others…

Jade tells me it's my turn.

"I'm Cipher," I say. "This is my first time in a tribe."

"How do you know?" Jade asks.

"Because I came from Red, and Blue before that."

A murmur spreads around the cave.

"Three colors!" Jade looks approvingly to Violet. "You were right. He may prove to be worth my first pick. You should have seen Baron's face! Even *his* hard eyes looked surprised. You're lucky, Cipher. I think Baron wanted you. Tell us, what kind of powers do you have?"

I meet Jade's eyes, but think only of Baron. He would have put me in a collar. He would have used my powers. But here, in this cave, no one has been collared. I could like the Eagles. We could beat Baron.

I turn to the group. "I control the wind."

The murmur grows again. I overhear them whispering words like, *Blue, wind,* and *Daniel.*

Jade slams the butt of her spear to the ground, making the group fall silent. "There's a story about a group from Blue invading our forest," she says. "The Lions tried to capture them, but a boy from Blue had powers over the wind. He even took away our leader, Daniel, for a time. What do you know about that?"

Everyone's gaze shifts from Jade to me. Her explanation is about right. I came to Green when Abram and Sarai sent me out from the Blue Tower to capture from other towers. They called it the Hunting. Helena's servant from Green betrayed us in the forest. We almost lost Emma, but instead we gained Daniel. He wanted to be caught. He sailed with us back to Blue and spoke with Abram and me. He looked into the Sieve to see what I saw.

The group is waiting, watching me.

"That was me," I say.

"Prove it," Jade says.

I glance at Violet, but she only nods for me to do as Jade has said. Looking out at the cave's opening, I pull thin threads of air and weave them into a contained breeze. The air blows into the cave and ruffles the feathers at the base of Jade's spear. The others let out a collective sigh of amazement. But I'm not done. I weave more, using dozens of threads to send a sharp gust of air through the cave. Hair blows, pebbles slide on the ground. Then I release and everything falls still.

All eyes are on me, filled with wonder.

"We can use this," Jade says.

# 13

THE THREE SUNS shine into the nest as they set. Flecks of green and gold stone sparkle on the cave wall. The Eagle tribe talks about what they've learned before in the forest, and how to get food without getting caught. Jade says that the biggest threats are the Lions in the jungle below the cliff, and the Wolves in the forest above. The Wolves and Lions wake first in the tree, so they stake out the best territory. The Snakes stay mostly to themselves, trying to hide closer to the coast.

When darkness falls, the cave grows cool and quiet. The stone feels heavy around us, enclosing us, protecting us. Jade assigns everyone things to do. Violet and I get the night's last watch.

Violet says we should get some sleep until then. She leads me deeper into the cave where the path seems to reach a dead end. She squeezes through a slender gap in the wall. It's very dark. There's a soft trickle and pitter-pat of water on stone from the other side. It makes the hairs on my neck stand up.

"Come on," Violet says, her voice echoing lightly. "It's

just through here."

I take a deep breath and force myself into the gap. The rock walls press tight around my sides. But then I pop out the other side, into a medium-sized room with a small beam of starlight shining down onto a pool of water. The light makes me think of Emma. I hope she's not with Baron, but if she is, it's only more important that I find her. Maybe we could talk through the stars.

I focus on the light. *Emma?*

There's no answer.

"This is Min," Violet says to me. "Min, Cipher."

"Nice to meet you," says a girl who emerges from the shadows. Despite the lone ray of light, it's still too dark to see her expression.

"Min's on water watch," Violet says.

Min comes to my side. "The beds are ready," she whispers. "I'll show you."

"What is this place?" I ask as we follow her silent footsteps.

"This is where we get our water," Min says. "It drips through the stone. It's also the innermost room. The safest place. When we're attacked, this is the last stand." She makes this sound as common as eating breakfast.

"How often are we attacked?" I ask.

"Every time. But don't worry, the attacks usually start around day thirty, when food is running low."

"Fear doesn't help anything," Violet says.

"Easy for you to say," Min replies. "Not all of us get to go out hunting. We rely on you to bring back food. And we always lose hunters. Just wait. You'll see. At first one won't come back. A snake bite might take one. A lion's trap another. That means less food. And empty bellies make us reckless."

"No need to worry about that," Violet says, laying on a pallet of straw by the wall. "Get some sleep, Cipher. Min will keep an eye out."

It can't be as bad as Min makes it sound. "Have we ever *not* been attacked?" I ask.

Min shrugs. "I don't know. It's been four Jubilees since I was wiped. Last time the Wolves caught me, but let me live. Now I'm back here again…on water duty…"

"Enough," Violet says from the ground. "Sleep."

I lay down and settle into another soft pallet of straw. It feels as safe as a place can be. I try again to speak to Emma through the starlight, but no response comes. I wish I could have asked her how it works. I *will* find her.

When Violet wakes me, the cave is still dark and quiet, except for the drip-drip-drip. We make our way through the cave to the ledge where the vines hang down from the cliff's edge above.

Jade is there, looking out with her legs dangling over the edge and her palms on the ground. The feathered spear and the bag lay by her side.

Violet and I sit with her. "We'll watch now," Violet says. "You should sleep."

"What, and miss the sunrise?" Jade muses. "Never know when it'll be your last as an Eagle. That reminds me, I'm sorry about your friend, Lily. Baron picked her for the

Scouring tribe."

My jaw clenches. "What about a girl named Emma?"

"Sorry," Jade shrugs, "who's that?"

"Long blonde hair, blue eyes," I say.

"The leader of the Lions picked a girl who looked like that," Jade says.

"Hank picked her?"

"Right, that's his name. The girl you describe was his first pick, but then Baron chose her for the Scouring. I chose you next—the leaders always pick in order, Wolves, Lions, Eagles, then Snakes—so it's odd that Baron did not send you to the Scouring. He usually plucks the strongest from the other tribes, but keeps his best."

"He's ruthless," Violet says.

"Aye, but you can't doubt his results."

"It's time to fight back," I say.

Jade shakes her head, looking like a tired predator in the day's first gray light. "Last time we tried that we lost all but two of us. I bet he's already captured some Snakes. His pack is always growing." She pats the bag beside her. "We'd need a little army to even try fighting them."

"How many?" Violet asks.

Jade turns to her, then to me, smiling. "Bring back one, that'll be a start."

"We will," Violet says. "Cipher and I can work together."

"Eager," Jade says. "How about you, Cipher?"

"I'm good at catching people."

Jade laughs lightly. "So I've heard. But the forest isn't

the Scouring."

I gaze out at the jungle below us, which undulates like a lush velvet sea. "The wind still blows in the trees."

"Aye, but sometimes it's better to hide." Jade looks to Violet. "Can you teach him?"

"I taught Lily," Violet says.

"Good." Jade rises slowly and lifts her spear and bag. She reaches inside the bag and pulls out a gleaming metal object. At first I think it's a weapon, but then I see the clasp. It's a collar, dull in the grey light. A shiver runs down my spine.

"Take it," Jade says. "Bring back a captive and some food. I'll take your watch. I was going to stay up anyway."

"For the Eagles." Violet takes the collar and ties it to a leather loop on her shorts. The metal hangs like a lifeless chrome snake by her thigh.

"Fly high," Jade says.

Violet grips one of the hanging vines and gives it a sharp yank. It holds. She repeats this process for four other vines, then picks two and begins sliding down them. When her head is level with the cave's floor, she looks to me. "What are you waiting for?"

I step to the edge of the cave and grab one of the vines. It feels firm when I put my weight on it. Following Violet's lead, I test a few of them and pick the thickest two. I coil one around my leg once, grip a vine tightly in each hand, and step off the ledge.

Inch by inch I lower myself. Muscles clench and release, willing me to hold fast. Below, Violet rappels off the cliff face and back. Past her it's a very long way down. I should preserve my power, but I can't resist using the wind to steady my descent.

I keep sliding, slowly, until the vine ends. We're still forty feet from the canopy below. More than that from the ground, which we cannot see through the trees.

"We have to climb from here," Violet says from below me. Her hands and feet hold fast to rock wall, like they're covered in glue.

"You could have warned me about this."

"Would you have come?" she asks. "Follow my path. I know the easiest way down."

Nothing about it is easy, but I do as she says. The grey morning light has turned to day. Though we are still in the cliff's shadow, heat wafts up from the jungle—sticky and wet. It makes my hands slick. I draw more of the air, enough to control a steady breeze. It blows against my back, pressing me snug against the cliff and drying my hands as I climb down, one hold to the next, grip never relaxing.

We finally reach the vivid green canopy. Violet sits on a branch that presses against the rock wall, with nowhere to grow but sideways. She uses a thick waxy leaf from the tree to fan herself off and scatter the bugs clouding around her. I release the air and take a deep breath as I sit on the branch. My mind and my body throb. I rub my calves, massaging out aches and cramps. The moist heat makes my clothes stick to my skin. Bugs swarm around me, buzzing into my eyes and ears. I summon the air again, blowing them away from us with a gust.

"We have to keep moving," Violet says, fanning her leaf in front of me. "Sometimes the Snakes are near here, and there's a little waterfall that spits mist. It'll keep the bugs away."

She swings away along the branches. We're at least thirty or forty feet above the ground. There's no way I could keep up with her without the wind. Many times I slip or lose my balance and have to use a gust to make my body hit a branch instead of falling through a gap and tumbling and crashing to the ground. The effort is exhausting.

She stops by a clearing, where mist sprays over me and forms minuscule beads on my skin. The thin waterfall begins so high on the cliff above that almost all the water evaporates before it lands. And the landing is not ground, but the sea. It feels like we've reached the edge of the jungle.

"What's past here?" I ask.

"Only sea," Violet says. "At the cliff above, the river that feeds this waterfall separates Green and Red lands. It runs through a steep canyon, with cliffs rising to Red mountains and dense forest on our side."

"So we could enter straight into Red's land?" I ask.

"I don't know. Why would we ever want to do that?" She points toward the waterfall. "See that cave?"

There's a dark opening at the rocky base of the waterfall, with ferns and other thick-leafed plants surrounding it, licking up the mist.

"It's perfect for Snakes," Violet says.

"How do they get down here from the cliff?"

She shrugs. "They're Snakes. Lots of secrets."

"So we're supposed to catch one?"

"Or more. But first you need to learn to hide."

# 14

SITTING BESIDE ME, high in the tree, Violet explains each step in detail. First she gets her breathing under control. Then she studies her surroundings—every branch and leaf, every shadow and movement. The important thing is the light, she says, the way it shines. All attention must be drawn to it, just as it is to the air when I weave it. Last, keeping her body perfectly still, she remembers something joyous from her life before.

"A time when you felt truly content," she says. "If the feeling is strong, you can move while you are invisible, and even make others disappear by touching them. Watch this. And don't move."

She goes through each step, breathing, looking carefully around her. Her gaze becomes distant and her face serene. It takes only a few seconds. And then, in a blink, she vanishes.

Something soft touches my arm. Her hand. Staying still, I look down at the spot. I can't see my own body. I quickly raise my arm, lifting Violet's with it. The motion instantly makes us appear again.

"Now you try," she says.

I do everything exactly as she said. It's not so different than weaving the air. My focus is complete. My breathing steady. But there's a problem.

"I'm sorry, I can't do it," I say. "I don't remember feeling content."

"You're overthinking it," Violet says. "It doesn't have to be anything special. You don't have to have everything together. It's just a sense of peace inside. I usually think of a time when I was a young girl, about the same age as I look now, kneeling in a cathedral, with the smell of incense, and all the light and the beauty were more than I could hold. It was just a little moment of quiet amidst the storm of the world." She pauses, studying me. "Can't you remember anything like that?"

"I'll try to think of something."

And I do try. For the entire rest of day. I go over and over the distant memories that the fruit revealed to me. I go over the most recent memory of visiting Susan's family estate in the mountains. In every vision of the past I'm wanting something. More money, more strength, more fame, more appreciation, more…everything. Dr. Fitzroy was not a content man.

As darkness falls, the heat relents and the insect chorus rises. Their chirping and squealing never quite settles into a steady rhythm, keeping me on edge. Violet volunteers to take first watch. I wedge between two thick branches and sleep. In my dreams snakes race across the jungle floor, chasing small animals, biting and coiling around them before swallowing them whole.

It's light when I wake up. Violet sits hunched over with her back to me. I yawn and mumble, "You were supposed to give me a turn."

"You needed the sleep." She turns to me and holds out a folded leaf filled with fresh figs. "I picked these from the next tree over. Eat up."

"Thanks. You want me to watch now?"

She blinks. "Yes, I might sleep a bit. Stay alert. Snakes can climb trees."

The figs are delicious, filling my empty stomach. Violet dozes on and off throughout the day. The waterfall sprays mist. The birds and bugs swoop and sing.

It is growing dark again when I spot a boy beneath us. He crouches, then moves silently, then crouches. He has wild brown hair and a bow and quiver strapped to his back. The mark on his hand looks like a lion. His head swivels side to side. He hasn't glanced up, yet.

I gently nudge Violet. "Look," I whisper.

She sits upright, immediately alert. She spots the boy and puts her hand over mine. "Don't move," she whispers.

Her face concentrates. Then disappears.

The boy moves forward again. He looks up, straight at us, then looks down and continues ahead. Violet lifts her hand and lets out a soft breath.

When the boy comes closer to the water's edge, he drops to the ground and crawls. He stops by the waterfall, behind a huge boulder. He studies the cave opening for a long time. He has a better angle to see inside than we do.

He stays there until it's so dark we can't see him.

"What's he doing?" I whisper.

"Hunting Snakes." Violet's voice is so soft I can barely hear it over the bugs.

"How did he get a bow and arrows?"

"There are a few in the forest after every Jubilee. Wolves and Lions take them. Quiet now," Violet whispers. "There's probably more coming."

Neither of us sleeps. The night passes without any interruption of the chirping.

In the morning, the same boy returns—though we'd never seen him leave—and this time he's not alone. A pack of six kids sprints below us and charges straight into the cave, wielding staffs.

We hear a sharp, piercing scream from inside the cave, followed by more shouts that make the bugs fall silent. Moments later a boy emerges from the cave dragging a motionless body with a collar around its neck. Then more come, some walking, some limping. They return our way, on track to pass right underneath us.

"Wait, be ready," Violet whispers.

The first boy, the one with the bow, approaches below us. He's looking back at the others rushing toward him.

"Here!" he shouts. "Over here!"

A fair-haired boy veers toward our tree and the boy who shouted. He hauls someone with him, holding the person under the shoulders and letting feet drag behind. When he reaches the boy under our tree, he drops the body and bends over, leaning on his knees and breathing so heavily we can hear it above.

"That's…one Snake!" he pants.

"And the others?" asks the boy with the bow.

"I think we got seven. Lost one…into the deeps. Can't go there."

"Hey, seven for one! I'll go back to help."

"Thanks," the fair-haired boy says, standing up straight again. "I'll wait with this one…catch my breath."

The boy with the bow turns and lopes off toward the cave again. Under our tree, the captured boy wears a collar around his neck and has a sinuous snake symbol on his hand. The other boy crouches with his hand by his side, showing a lion.

"Now," Violet whispers, pointing down. "Those two."

"How?" I ask.

"Your wind. Do it silently."

I should be able to do it, but it's a lot of power at once. It would be like when I saved Marcus and Seymour from going over the waterfall in Red. That took everything I had. It knocked me out. And this time it would leave us with two bodies stuck in the top of tree.

"If I get them, then what?" I ask.

She lifts the collar, which still hangs by her side. "Just get them up here."

I nod and summon the wind and weave it into two shapes: a huge net and a ball the size of an apple to gag them. Taking a deep breath, I quickly stuff the gag into their mouths. They twist and shake wildly but don't make a sound. I wrap the net tightly around them and lift, lift, lift.

It takes a massive burst of energy to get them off the ground. They rise but bump against a thick branch.

The power slips.

My hand grabs instinctively for Violet's. Through our touch I pull on her energy, weaving thin threads of green into blue.

It's enough. The boys rise faster, momentum helping me. I move them up, shifting left and right of branches, until they reach our makeshift nest at the top.

My head spins, but I cling to enough power to keep the boys quiet and still. They look at me with wild, terrified eyes. Violet lunges forward and snaps a collar around the Lion's neck. He suddenly goes rigid, sitting up straight and attentive to Violet.

"You can let go," Violet says to me.

"You sure?"

She nods. I release her hand, then the power, bit by bit.

The boys hold their position, and their silence. Still my head spins violently from the effort. I take deep breaths, trying to pump oxygen into my brain.

"Follow me," Violet says to the three of us, then swings away through the trees.

# 15

IT TAKES THE whole night to get back to the cliff, and the whole morning to climb back up to the nest. The two captives do whatever Violet tells them. They don't look happy about it, but they don't seem to have any choice. I'm not sure how much choice I have, either, if I want to make it back to the Eagles' nest. At least Violet listens to me when I ask for a few rests. She doesn't let the boys talk.

When we reach the ledge that leads into the nest, Jade greets us and appraises our catch with bright green eyes. "Nice work. Two on your first hunt."

"It was Cipher," Violet says.

"And Violet," I add. "She kept us hidden."

"You make a good team." Jade studies me. "But you'll have to go out on your own next time."

"Why?" I ask.

"We've lost sixteen since you left."

"Sixteen!" Violet says. "What happened?"

"The Wolves attacked. We fought them off, but many of ours were collared and taken. One fell out of the nest during the fight. Another four went hunting and haven't come back."

"They still might," Violet says. "We did."

"Aye, but not all know their way around the forest like you." Jade motions for us to follow her. "Let's get you some food."

Jade leads us into the main room, where the same red-haired boy from before sits beside a small fire. It smells like roasted meat. She tells the boy to take the servants away. Our captives follow him out of the room with their heads bowed.

"What's cooking?" Violet asks.

"You're in luck," Jade says. "Stephen killed a snake."

Stephen returns with a proud smile on his freckled face. "Twenty foot python," he says. "We hauled it up here with vines. Should feed all of us for a couple days."

We sit around the fire. My stomach revolts when I'm handed a piece of snake meat. The long round body lays half uneaten outside the fire. Something about a creature without legs makes my gut do cartwheels. But I close my eyes and try a bite, imagining it's chicken. In the battle between hunger and taste, hunger wins.

Jade explains that the Wolves have taken control of the forest above again. There haven't been many reports from the jungle, but based on what we saw, the Lions wiped out most of the Snakes. Again the tribal battle is down to Wolves against Lions, with a few Eagles and Snakes trying to survive. Most of the fighting centers around the only real path down from the cliff. It is near the largest waterfall. Other than that path, climbing down on vines and rock is the only way. Jade says the Wolves will have to go to the jungle eventually. Food always runs out first in the forest above.

"Want me to scout the forest again?" Violet asks Jade.

The leader shakes her head. "This attack was different. The Wolves came with full force, like they were searching for something or—" she glances at me—"someone. We can't just stay in this cave. We might hold off another attack, but I won't have us starve in here again. We're going to fly out on our own."

"That's suicide," Violet says. "No one can survive alone out there."

"Not alone." Jade looks to where the collared captives were led away. "We have four servants. Each of us will take one. We'll hunt from the trees. If we get some numbers back, we can always return here."

"Unless another tribe moves in."

"Why would they?" Jade asks. "There's no food. You know how the Wolves and Lions like to roam, and there aren't enough Snakes to worry about."

Violet sighs. "You're the leader. When do we leave?"

"Tomorrow at first light. And check back in five days."

"Very well," Violet says. "Pass the snake."

As we eat, Jade says it's important for each of us to tell the others about our pasts. That way, if one of us doesn't survive and gets wiped before the Jubilee, we can help that person remember. Violet, Jade, and Stephen give only brief stories of their pasts, as they seem to know each other well already. Violet was a Roman servant, as she'd told me before. Stephen was a European monk in the Middle Ages. Jade was an American judge in the 1900s. When I tell them the basics about my past—an American neurosurgeon who somehow died and woke up in the Blue Tower—Jade tells me that she lived in Chicago, too. We try to find some connection, some way our paths might have crossed on Earth, but we don't. Maybe it's just coincidence.

With our stories and meal finished, Jade leads us to the servants deeper in the cave. They are held in a makeshift prison of thick branches wedged between the cave ceiling and floor. Behind the bars are three boys and one girl. Each one wears a silver collar around the neck.

"Why the bars?" I ask. "Don't they have to obey when they wear those?"

"Aye," Jade says, "but better to take every precaution. Orders can be circumvented. You must give your commands clearly."

"I've had a servant before," I say.

"Good, because you get last pick this time." Jade turns to the servants. "Some are easier to command than others. Violet, which one do you want?"

"Him," Violet says, pointing to the fair-haired Lion that we caught.

"And you, Stephen?" Jade asks.

"Him." Stephen points to the Snake we caught.

"Very well," Jade says. "I'll take the Wolf girl. That leaves the other Lion boy for you, Cipher."

The one she points to keeps his head down.

"What's his name?" I ask.

The boy looks up. His skin is pale and his cheeks are paunchy. Not what I'd expect from a lion.

"Doesn't matter," he says.

"Nice name."

"Come out, Polo," Jade says to him, pulling away the branches that barred them in.

He moves reluctantly, but does as she says. He kneels at her command. With a look of concentration, she reaches behind his neck and releases the clasp. She hands the slender metal device over to me cautiously, like it could bite.

"Put it on him," she says.

I place the collar around the boy's neck. It snaps shut.

His feelings suddenly rush into me. And he feels…dangerous.

# 16

WE SPEND THE evening in the nest, readying to head out the next morning. I use the short time before sleeping to learn what I can from my new servant, Polo. I command him to tell me everything he knows about the Lions. He says their tribe has set up a base on the far side of the jungle. It's more than a day's journey away. It has wooden stakes for a defensive wall. The leader is Hank. He sends out hunters in pairs, and he gives them a lot of discretion. They spend their days out in the jungle, setting traps and catching whatever food they can. The traps are everywhere, from hidden pits on the jungle floor to rope triggers high in the trees. Polo says he knows how to spot them.

Clouds cover the sky in the morning. Jade, Violet, Stephen, and I say somber goodbyes and wish each other luck. Jade and Stephen and their servants go up, toward Wolf territory.

Violet goes down, toward the jungle and the Snakes. As she leaves, she tells me to keep searching for a content memory. "I know you'll find one," she says. "See you back here in five days."

Polo and I are the last to go, climbing down the vines and the cliff and then heading toward the Lions. I figure if I make it to Hank, he'll help me out—no matter what tribe I'm in. And Polo, dangerous as he might be, at least knows his way around the jungle.

*Lead us to the Lions' base*, I command him. *Stay in the trees, stay alert, and avoid any and all danger. Warn me immediately if you see a threat.*

He grumbles but does as I say. The one thing I can't command is his feelings. They continue to pour through the link, in waves of anger, frustration, and contempt. But we make steady progress all the same, advancing through the canopy branch by branch. After an hour or so, the constant cloud of humid heat and buzzing insects drags on us like iron weights. I summon a stream of air to cool us and keep the bugs at bay. It tires me, but it's worth it.

When it grows dark, Polo asks if we can stop. "Not safe at night," he says. "Can't see the traps."

So we stop. I order Polo to keep watch and wake me if anything comes. Maybe it's wrong to make my servant stay awake after such a taxing day. But this isn't like the last time I had servant—with Emma in the Blue Tower. I don't have safe, comfortable quarters. I don't have a steady supply of food. If I'm going to survive to see Emma again in the Jubilee, I'm going to have to use my servant.

Sleep comes easier than I would expect while hiding in a tree with other tribes roaming the jungle below. Maybe it's the chirping bugs that lull me to sleep, or just the exhaustion. In my dream I stand beside Marcus, my friend from the Red Tower, facing snarling lions in an arena, with no armor or weapon. I wake up before the lions charge.

It's still night. Polo sits in the tree beneath me. The faint light reveals dark circles ringing his eyes. Through the link, he feels overwhelmingly tired. I give him permission to sleep. After a few twists and turns, he settles in against the trunk and dozes off. I listen to the bugs.

After a while the birds start to awaken. The slivers of sky showing through the leaves become gray. My stomach rumbles. I take out the leftover snake and force down a few swallows.

Polo stirs and spots the food. "Can I have some?"

I shake my head and put the rest away. "Show me how to get more."

He scowls. "Flora or fauna?"

"Which one's easier to get?"

"Take my collar off and I'll get you however much you want."

"We can't eat the collar."

"Ah, but we can trade it," he says. "I was a merchant, on Earth. I traveled the world, from Italy to China and back. I brought many treasures with me. Gemstones the size of my fist." He holds up his clenched hand. His eyes have a hungry look to them.

"We can't eat gems, either," I say.

"If what you have is rare, you can buy anything you want." He rubs his fingers along the metal link at his neck. "These are most rare and valuable here. I once traded one for a whole hog."

"Sorry, it's not for sale. I'll take any food you can get. Now show me what's easiest to find."

Polo motions for me to follow. He scrambles halfway down the tree and pulls back a dense fold of green leaves, revealing a small nest with four round eggs. "Breakfast," he says.

I eat three eggs, raw, and let him have one.

"It doesn't seem so hard," I say. "Why is everyone so concerned about food?"

"We have many days before the Jubilee. There is food in the beginning, but about halfway through, the food runs out."

"What happens to it?"

"It is eaten," he says. "No eggs, no fruit, no animals remain. Nothing new comes. Only predators."

"Why does this happen?"

Polo shrugs. "It's the Green Tower. You learn to survive."

"I see." Nothing like putting us in the wilderness without enough food to make us fight. Even the Red Tower was more civilized than this.

We press on. Swinging and jumping, branch to branch, we make our way through the canopy. There's no sign of another person. Only the birds and an occasional monkey keep us company. After a few hours we reach a fig tree. I stop to fill my bag with them.

"Can we rest here a while?" Polo asks. "We're close to the Lions' base."

"How close?"

"Less than half a day at this pace."

"Just gather what we can carry. I want to set eyes on the base before we stop."

He rolls his eyes but does as I say. He doesn't have a choice. We both fill our bags to the brim with figs. The load slows our pace, but it's worth it. I could survive a few days just on the figs we've collected.

After another hour of moving through the trees we reach a stream. It's so narrow, and the canopy so thick, that we could cross the water without setting foot on the ground. Polo tells me that if we follow the stream uphill, we'll reach the base. "The water's fresh and cool," he says. "A good place to camp."

He looks and sounds innocent, but there's something new in his feelings—a subtle excitement, like a gentle boil, that makes me worried. But I am thirsty. The figs leave a sticky residue in my parched mouth. And our waterskins have gone empty.

"You climb down," I say. "Refill our water, then hurry back."

This time Polo doesn't grumble. He smiles, takes my waterskin, and happily slips down out of the tree. He moves in a low crouch, very quietly, toward the bank of the small stream. As he kneels down by the water, I try to watch everywhere around us at once.

There's no motion. No sudden attack.

As Polo drinks, the feeling through the link is pure delight. Maybe it would be nice to have firm ground underfoot and fresh, cool water running down my throat.

I climb silently down the tree and join him. Still no one is in sight. The birds and bugs chirp noisily. They would go quiet if a threat was near. But all is normal. The ground feels assuring after a day and a night spent in the trees.

Polo finishes drinking. I command him to keep an eye out, then dip my hand into the water. It's crystal clear and flowing steadily. It makes me miss Blue, where we had more water that I could ever want. I lift a handful to my lips and drink it down. Then another and another, until my belly is full. Polo waits for me, leaning content against a tree as he watches the jungle around us.

We move away from the creek together. The tree that we dropped from doesn't have low branches. Polo points to a large banyan tree fifty feet ahead.

"Let's climb that one," he says.

It's not far, and it will be much easier to climb. I agree and we head toward it together. The soft, decaying ground thuds with each footstep.

Until one thud gives.

The whole jungle floor seems to give. There's nothing to grab as I fall and land with a crash. I spit dirt from my mouth. My ankle groans as I try to stand. The same ankle I hurt last time. The one that had healed. But it's the noise that holds my attention.

Laughter.

Above I see Polo's face gazing down at me. He's cackling like a giddy toddler. He *feels* triumphant. The hole is twenty feet deep. The walls are steep. Too steep to climb.

He led me straight into a trap.

# 17

POLO STILL WEARS the link around his neck. He's still the servant. I'm still the master, even if I'm at the bottom of a twenty-foot deep pit. As long as no one finds us, this should not be a problem. Polo must help me. I order him: *Do whatever you can to get me out of here as soon as you can. And don't let anyone see you.*

His triumphant feeling becomes anger again, but with lingering traces of amusement. His face disappears from view, leaving me alone.

I can't shout for help. I can't climb out, especially not with my hurt ankle. So I sit and eat a fig. It's dark and warm, and the jungle bugs leave me alone. I have nothing to do but wait, so I focus on Violet's advice. There were so many bad decisions in Dr. Fitzroy's life. Were there any good ones? What joyful, content moment can I remember to make myself disappear the same way Violet does? Nothing comes to me.

There's a flash of emotion through the link. It feels...triumphant.

*Tell me what happened,* I command Polo.

But I immediately realize he can't answer. It's not like talking to Emma through the stars. I can give commands through the collar, but he cannot talk back to me.

*Do nothing but help me!* I command again. *Come back now!*

This command sets his feelings aflame. But only for an instant. It's a flash of anger like lightning, and yet when it's gone the same sense of secret triumph remains. I start to worry. I should have been more specific with my commands.

The sound of laughter makes me rush to me feet. A moment later five faces are looking down at me. It's Polo and four other boys. They're smiling, positively gleeful.

"Throw him the rope!" one of them says.

Moments later a vine drops into the pit. The end lands by my feet. I stare down at it like it's a snake.

"Come on!" a boy says. "Grab it!"

It's a logical command. Grab the rope and get dragged out of the pit. Who wants to stay in a pit? Maybe someone who expects to be killed or, maybe worse, collared once he's out.

"What then?" I shout up.

"We'll barbecue you!" a boy shouts back.

"Look at him," another says. "He believes it!"

The five of them burst into laughter. It should make me angry. But instead I feel what Polo feels, and there's something good in it—camaraderie with these boys.

I grab the rope. They all have to pull together to drag me out. Once I crest the edge, I brush myself off and calmly face them. They have me surrounded, and each one wields a long staff. Two of them have bows at their backs. Running won't work. But a blast of wind might. They might be ready for that. Polo could have warned them.

*Be still, silent, and ready to defend me*, I command Polo. His teeth clench. His hands curl into fists.

"Who are you?" I ask the boys.

One of them steps toward me. He's a head taller than I am, with wild brown hair, stern eyes, and a bow across his back. A gentle wind blows through the trees and ruffles his hair. I recognize him as the boy who led the attack against the Snakes, but this close, I also remember that he was with Baron when he collared Lily and me. Now, as the boy crosses his arms, I see a lion, not a wolf, on his hands.

"I'm Fugger," he says. The other boys snicker behind him when he says his name, but he ignores them. "You're in Lion territory."

"I'm Cipher. I know your leader, Hank. He will want to see me."

"I don't report to Hank," Fugger says.

"Baron?" I ask.

Fugger spits. "Didn't pick me this time, so I'm my own boss." He looks to Polo. "Take off his collar."

"And then what?" I ask.

Fugger shrugs. "We'll let Polo decide. He brought you here."

The feeling from the link is pure, greedy excitement. Polo will turn and snap the collar right around my neck. I'm not going to let that happen.

*Attack them*, I order.

Then I summon the air. In an instant a gale force wind blasts the boys back, just as Polo leaps at them, punching and kicking. Sticks and leaves whip through the air. I run away as fast as I can, hobbling on my ankle but with wind at my back. All I have to do is get up into the trees. There, with the wind, they'll have no chance of taking me down.

I charge for the closest tree I can climb. Glancing back, I see three boys running after me, but they won't reach me in time. I start to scramble up the branches, but something hits me.

Pain. Falling.

My face plants into the wet jungle ground. My leg screams. I grab at my thigh, where an arrow protrudes and blood gushes down my bare skin.

A shadow moves over me. It's Fugger, with a bow raised and an arrow notched. How did he move so fast? Through the pain and the dim light, I make out a snarl on his face. This time the arrow is only a foot away from my throat.

"Take off the link," he demands.

Two boys hurry to my side, holding Polo as he twists and fights to get free, to attack them. A third boy joins and together they force Polo's head forward, bowing over me.

"Now," Fugger says, "or I'll shoot."

I don't doubt him.

But I still have the wind. I reach for it, but my vision blurs as my leg throbs in pain. The threads slip away.

"Now!" The arrow is still pointed at my throat.

The boys shove Polo's head closer. There's a bloody

scratch on his cheek, sweat on his forehead. I reach hesitantly behind his neck, prodding the link. I close my eyes and take a deep breath, focusing on the seal within the silver metal. I funnel a tendril of air and blow into the spot, pressing my fingers hard against it at the same time.

The collar snaps open and falls to the ground. Polo jumps up with his arms raised and lets out a triumphant shout.

"Goodbye, Eagle," Fugger says, then he fires the arrow.

# 18

AN OLD MAN with a long beard and bushy eyebrows sits cross-legged in front of me on the wooden floor. I sit up and rub my bare arms, as if feeling them for the first time. I wear soft brown shorts and a vest. The old man wears a dark, velvet green robe. A gnarled staff lies beside him. Behind him and around us, everything is green and alive. Leaves blow gently in the wind.

"You've had a tough start," he says.

"Who are you?" I ask, surprised by the young sound of my voice. "Where am I?"

He holds out a bright red fruit. It looks like a little heart resting on his wrinkled palm. "A friend earned this for you. Take and eat and know."

I am confused, but he sounds gentle and friendly. He moves the fruit closer. The smell is sweet, irresistible. I take it and lift it to my lips.

The moment the first drop of juice goes down my throat, my hands go to my neck. The boy. Fugger. He shot me with an arrow. *He killed me.* The pain only lasted a few moments, but it was so bad that the memory of it makes me retch.

"Sorry, Cipher," the old man says, patting my shoulder softly. "You're okay now."

My breathing steadies, and I fight my way out of the memory. My neck has no wound or scar. There is no real pain. It's only a memory. And from that memory extend other paths into the past, through the Red Tower and back to the Blue Tower, through the Scouring and back to my mother and to Emma. Each path is like tracks through freshly fallen snow, showing how I got to this moment. The path from the world before is darker, frightening. My name was Paul Fitzroy there. I died on Earth, somehow, and the last thing I knew, I died here. Emma probably earned the fruit again. She's done that before, I remember. I remember it all.

My body looks just as I did when I woke up beneath the Blue Tower, except now there are scars on the backs of my hands. One from the Blue Tower. One from my mother, before she left the Red Tower and went up through White.

My fingers run slowly over the scars. "Why are these still here?"

"They point to the future," Daniel says. "Not your past."

"What future?"

Daniel laughs softly. "Not even I can tell you that. In our present state we cannot grasp the fullness of time. But know that all of this, and all of the earthly past, will be rolled up into forever. No drop of what has happened will be lost or wasted. Even the agony will turn to glory."

"Why does it have to hurt so much?"

"Because the world had that much darkness."

My memories leave no doubt about that, but his words make me pause. "*Had?* Isn't the world still there?"

"Perhaps…" Daniel's fingers graze idly over the bumps of his gnarled staff. "I have seen signs of darkness here. The end approaches."

He said something like this before. "The end of what?"

"Of time's domain," Daniel says solemnly. "In its fullness, time will stop passing in moments and exist only as the present."

I shake my head, not understanding and not comforted by his cryptic words. "I just want out of here."

"You can't earn your way, no more than you earned those scars." His penetrating eyes look down at my hands. "You've been told this is a process, and so it is. You are being scoured. There are stains left to be cleansed."

"So why can't I go back to the Scouring? Don't you want Green's numbers to rise?"

"In time…but you are not ready."

"Don't you know what I did in Blue and Red?"

"Yes…" He points at my chest. "And I know what was done *inside* you. The towers each have their own rules and purposes. Here the leader of the tribes chooses who enters the Scouring. There is no other way."

"Why…?" My hand goes to my throat again, where the arrow struck. "You want to make us fight? To kill each other? It's wrong!"

He remains calm. "No one makes you fight."

"You put us in tribes. You give weapons!"

"Bows are useful for hunting food, are they not?" He sighs. "Giving sets you free. I do not hide this truth, yet it is a hard truth to swallow. Those who have long thirsted for more and more are difficult to quench. Tell me, Cipher, have you learned to use Green's power yet?"

"To go invisible?"

He nods. "That is one way to describe it."

I remember Violet. She told me to think of a joyous memory and nothing came. My head falls to my chest. "No, I can't think of a content memory."

He squeezes my shoulder, drawing my eyes up to meet his. "There is more good in your past than you know."

"Then why haven't I seen it?"

"You draw closer," he says. "For one as stained as you, you must look through the lens of more colors to see more light. Green is your third. Light should begin to appear."

Light. I remember my mother going up through the dazzling column of light, the White Tower. "Is that what it takes to leave here?"

"For some, yes. Others require only one or two more facets of the prism."

"You mean Genius, Passion, Healer, Provider, and...?"

"Black's facet is not for me to reveal." He suddenly sounds more like the other leaders—Abram, Sarai, and Rahab—full of mystery. Except he gives the fruit that reveals the past...

"Why does Green give memories back so easily?" I ask.

"The Provider gives as each person needs. You have always needed much and thirsted for more. But you have always been capable of much."

His words, though said softly, sting like an accusation. "Rahab told me my power came from not living up to my potential, on Earth."

"This is true. As I said, however, the light from your past may soon begin to shine through the stains."

"I hope so."

He smiles. "Yes, always hope. A great tree may die and fall to the ground, but as it decays, new life will grow." He taps the scar on one of my hands. "Death has been defeated here. You believe that now, hmm?"

"Maybe, but…" The thought of death reminds me of the pit full of bones beneath the Scouring. It was so dark there. It felt like death. "What about the pit?"

His brow suddenly furrows in anger. "Do not speak of this! Rahab should never have let you go."

"What do you mean? I made it through…"

"A great mercy!" Daniel snaps. "Never test the Colorless One! Never visit the pit! It could bring a fate *worse* than death."

"But—"

"No!" He holds out his hand and my mouth instantly shuts, sealed tight. "I've told you there are signs of darkness. The leaders are attending to this. I will speak no more of it, and you will *not* ask again." His voice is steel, but his eyes soften as he slowly lowers his hand to his lap.

My mouth gapes open, shocked. What are the leaders

attending to? The pit? *The Colorless One?*

Daniel sighs. "I am sorry. I am afraid you will learn more about this. But you are not ready yet. The point I was making was one of hope. You cannot die here, hm?"

I choose my words carefully, still shaken by Daniel's reaction. "Not for long?"

"Precisely. It is not permanent. It is a cycle of *life.*"

"But if it's a cycle, how will it end? You said before that millions could come—wiped and remembering and dying and starting again."

"That has long been true. Now it is not so clear. If the world has truly ended…well, no need to guess about such things. Each day has enough trouble of its own, eh? It will remain so until the way finds you."

"What way?"

He smiles. "What's the best thing you can imagine?"

He asked me this before, when he came to the Blue Tower and talked with Abram and me. "Last time I told you it was a place full of love."

"Yes, still true. That is part of it."

"So how do I get there?"

"That, my friend, is the wrong question. You bear the scars. Find the others like you and, together, ask, *how did we get here?* If you learn that, the way will be close."

There's only one other person I've seen with a scar like mine. "You want me to talk to Baron?"

Daniel nods. "This will be far more difficult than you think, painful even, but it is…necessary. Now, it's time to join the others. The Jubilee begins."

He doesn't wait for me to reply. He simply vanishes, as he has before. I stand, feeling as confused as ever about these towers, and wanting more than ever to talk with Emma. If anyone can help me make sense of this, it's her. We went through the pit together…

I follow the sound of a crowd, which leads me down a series of branches and ladders until I come to the vast platform at the center of the Green Tower. Dozens of dirty, gaunt shapes are gathering and feasting. Everyone will be here, even Baron and the boy who killed me.

# 19

SCANNING THE CROWD, I spot Fugger across the platform. He's with Polo and the other boys who attacked me. Seeing them makes my blood boil, but I avoid them. Daniel and the Hunter won't let us fight here, and they are only a distraction from what matters.

A familiar face rushes toward me: Hank. He sweeps me into a bear hug, like usual. His body does not feel as thick or as strong as I remember.

"Cipher!" he says. "You remember, right?"

I nod. "Daniel gave me the fruit again."

"Oh man. Must have gone bad out there. I looked for you and asked around about a boy using the wind, but there was no sign of you. What happened?"

"A boy in your tribe killed me."

"Who?" Anger fills Hank's voice.

I glance toward the group of boys across the platform. "His name was Fugger."

Hank grimaces. "Jakob Fugger…"

"You know him?"

"He was the Lions leader before me. He was a very rich

man on Earth. He's ruthless, but talented. I picked him last time for the Lions thinking he'd help us win. It was a terrible decision. Right from the start he set up his own rival Lion tribe. They captured a bunch of Snakes, then claimed part of the jungle and did whatever they wanted. One night they snuck into my camp and stole my collars. I think he traded them to Baron for food. I was left with only two Lions by my side at the end. We lost the few we captured. Things were rough, but hey, we made it. How'd he get you?"

"It's a long story," I say. "Let's get some food and I'll tell you."

Hank bobs his head in agreement and walks with me to the nearest table. We fill our plates from the feast. My body feels completely empty, which it must be, since I apparently slept or didn't exist or whatever from the time I was killed until the Jubilee—many, many days.

I tell Hank about the Eagles and how we left the nest with a servant each. When I tell him Polo was mine, Hank's fists clench.

"He'd trade his own mother for a buck," he says.

"Is his mother here?" I ask.

Hank laughs. "No, just a saying from my time."

Violet and Jade spot me and approach with smiles. They have tears in their clothes and cuts and scrapes over their limbs, but otherwise look about the same as when we last saw each other.

"You're here! You weren't wiped!" Violet says. "Jade and I made it back to the nest and hoped you and Stephen would come. I even went out searching, but there was no sign. What happened?”

I recount the saga about how Polo led me into a trap and Fugger shot me with an arrow. The last part still makes me wince.

“Sorry to hear that,” Violet says. “But hey, at least you’re not waking up blank slate with a new tribe. Daniel must have given you the fruit.”

“Yeah, he said a friend earned it for me.”

“A high honor,” Jade says.

“It must have been Emma…” Hank shakes his head in disappointment. “She was my first pick for the Lions, but Baron chose her for the Scouring.”

“It is his right as the tribal winner,” Jade adds. “He chooses all twelve, and he can pick anyone except the other tribes’ leaders. He usually sends the strongest from the other tribes into the Scouring. It’s one of the reasons why he always wins.”

“All roads go through Baron,” Hank mutters. “Anyway, Emma must have caught someone from another tower. That’s the only way Daniel would let her pick who to give the fruit to.”

“You’re lucky,” Violet says to me. “Now that you remember, you can improve.”

“Aye, you made a fine Eagle,” Jade says. “We will do better next time.”

“Not just better,” I say. “We will beat Baron.” As I look from Jade to Violet to Hank, and remember Daniel’s words, I suddenly have an idea. “Why don’t we agree to work together, no matter what tribe we're in?"

"Fine by me," Hank says. "We're all gonna be starving in the woods as long as Baron's in control." He smiles at me. "And we need to get you back in the Scouring."

Jade studies Hank warily. "The Lions have stolen many of my Eagles."

Hank puts his hand over his heart. "I swear. If I'm the leader, we won't collar a single one of you."

"Violet, what do you say?" Jade asks.

"If Cipher believes him…" Violet looks to me.

"You can trust Hank," I say. "We have to try it. We have to shift the balance against Baron."

"So we fight Wolves, but not Lions…" Jade crosses her arms, as if considering it. "You think you'll be a leader?"

"Even if I'm not, I'll fight with you and Cipher." Hank holds out his hand to Jade. "You agree to do the same?"

She stares down at his hand, then slowly extends hers and they shake. "It is agreed."

Violet joins the pact and, as the light fades, we feast together and make plans. We decide to split up when we leave the tree, so Baron won't have a single target, but then to find each other in the forest and combine to attack the Wolves. As long as two of them are tribe leaders, we'll outnumber him.

Later in the evening, Baron passes us with his entourage. There are least twenty boys and girls trailing behind him like he's some kind of king. They all have wolf marks on their hands. Baron still has a criss-cross scar like mine on his right hand.

Heeding Daniel's advice, I quiet my anger and follow after him. I wade through his group and tap his shoulder. "Hey, Baron."

He stops and stares at me with his granite eyes. "I saw you with Eagles and Lions. Think you're strong enough to be a Wolf now?"

A few laughs ripple through the group surrounding us. I ignore them. They can't do anything to me here. And I know more than Baron thinks. He wanted to pick me last time. "It's not about that," I say. "I was hoping we could talk alone."

Baron grins as he glances around his group. "No secrets here."

"It's about the scar on your hand."

His grin retreats. The granite stare returns. "A hunting accident. Nothing to talk about."

I hold out my hands, with the two scars facing up to him. "Mine aren't from hunting."

Baron glances back at his entourage. "Probably snake bites," he says. "Only an Eagle would let a Snake hurt it." As they laugh, he turns back to me. "Fly away, Eagle."

He walks off with the group following on his heels. Whatever he's hiding, I will find a way to make him talk.

When I return to our group, Hank asks me, "Spying on the enemy?"

"Just trying to figure out why I have these scars," I say.

Hank shrugs. "Can't help you there."

All other wounds and hurts go away, but not the scars. *They point to the future*, Daniel said. If only I had some clue about what I was supposed to do about it, and how a tyrant like Baron factors in.

When darkness falls and the glowing fairies fill the air, Daniel comes to the Jubilee as he did before. He walks slowly down the wide stairs, disappears and reappears a moment later just above us, with his staff lifted high. "Welcome to the Jubilee!"

He calls forward the Scouring tribe, which emerges from the canopy, descends the stairs, and stops before us. There are thirteen of them, and in the center, with her head held high, is Emma.

Daniel holds his staff out over the group. "You have fought well for Green," he says. "No one has been lost, and one has been captured from Black. This brings us to ninety-three."

As before, Daniel releases the Scouring tribe into the crowd and announces that it is time to name the new leaders. Baron strides up the stairs and stands by Daniel's side, composed and confident. As he lifts his hands in victory, his tribe howls among the crowd.

"The Wolves captured twelve," Daniel says, quieting the crowd and looking to Baron. "And you lost five—one to the Lions, and four to starvation. Is there anything you would like to say for yourself?"

"It's better to join me than fight me," Baron says.

"Is that all?" Daniel asks.

Baron nods, and a moment of awkward silence passes between them, with the crowd watching on.

"Very well," Daniel says. "Next is Fugger, who caught

seven, then Jade and Violet who…” Daniel continues to speak, but the words hardly register. My thoughts race as I watch the leaders move to join Daniel and Baron on the stairs. Hank will not lead the Lions. Fugger will. But if Jade and Violet pick their tribes well and we work together, we can still stop Fugger and Baron.

“…and drink deep of the Provider’s bounty,” Daniel’s words fade as everyone rushes toward the trough of amber liquid. Even Hank, who stood beside me, draws forward without saying a word, as if unable to resist the sap. I also feel the tug, remembering the enticing bittersweet taste, but then I see Emma. She approaches me through the crowd, smiling, and we embrace.

“I had the fruit again,” I say. “Thank you.”

“I am glad I could help.”

“How was the Scouring?”

“Quite hard,” Emma says. “We had to enter it several times. Black and Red and Blue remain very powerful. Yellow stays close to their gate, entirely defensive. We had to be cautious.”

“But you got one from Black?”

A corner of Emma’s mouth turns up. “Some here can go invisible. We snuck up, and I caught her with fire.”

“Impressive. I wish I could have been with you.”

“Me too. We would have caught many more.” Emma hesitates. “But you were in the forest. Did you see Oliver?”

“No. I didn’t survive very long…”

“Oh dear,” Emma says. “I worried about that. I searched for you through the stars, but I could not find you. Was it bad?"

"An arrow to the throat." I grin like it was no big deal. "I'm okay now, thanks to you."

"This place has its perks," she says, grinning back. "Maybe we will finally get to be together, in the same tribe this time."

"The leaders get to choose," I say. "But only the first leader chooses who goes to the Scouring. I think it's been the same boy, Baron, for a long time. He's the one who sent you to the Scouring. I have to find a way past him so we can work together again. We can't leave it to chance. I heard some troubling things from Daniel."

Her blue eyes widen. "What?"

"It was about the pit. He said—"

My lips suddenly freeze shut. A hand clasps my shoulder, and Daniel is there. He told me not to speak of this. But...how did he know?

"The sap," he says.

"May we please talk a little longer?" Emma asks.

"No, it is time." He points his staff to the amber liquid.

Emma's shoulders slump. She takes my hand and we move to the trough together. When I kneel and lift the sap to my lips, they open easily.

# 20

SUSAN SAYS SHE likes the house. Who wouldn't like the house? It's a mansion with an uninterrupted view over Lake Michigan. The stone and timber facade is classic Tudor—just my wife's style. It's not new, which is a little disappointing, but even we have limits. You can't exactly invent a new plot of land this close to Chicago. You have to deal with what's there. Unless you want to tear down a perfectly good mansion. It's tempting, but it's also nice to identify your home as the one built by a tycoon like Oliver Chamberlain. *I'm just a doctor*, I practice saying in my head, with a dose of humility, *but lucky enough to live in you-know-who's home.*

"Are you listening?" Susan asks.

"Yes, of course," I say, though I was not. She knows when I'm not listening. After seven years of marriage, she can tell by the look on my face when I'm lost in my own thoughts. It happens a lot. I'm past being annoyed by how well she reads me.

"Tell him again," Susan says to the realtor showing us the house. "I'll take Benjamin to the back. He wants to see the pool."

"Absolutely!" the man says, like someone who's had too much coffee. "Paul, I've been thinking of what you said about your study. You've got to come see this. There's a secret passage!"

"Secret! Secret!" Benjamin bounces on his little legs, his big brown eyes beaming just like Susan's used to when we first met.

"No, honey," Susan says gently. "Daddy needs some space to think."

Benjamin takes her hand and waddles out of the room. Susan spares a glance back at me before leaving. Her eyes show hurt more than anger. She told me she wants me to make this decision *with* her—a joint decision about what's best for the family. It's hard to say no to that when it was her father's death last year—pancreatic cancer coming on like a storm, nothing a neurosurgeon can do but say sorry—that landed a Rockefeller family fortune on us. So I'll pretend. That's why I talk about this house like it's still a decision. It's a not a decision. I saw this mansion when I was seventeen, rowing on the lake. I decided then and there that it would be mine someday. At the time I was naive. I thought being a doctor would be enough to afford it. Being a doctor was instead the gateway that put me in the running for a woman like Susan from one of the richest families in the country. Hey, whatever, it worked. Here I am, and I'm buying this house. If I need to make it look like a decision *with* Susan, so be it. I've gotten used to putting on a show.

"See, Dr. Fitzroy?" the realtor taps my shoulder. "Paul?"

I realize I've been standing at the window, staring outside, while he blabbers on about various details. A forced smile returns to my face. "Sorry, Mike, just admiring the view. Could you tell me that last part again?"

"Yes, come over here and I'll show you." He walks to the wall of books in the study, rising twenty feet high. He runs his hand over the spines of old, embossed tomes. Dickens. Dostoyevsky. Joyce. Authors I'd never find time to read.

He pauses and glances to me. "Care to guess which book holds the lever?"

I quickly scan the titles. "Tolstoy?"

"Not bad, but remember, the former owner had quite some struggles with Russia. He had family in England. He yearned for the British golden eras."

"So...Dickens?"

The realtor laughs. "Not quite golden. Here, try this one." He points to *Paradise Lost* by John Milton. Then he steps to the side.

I try to pull the book off the shelf, but it sticks.

"Pull down from the top," the man says.

When I do, the book tilts as if fixed and rotating. There's a metallic click. The whole shelf swings in smoothly, revealing a spiral staircase going down.

"Go on," the man says, having produced a flashlight and shining it in front of me. "There's a light switch at the bottom."

The stairs lead down to a sitting room. There are leather couches, a pool table, and a long oak bar. The yellowish bulbs dangling from the ceiling give the room an eerie glow, like this was some sort of war bunker before being converted to a gaming lounge. At the far end of the room a hallway leads into darkness.

"What's down there?" I ask.

"That's the best part." He holds out the flashlight. "Here. Lead the way."

We walk together down the long hall. The floor is black marble. The walls and ceiling look like metal. At the end there's a door that looks like it belongs in a submarine. A wheel at the center looks like the only way to open it. Maybe this really was a war bunker.

I hand the flashlight to the realtor and twist the wheel. The door swings open silently and light blazes in. I step outside and find myself almost at the shore of the lake. The mansion looms behind me.

"Impressive, right?" the man asks. "Now, see if you can detect the door."

He pushes the door closed. The metal is entirely covered in ivy, which blends in perfectly with a large garden of ivy spreading around, underneath a row of ancient oaks.

He opens to the door again. "Couldn't even see it, could you?"

"It is well hidden," I say. "Why was it built like this?"

"With this access to the lake and this entrance, you could sneak almost anything inside. The Chamberlains were here during the Prohibition. You can imagine what they used it for.”

*You could sneak anything in.* “How many people know about this?”

“Almost no one. It’s in the deed that this is to be kept secret from everyone except the owners and partners of my realty company. We’ve been in business a long time.”

“So why are you showing it to me now?”

The realtor smiles. “Because I’ve been selling homes a long time and I know the look of a man who’s made up his mind.”

Maybe I’m more readable than I thought. I decide not to debate him. This could be leverage. “We haven’t talked about price.”

“There’s no home like this,” he says, with a wink like he knows what’s in my wallet. “Let’s not let little details get in the way of what you want.”

<h1 style="text-align:center">21</h1>

SOFT, DAPPLED LIGHT filters through the leaves and shines onto the wooden floor and my young body. The mansion and Dr. Fitzroy are gone, except for the traces—or stains—that course through my mind and suddenly connect. Susan's father was Jonas Rockefeller. When Baron collared me, he asked me what I knew about John Davison Rockefeller, the patriarch who earned the fortune that I was spending on a mansion. Does that mean Baron knows about me? Or could he have been *the* Rockefeller? Daniel wants me to talk to him. This must be why.

"Everyone up! Time to fly!" Jade stands tall by the door, holding her staff and surveying us like a golden eagle over its nestlings.

I look down and see the familiar scars and mark of an eagle on my hands. My heart sinks as I glance around the room. Most of the boys and girls around me are unfamiliar. Some wear blank expressions. There's no Emma, no Hank. Maybe Violet managed to pick them.

Jade orders us to form a line, then quickly assigns newcomers to those who have been Eagles before, including two to me. She tells everyone it's time to move out, as quietly as we can.

The two wide-eyed girls assigned to me wait at the back of the line, watching the tribe file out. As I approach them, I recognize one is Min, the girl who had been in the starlit cavern before. The blank look in her eyes, and her assignment to me, confirm that she didn't make it back to the Jubilee alive.

"Where are we going?" the other girl asks.

I start to answer, but stop when our eyes meet. Sad eyes, rounded shoulders. "Shelley!" I say.

She smiles faintly, though it doesn't reach her eyes. "Hi Cipher. Thought I recognized you."

"Did you get caught from Blue?"

She shakes her head. "Black."

The word sounds ominous from her lips, but it seems better than the alternative—getting wiped. She must be the one Emma caught. "How much do you remember?"

"I ate a fruit. It showed me more than I wanted…"

"Hey," Min says, pointing past us. "Shouldn't we be going?"

Everyone else has left.

"Yes, let's keep up," I say, before sprinting out.

The line of Eagles is ahead of us, crossing a long, swaying rope bridge. We race after them and catch up just as they cross a platform and reach another bridge. Down and out, down and out, we move through the giant tree's branches until we reach a long ladder leading down to the forest below.

I don't think I'll ever get used to the height. I summon the wind as a brace and clutch each rung of the ladder like my life depends on it. The vertical vines swing and jostle with the steps of our tribe. No looking down. No falling.

When we reach the forest, Jade and the others are waiting in a shadowy clearing beneath the trees. Shelley and Min stay close. They eye the forest warily, neither one saying a word. It's very quiet.

Jade motions for us to follow her. We make it only a few paces before shouting rings out beside us.

"Run!" Jade shouts. "To the nest!"

Another tribe charges from every direction. Metal collars clink as they close around us. I see one hand, with a lion mark, snap a collar around a neck. As the Eagles scatter, I funnel the wind. It's hard to use it in the close, chaotic combat. Jade disappears, then reappears behind a Lion and bashes her staff into him, knocking him flat. She darts into the darkness of the trees, with two Eagles, and then two Lions, trailing. I follow them. Shelley and Min are still with me, within the protective wall of air.

There's a scream to our right. Metal clinks together. The sound of fighting fades behind us.

I feel the boy before I see him. He rushes into the current of air, with an open collar a foot from Shelley's neck. Just as he readies to snap it shut, I blast him back with the wind. He slams into a tree and slides to the ground, motionless.

The forest is still. There's no sight of Jade and the others.

Shelley looks pale, with her hands cupping her neck.

"You okay?" I ask her.

"I…know what the collar does."

"Yes, it's the same here." I remember that Shelley had a servant when I first met her in Blue—a servant from Green. She had become very strong with the wind and reached Fourth Class. We'd fought together. It seems like forever ago. "Why didn't you use the wind?" I ask.

She looks down. "Black took my power away."

I swallow, not knowing what to say. Then a shout to the left makes us turn. It sounded close, but there's nothing to see beyond the forest shadows.

"We should go," I whisper.

Shelley and Min follow me. Moving fast, trying to follow the direction Jade went, it doesn't take long to get completely lost. Birds sing cheerfully around us, as if oblivious of the struggle. The wind rustles the leaves. The occasional sound of shouting is the only compass. We go the opposite direction, wherever it may lead. I maintain the protective wall of air around us, along with a steady wind at our backs.

Minutes pass. Maybe an hour. A sheen of sweat covers me. We slow when we reach a small opening, where a beam of sunlight manages to pierce through the canopy. The light reflects brightly off two eyes and the largest set of antlers I've ever seen. I move forward quietly, but the stag's eyes study me as if unafraid and curious. I move to within thirty feet. Twenty feet. I step into the sunlight.

*Follow me.* It's a voice in my head, and somehow I feel

that it's from the stag. But that's impossible.

I glance back at Shelley and Min. They're staring right at the stag. I'm not imagining it.

"Let's follow it," I say, and they don't protest.

When I turn back to the stag, the amazing creature blinks and bounds off into the woods.

We charge after it, twisting and turning to avoid trees and branches. It's far faster than we are, but each time we lose sight of it, the stag appears a moment later, as if pausing to wait for us. Then it bounds off through the forest again. We continue like this for a long, long time. The forest grows darker, shadows longer. My lips become parched. Legs ache. Stomach groans.

After a long chase, the stag bounds off and does not appear again. I stop and lean over, with my hands on my knees.

"I think it's gone," I say.

"Where are we?" Shelley asks.

"Look!" Min calls out. She stands ahead of us, pointing through the trees. "It ends!"

We go to her and soon reach the end of the forest. It's the cliff. The Eagle's nest could be close to here. Maybe the stag was trying to lead us here, to help us. The suns have set below the horizon and the last light retreats quickly. The first stars appear in the midnight blue sky.

"Let's follow along the edge," I say. "The nest is somewhere near the top of this cliff. Anyone who survived the attack would go there."

We stay close together, moving slowly and carefully

along the top of the cliff. I study the ground for vines going over the edge. It's a slender hope, to recognize it when I see it.

I'm on my knees, inspecting a vine that runs over the ground, when I hear the voice.

*Finally, I found you.* It's Emma, in my mind, urgent.

Gazing up into the stars, the light pulls me with it, racing high above the vines and the forest.

*You okay?* I ask.

*I'm with the Wolves. Baron collared me. A pack is following you! Look!*

The starlight shines down into the forest, through a narrow gap between trees not far from me. Five shadowy figures are lurking forward along the forest floor, ducking from tree to tree, moving in a single direction, as if with a single purpose. They disappear again into the darkness.

*Hurry! There's no time.*

I'm kneeling by the edge of the cliff. The ones approaching us are very close.

*What should I do?* I ask.

*Run! Along the cliff. Sorry, trees blocking…*

*Wait.* "Wait," I say.

But the starlight has retreated, looking a million miles away above me.

"Wait for what?" Shelley whispers beside me. Her expression, only faintly visible in the dim light, is one of confusion and concern.

"Emma told me we have to run."

"Emma?" she asks. "What are you talking about?"

"No time to explain. You, Min, go that way." I stand and point in the direction we had been heading along the cliff. "Go as fast as you can. If you find a thick set of vines—lots of them—try following them down the cliff."

"What about you?" Shelley asks.

"I'll be fine. I still have the wind. Now, go!"

She and Min turn and move briskly along the cliff. They won't be fast enough to get away if the other tribe sees them. But I can handle a few attackers. It's time for a diversion. I sprint the opposite direction and start to shout.

"Wolves, Wolves, come and get me!"

*Hush!* Emma demands. *What are you doing!?*

*Distracting them.*

The trees grow closer to the cliff, blocking the stars and Emma. I sprint forward, focusing on each step, dodging branches and leaping over roots, always close to the cliff. Fast as I'm running, it's not fast enough. The other tribe howls behind me. The Wolves are coming, drawing closer with each step.

A deep, rumbling roar grows louder ahead of me. A silver line appears through the trees. A river. A waterfall. A deadend.

The shouting is very close. Footsteps pound behind me. I wheel around to face them, funneling the air. Five figures appear through the trees. They crouch as they approach. They wield staffs. I wield the air.

"There!" someone shouts in the distance. "I see him!"

On the opposite side of the river bank, across the churning rapids, another group emerges. I can't tell who they are in the darkness, but I can see one of them raising a bow easily enough.

I form the shield above me, focusing on the five attackers that are closing on me. I can hold them all off. I take a step closer to the cliff's edge.

The archer across the river draws the string. Another archer has joined and does the same. The arrows fire.

I weave the air to move them in mid-flight. Not much. An inch. Then two. It shifts the trajectory enough. The arrows stab into the dirt beside me.

"Fire again!" someone shouts.

The archers raise their bows. The four others are closing fast, only a stone's throw away. Wait, there were *five* of them. Where's—?

The blow hits me in the jaw.

I'm down, flat on my back. A boy looms over me, as if appearing out of nowhere. Arrows soar straight at us. I manage to flick just enough wind to make them hit the ground around us.

I channel the wind to blast him away, but he slams his fist into my nose. Stars erupt. The power is gone. He pins me down, knee on my chest. My head hangs over the cliff's edge. His granite eyes lock with mine. It's Baron.

I try to speak. "Are you Rockef—?"

He punches again, silencing me. "I saved one for you."

A flash of metal catches the starlight. He holds a collar.

*No! No!* Emma's voice echoes in my mind like thunder, joining the sound of the waterfall. This can't happen.

I wedge my elbows up, leaning back and away, my

shoulders slipping over the cliff. Baron presses closer to snap the collar shut. Closer, closer, but then he suddenly jerks away and shouts in pain, grabbing at an arrow that has stabbed down into his shoulder.

The moment his weight lifts off me, my balance is lost. Gravity drags my body over the cliff.

# 22

I FALL TUMBLING in mid-air, screaming into the gusting wind. My arms and legs flail like broken wings. Moisture from the waterfall sprays over me.

*Wind!* Emma shouts it in my mind. *Use the wind!*

I try as I plummet down, down, down. But everything blurs. Air blasts into my face. Wind whips in my ears. Threads of blue flash and swirl, dizzying against grey cliff, black sky, and dark jungle below.

Emma shouts again. *NOW, WIND!*

I'm halfway down. Seconds to death.

*WIND!*

For Emma. Focus, focus.

Blinking through the wind and the moisture in my eyes, I isolate a single blue thread and seize it, fighting to hold on, like trying to grab a balloon as it deflates and jerks about. Another thread. Another. Blue weaves into blue. A net forms beneath me.

*YES, SLOWER!*

But it's too late. I see fish under the water. A boulder rushes up, up, up. My head hits.

In the blackness there is only quiet.

Everything is still.

"There now," says man's voice. "You'll be alright."

I sit up and rub my bare arms, as if feeling them for the first time. I wear soft brown shorts and a vest. The man kneels beside me, his face shadowed. We are in a small, wooden room. The light is dim.

"You'll start with a tribe in the morning," he says.

"Who are you?" I ask, surprised by the young sound of my voice. "What is this place?"

"I am the Hunter. This is the Green Tower. Your new tribe leader will tell you more. Have a sip of this."

He holds a tiny cup to my lips. A sticky liquid pours into my mouth, bittersweet and intoxicating.

Again the blackness comes, and with it, the quiet.

Something pulls at my arm.

"Daddy! Daddy!"

It's my son, Benjamin, trying to drag me out of bed. He wears pajamas with pictures of little reindeer all over them.

"Get up, Daddy! Santa came!"

He keeps pulling until I reluctantly rise from the silken sheets. My gaze passes over a book on the nightstand. My feet slide into velvety slippers by the bed. They show the letters, PF. My initials. Paul Fitzroy. I'm a doctor. This is my home. Our new mansion by Lake Michigan. Outside the wall-to-wall window, past an ancient towering oak, the water glistens in the morning light.

Another tug at my arm. The little boy pulls me like an earnest tugboat dragging a tanker ship.

"Come on, Daddy! It's Christmas!"

"I let you sleep as long as I could," says my smiling wife, Susan.

We pass her through the bedroom doorway. She follows after us.

"Coffee?" I mumble.

"It's brewed. I'll pour you a cup. You go ahead with Benjamin."

He leads me into a cavernous room with a pine tree twice my height in the corner. Dozens of colorfully wrapped boxes lay under the tree. Benjamin begins picking them up, one by one, and shaking them. He asks me what's inside. I don't know. Susan picked them all out. But he guesses each one.

Susan comes with the coffee. The smell wakes me up a little. She sits with me on a leather couch and tells Benjamin he can open a present. He rips off the paper and pulls a toy racecar out of a box. He begins zooming around the room with it, as if he's entirely forgotten the other gifts.

Susan squeezes my hand. "I'm glad you decided to stay."

"Thanks," I say. "Who needs another conference?"

"It means a lot."

Zooming noises race around and around the couch. Suddenly it's quiet.

"Benjamin?" Susan calls out. "Want to open another one?"

There's no answer. Only a subtle, shuffling sound behind us.

Susan is up in an instant. I follow her and see Benjamin on the floor behind the couch, shaking and convulsing uncontrollably. It's another seizure.

"No, please God," Susan moans. "Not again."

"Call 911. Stay with him." I rush to my cabinet of medicines, thoughts racing about the brain and the possible diagnosis. I stand before the shelves of pills and serums. There's everything a doctor could want. Grabbing a bottle and a needle, I hurry back, confident that I can stop the shaking, but with no idea how to prevent it from happening again. I'm kneeling over my son, my helpless Benjamin, when darkness falls.

"Hey, wake up!" something pulls at my arm. "Up!"

I'm pulled to my feet. The boy in front of me is my size, with golden blonde hair and bright blue eyes. He wears brown shorts and a vest, just like mine. I look down at his hand with a wolf head imprinted on it. My hand bears the same mark, over a deep scar. The scar wasn't there in the vision, when I was a man named Paul Fitzroy. But the scar was there when a man who called himself the Hunter woke me up and poured a sticky liquid into my mouth. From the recesses of my mind, I know what diagnosis Dr. Fitzroy would give me: mental whiplash, with a risk of schizophrenia.

"Baron let you sleep," the boy says, "seeing as you were wiped, but now we have to go." He drags me toward an open door. "Baron says we must be the first tribe out. He ordered me to make sure you come."

"Who are you?" I ask.

"Baron calls me O," the boys says, fingering a metal band around his neck.

"Who's Baron?"

"You'll see. Come on!" He drags me out of the room and down stairs carved into a thick wooden branch. We're in the middle of a giant tree. We reach a platform and hurry toward a group of others. They're waiting in a line, dropping one by one into a hole in the center of the platform. Two boys stand watching the line pass.

As we reach the back of the line, O tells me, "That's Baron. The leader of the Wolves. He's not so bad as long as you obey. The boy beside him, with the wild hair, is Fugger. Don't mess with him."

The line moves forward and we pass in front of the two boys. Baron eyes me calmly, with his hands clasped behind his back. "Welcome to the Wolves, Cipher. Help us get out to our camp safely and you'll be rewarded."

I stare back blankly. Why did he call me Cipher? He sounds so confident, so powerful, but the way he looks at me gives me chills. Before I can formulate a question, O pulls me away to a ladder that leads straight down. It reaches another steep stairway, then another. O moves quickly above me, leaving me little choice but to keep going down.

We reach the bottom and hurry out of the tree's immense trunk. An open grassy area surrounds us, and forest beyond that.

"Stay close when we run," O says, grabbing my hand tightly again. "Looks like we beat the Lions out, but they'll come soon."

"Lions?"

He doesn't have time to answer. Baron exits the tree beside us and takes off running toward the woods. Our group sprints after him. All of us have the same mark of a wolf on our hands. And all but three or four wear collars around the neck. I wonder why I don't have one.

The forest becomes thicker and thicker, slowing us down. We reach a thin, gurgling creek and everyone stops to drink. Baron and Fugger stand on guard. They have somehow found bows, which they each hold with arrows at the ready. I kneel and cup water in my hand. Then I hear a stick snap behind me.

"It's the Lions!" Baron shouts. "To me!"

O springs up and pulls me toward the others. They form a straight line in front of Baron, each standing defensively with matching metal bands around their necks.

"Behind me," O says urgently. "Baron told me you have some kind of power. Use it."

A dozen others are charging at us with staffs. There's a scream, and two of them fall to arrows. The others slam into our line. Shouts of fighting and pain erupt around me. A boy swings his staff at O, knocking him to his knees. Then the boy comes at me.

*Some kind of power?*

I try to duck but it happens too fast. No power helps

me. The boy's staff slams into my bare neck and something cracks.

When I come to, my body feels impossibly stiff. Nothing will move. Not even my toes. I can't lift my head. But my mind works well enough to give a new diagnosis: paralysis. All I can do is stare straight up at a dense green canopy. It is moving. Or I'm moving. Up and down slightly, and parallel to the ground in the same direction my head is pointing. A few stars appear among the leaves.

I swallow nervously, my throat bone dry. A word comes out like a whisper, "Hello?"

*Cipher!* A girl's voice immediately comes to my mind, as if answering my question from the stars above. *Are you okay?*

*No,* I reply. *I can't move. Who's Cipher? Who are you?*

*Oh no. It's me, Emma.*

*Sorry, Emma…?*

*Where are you?*

*I don't know…in a forest.*

"Hello?" I croak again, a little louder this time.

"You hear that?" It's a boy's voice, coming from below me.

"Nah, just the wind," another boy says.

*Quiet,* the girl says soothingly. *No need to speak. I can hear you. It is going to be okay. You are with the Wolves. You must have gotten hurt. But Baron's servants are carrying you.*

It comes back to me in violent, confusing flashes. Benjamin had another seizure. Then a boy named O guided me out of a giant tree. We joined the leader, Baron, and others with wolf marks on their hands. A group called the Lions attacked in the forest. None of it makes sense. I start to panic.

*What is this place?*

*The Green Tower*, the girl says. *Just try to survive until the Jubilee. I will earn you another fruit. You will get your memories back, Cipher.*

She keeps calling me Cipher. The Jubilee? The fruit? This isn't a dream. It's a nightmare. I can't move. I need to wake up. I scream.

*Oh no*, says the girl's voice. *What happened?*

It's suddenly quiet. The movement stops.

"Hello?" I say.

"Baron said no talkin'," a boy says.

"So shut him up."

I hear a footstep, a heavy breath, then I'm lowered. A figure appears above me, the face hidden in shadows.

*Cipher, are you still there?*

There's a blur of motion and something hits me on the head. In a flash of pain, the man from my vision, Paul Fitzroy, tells me he can solve this, surely he can. No problem is too difficult for him.

# 23

"CAN YOU FEEL THAT?" It's a girl's voice, whispering, very close.

No. I can't feel anything.

"How about this?" she asks.

I manage to move my head very slightly, side to side. There's no stiffness, no pain. My head feels like it's separated from my body. Like there's nothing below my neck. A makeshift roof of sticks is above, blocking any view of the trees or the sky.

"So not this either?" she asks. There's a pause. She speaks to someone else: "It's what I thought. He's paralyzed from the neck down."

"Can you fix him?" a boy asks. "He's worth more to me alive."

The girl breathes deeply. "Yes, it'll drain me. And him. You'll need to keep us safe a few days while we recover."

"Fine," the boy says. "Do it."

Footsteps move away.

Thin hands come to my cheeks and a face appears in front of me, upside down. She has copper skin and dark, hawkish eyes. Her black hair is pulled back and flowers and leaves are woven into a braid that hangs down beside me. Her hands feel warm and secure, holding my head in place.

"This will feel cold," she says.

*Cold? I can't feel anything.* Panic forces soft words out. "What will?"

"The healing."

"Who are you?"

"Do you know who *you* are?" she replies.

"Um…a doctor? Named Paul?"

"Interesting. I thought you were Cipher." Her lips press tight as she focuses. "We will talk when we wake up. Now, ready."

Her fingers press firmly against my temples. Her eyes close. A shocking force courses through me. Freezing. Colder. Burning. Colder.

My mouth gapes open. My back arcs off the ground and I suck in all the air of the universe before I collapse, motionless again.

My body feels like ice when I come to. Muscles ache and shiver. Teeth chatter. I sit up and hug my knees into my chest, trying to feel my toes and marveling as they move. Every part of me can move. There's no pain, only cold.

"Here, this'll help."

A girl sitting across from me holds out a bowl of something that steams. It's the same girl, the one who sent the force into me, who…fixed me.

I take the bowl and huddle over the steaming liquid. Warmth enters as I sip. Breaths come fast and shallow. Another gulp goes down. The heat feels like paradise.

"Not so fast," she says with a soft laugh. "You're still in shock."

"What…did you do?" I ask.

"I healed you."

"How?"

"I was in Yellow. A long time. There we learn the Healer's ways. But now I've been here, in Green, even longer. Baron wanted a healer in his tribe. You should have seen the arrow wound I healed before the last Scouring. He would have died if not for me."

"What do you mean—Yellow, Green?"

"I see…" She rises slowly. "I'll get more soup. There's much to tell you."

She goes to the door of the shelter, where she says something to someone outside. The shelter is made of sticks tied together by vines, leaning against another wall of wooden stakes driven into the ground. The floor is dirt. Sunlight peeks through slender gaps in the makeshift walls and roof. Through the gaps in the door I can see the forest beyond. It is lush and green and alive with the sounds of chirping insects and birds. A gentle breeze blows through the shelter and cools my skin. I somehow feel the wind *inside*, like it's tickling my mind.

A boy opens the door and hands the girl two wooden bowls of steaming soup. The door closes. The boy stays just outside, like he's on guard.

The girl sits down in front of me, placing the bowls on the ground. I don't understand how she healed me. She's not like any doctor I remember.

"Who are you?" I ask.

"I'm Seneca." She motions to the soup. "Please, eat. It's been days since you've had anything more than water and the bits of acorn paste I could squeeze between your lips."

As I slurp down soup, she tells me a story. She says I'm in the Five Towers, that my name is Cipher. Apparently I'm rather notorious in this place. She says I started in the Blue Tower, then went to Red, before coming here, to Green. She points out the criss-cross scars on both my hands. She says there's only one other boy in Green with scars like that, and he's the leader of our tribe, the Wolves. Everyone thinks it has something to do with the battle between the towers called the Scouring. Other towers have thrived when I led them, because I have some power over the wind. It has to do with my past.

"I still don't understand." My fingers idly trace the scar on my hand. "I had a vision that I was a man named Paul Fitzroy. He had a family. A son who was sick."

"That must be who you were on Earth, before you died and came here," Seneca says. "I don't know that story."

"I...*died?*" It seems impossible. I am breathing. My young body was hurt, but healed. My heart beats. And yet...the memory of Paul, and my son...it felt so real.

"I know it's hard," Seneca says. "We all go through this. Give it time to sink in."

I don't like it, but her explanation is plausible—and better than losing my mind. "Why is this happening?"

"The leaders say we must remember, and be scoured."

"How?"

"You get some memories back from the sap at the Jubilee," she says. "You get it every fifty days in the Green Tower. The Jubilee is when our young bodies are made whole again, and the forest is reset. A clean start. Except for memories. The sap only restores bits and pieces. But if you've had the fruit and told others about your past, they can help you remember…if you happen to be in the same tribe."

*The Jubilee. The fruit.* The girl who spoke in my mind, Emma, talked of these things. "What's the fruit?"

"It's small and red and irresistible. Daniel gives one to each new captive from another tower. He says it is from the Provider. It restores whatever memories you gained in other towers before coming to Green. But you usually get the fruit only once, when you first arrive."

This sounds promising. Emma told me she would get me *another* fruit if I survived. "What if someone else gives you the fruit?" I ask.

"Only Daniel has the fruit, unless…" she leans forward, studying me. "Wait, how did you hear about that?"

*A girl told me through the stars.* It almost makes me laugh to think of saying that. "I…heard some people talking about it."

"It's very rare," Seneca says. "If the leader of the

Scouring tribe manages to capture more from other towers than those who are lost from Green, then that leader gets to pick one and only one person to get the fruit at the Jubilee. Otherwise you have to build up slowly, from the sap and whatever others remember about you."

That must be what the girl Emma had in mind. I wonder why she would do this for me. Whatever the reason, it gives me some hope. I just have to survive.

"So the Jubilee is in fifty days?" I ask.

"Not quite that long. You were unconscious several days. But trust me, it's going to feel like a long time by the end." Her voice is grim, like a jaded veteran.

"How did you get here?"

"I started with the Lions this time, but the Wolves caught me...again." Her slender fingers slide along a silver collar around her neck. "Now I heal for him."

"How did they catch you? With the collar?"

"Not *they. Him*. Baron. He uses his collars to control everyone he captures. His only weakness is that he doesn't have enough collars."

"Why does this happen?"

"The four tribes battle for control until the next Jubilee. It gets hard, and wild, out here. There's not enough food for all of us. We must hunt, and when we do, we are vulnerable. Baron and his Wolves are very strong." Her voice lowers. "His thirst for power knows no limit. So I obey, and wait until I can get my revenge."

Her tone, more than her words, makes it clear she's dangerous. But she helped me. My body still shakes, but at least my teeth have stopped chattering. Two bowls of soup are now empty beside me.

I point to the third bowl. "Is this one yours?"

"No, you should have it. You're the one who broke your neck."

My hand rubs the back of my neck. It feels straight, if a little weak. "The Lions, your old tribe, they attacked."

"We thought we'd catch Baron by surprise. It didn't end well… Life is nasty, brutish, and short in the forest. Same as it was on Earth, except not even death offers an escape here."

I rub my eyes, trying to understand. "I don't get it."

"It makes more sense when you learn more about who you were," Seneca says. "Would you like to know who I was? It might help."

"Yes, please." I sip the soup, and she speaks.

"Some of these words and places may be foreign to you now, but when the Jubilee comes and you remember your past, remember this story. It will become clearer then. I was born on a ship. My name was Mary Jemison. We were traveling from England to the new world, America. My family went to the frontier, the mountains. Pa and Ma built a nice wooden home in a valley. My sisters and I worked hard. Gathering fire wood, planting corn, even learning to read a heavy black book that we'd brought from England. We were happy. Then the savages came. There was no warning. They attacked from the forest as the sun was setting. Pa had a gun. But there were too many of them. He killed three of them before they broke down our door.

They took his scalp off. They tied up the rest of us and took us away in different directions."

Her hands cover her face. She shivers.

"I'm…sorry—"

"It's okay," she says. "It gets easier every time I say it. When I first learned this I had only fear. The kind of fear that sank down to my toes and made it impossible to even move, just as it had been that night when they came. I couldn't even scream I was so terrified. I never saw Ma or my sisters again. All of this I saw in Yellow. But I've learned more in Green. After that terrible day, I began to grow in different soil. I married one of the savages. He was actually a kind, gentle man. His name was Sheninjee. Many of his people feared the white man and their guns. Feared and hated. Sheninjee took me away from that place in the mountains. We traveled north to his kin, the Seneca. When he became sick and died, I married again. My new husband, Hiokatoo, taught me more of their ways. I changed my name to Dehgewanus. There were some happy days. There was a kind of freedom in that life. But…the strong take what they can, and the weak suffer what they must. We, the Seneca, suffered loss after loss. Our land dwindled, taken and sold and swindled. I raised my family by a great lake. We did as well as we could. I shared with my neighbors. We protected each other."

She sits back, her hands planted on the dirt behind her. "That's what I remember, Cipher. Maybe you'll have memories like mine. Maybe better. Maybe worse. But your question was *why*, right?"

I nod, feeling sad and tired all over after Seneca's story.

"Sometimes, after the Scouring, there is a voice," Seneca says. "An incredibly powerful voice. And it says, *The fire will try your work. If your work survives, you shall receive your reward. If your work is burned, you must be purified.*"

"What's that supposed to mean?" I ask.

She shakes her head sadly. "I don't know, but I think these towers are like locks to a doorway, which we call the White Tower. I think we're all going somewhere, and this is the only way to get there." For first time since she started her story, Seneca smiles. "I wish I knew more. But I feel in my bones that it'll be somewhere far, far better than here."

# 24

AFTER MORE SLEEP and more bowls of soup, I'm finally able to stand and move about in the little prison. I bang on the door and ask to leave, but a boy outside says it's not allowed. Through slender gaps in the wall, I watch the tribe gather in the morning, as many as thirty of them. One boy gives commands before they head out hunting for the day. I sleep again.

When the forest grows dark, the hunters trickle back into the village, build a fire, and cook meat that smells delicious. They sing and dance around the fire like they're celebrating something. Maybe the food. The leftovers reach me the next morning. The meat's cold, but it beats acorn and mushroom soup.

Seneca visits often. During the second day she shows me how to work my sleeping muscles back to life. It's nice to have her company, but she does not stay long. She says she's been ordered to wait on a boy named Fugger. The way she says his name makes me think it is not a pleasant experience.

Two large boys take turns guarding the door, armed

with long wooden staffs. They wear silver bands like Seneca's around their necks. The door has a thick beam across it, locking it from the outside. The guards only open it when Seneca comes and goes. The guards also seem to have only half a brain.

"Hey, what's your name?" I ask once through the door.

"D," the boy says, keeping his back to me.

"Like the letter? What's it stand for?"

"Baron says it's D. He says to keep you inside."

D doesn't answer any more questions. I try talking my way past him a dozen ways, but he won't budge. A few hours later the other boy replaces him on guard duty.

"Hey, what's your name?" I ask.

"B," the boy grunts.

"Okay, B. Listen, I have to relieve myself." I hop lightly from foot to foot. "Come on, I really have to go."

"Go in there," B says.

"But I have to sleep in here. *Please?*"

"Baron says you stay," B says.

None of my attempts work. So I use a small hole in the ground. A little while later it starts to rain. It's miserable.

By the second night, I've decided to try escaping. I wait until everything is silent except the bugs. B, or D, I've lost track which one it is, sits by the doorway to the primitive shelter. He hasn't moved in hours. He must be sleeping.

The branches forming the shelter are thicker than my thigh—far too strong to break. Without a knife, I also can't undo the vine ropes holding it together. But after careful inspection, I find one stick on the makeshift roof that looks thin enough for me to snap. Keeping an eye on the sleeping guard, I break it. The crisp sound makes the guard stir, but after a few breaths he's motionless again. Using the stick, I reach through a small gap in the door and, inch by careful inch, lift the beam locking it shut. As soon as the beam is out of the way, the door easily swings open, creaking loudly as it goes.

I dash out toward the trees.

I make it three steps before something hits my legs and knocks me flat on my face. A foot stomps down on my back. Twisting, scrambling, I try to get free but only manage to see B or D swinging a staff down at my head.

When I wake up, Seneca is rubbing my head gently. Daylight streams through the cracks in the shelter. She tells me to rest, and not to try escaping again. She says Baron has been gone hunting, but he might come back with more collars. Or he could remove someone else's collar—someone more loyal to him—and put it on me. He's interested in my power, but he cares most about making sure no one in his tribe gets away.

Seneca leaves. I curl up on the ground and sleep.

I wake up in darkness, soaking wet, with rain battering the roof and dripping down like a waterfall. The downpour leaves me soaked and muddy and miserable. Seneca said that there's a way to remember our past and that the towers are like locks to a doorway, but it hardly matters when I'm trapped in here. The only doorway is sleep. I try to empty my mind. I toss and turn and do not dream.

The next morning, after hunting groups have been sent

out, Baron comes to the door of my shelter. This time both B and D are there, standing by his side. They grip their staffs firmly. Silver bands gleam at their necks.

"Hey friend," Baron says, leaning against the doorway. "Sorry to have kept you waiting. We had quite a hunt. Ready to join us?"

I'm speechless, hardly believing the casual friendliness in his voice. He's the one who ordered me locked up, who told Seneca I'm worth more to him alive. And now he says *sorry…join us?* A new energy swells in me, desperate for freedom. I glance out the door.

"Come, let's have a look at you." Baron steps to the side, clearing the way.

I resist the urge to run. Seneca said Baron is interested in my power. I have to use that, to learn more. I move through the door cautiously, half expecting B or D to forget I have permission and whack me in the head again. But they only smile dumbly at me. They're nearly as filthy dirty as I am.

"You haven't changed much." Baron eyes me curiously. He has brown hair, granite eyes, and the shadow of a mustache. He wears light brown shorts and a vest. There's no collar around his neck, but there's one in his hand, held casually at his side. His hand has a criss-cross scar like mine.

"Why would I have changed?" I ask.

"Ah, the loss of memory is such a tragedy. Shall we make the most of it?"

"What are you talking about?"

He holds up the collar in his scarred hand. "Want to try this on?"

I step back. B and D block my way.

"What do you want from me?" I ask.

"That's my favorite question," he says dryly. "How are you with a bow and arrow?"

"I'm not sure."

"Delightful. Let's find out."

Baron spins away and walks toward the center of the small village. B or D shoves me in the back, forcing me to follow. The trees around us stand so high and so thick that only a few spots of sky show through the canopy. There are four or five makeshift structures like the one where I'd been locked up. The other two buildings are better built, with sturdy wooden frames and thick, thatch roofs. One building is long and straight, low to the ground. The other is round, with a domed top. In the center of the village is the firepit, full of fresh wood to be burned. Two boys stand there, one wearing a link and the other not.

"Friends," Baron greets as he approaches, waving with the collar in hand. "It's time for a little competition. The loser gets to wear this. I'm afraid it's my last one. For now."

"What do you want us to do?" asks another boy without a collar. He's small and lanky, with long red hair. The three boys wearing collars—B, D, and another one—stand silently, on guard with their staffs.

Baron clasps the red-haired boy's shoulder. "The seasons are changing, Tom. Food is running out. We will need hunters who can shoot an animal on the move, or other tribes on the move. G, ready the target. D, the weapon, if you please."

The two guards spring into action. G moves toward the large, low building at the far side of the village. D enters the round building with the domed roof and exits a moment later, returning with a bow and a quiver of arrows.

"Those aren't their real names, by the way," Baron says to Tom and me. "But it's much more efficient this way, don't you think? We capture so many from other tribes it can be hard to learn all their names. This is a kindness, really, to help them understand their roles. You understand, right B?"

The large boy nods. His face is blank.

"See?" Baron continues. "You'll find that I'm a very kind leader. It's why our tribe always wins."

G finishes hanging a round piece of white wood on the wall of the distant building. Then he returns to our group. It takes him at least twenty paces.

"Very good," Baron says. "First one to hit the target wins. Who'd like to go first?"

"Me," Tom and I say at the same time.

Our eyes meet. He blinks in recognition.

"Cipher?" he says.

"You know me?"

"He knows you..." Baron says, clasping his hands eagerly. "This grows more interesting. Tom, why don't you take the first shot?"

The red-haired boy shrugs toward me, but then nods

and takes the bow and an arrow from D. He sets his feet. He raises the bow and notches the arrow. The muscles in his thin forearm tense as he pulls back the string. Keeping a tight hold, he lets the string go loose, then pulls again, as if getting the feel for it. A sheen of sweat covers his forehead.

"Five," Baron says.

Tom looks to him.

"Four."

Tom turns intently toward the target.

"Three."

He pulls the string.

"Two."

The arrow flies. It soars twenty feet over the building and disappears into the forest. There's a soft thud in the distance.

Baron grunts. "You're stronger than you look, Tom." He grabs the bow from him. "G, be a good lad and grab that arrow, won't you?"

G takes off in a trot toward the forest. Baron hands the bow to me, smiling widely. "Good luck, Cipher."

"Cipher," Tom says. "Do you still have your power over the—?"

D hits Tom hard in the gut, making him double over and fall to his knees.

"Sorry, Tom," Baron says. "I'd rather you not spoil the competition. Cipher, ready?"

I nod nervously.

"Five," Baron says. "Four."

I hurry into stance, copying what Tom did but lowering the bow, pointing toward the target as I notch the arrow, pull, and release on Baron's count of "one."

The arrow thuds into the building, five feet to the left of the target.

"Hey, not bad," Baron says, patting me on the back. "If we were hunting hippos, you might have hit something." He takes the bow, but this time he does not hand it to Tom. He pulls his own arrow out of the quiver. "It's like this, boys. Pull hard. Release smooth. Don't hesitate."

In one fluid motion, Baron fires an arrow. It flies straight and smooth and slams dead-center into the target. Baron hands the bow to Tom. "Don't worry. The second shot is always easier. That is the way to success. Make every next shot better. And the next better again. The slightest improvements, over time, lead to massive victories."

Tom does not hesitate. He readies the bow and pulls back the arrow and releases before Baron starts counting. The arrow stabs into the ground three feet below the target.

"Overcorrection," Baron says. "A common mistake. There are worse ones. Cipher?"

I take the bow. If there's one thing I've learned from Seneca, it's that I don't want to wear a collar. I can't lose.

*Pull hard. Release smooth. Don't hesitate.*

Baron's instructions race through my mind as I try to be still. The bow's flexible wood strains. The string pulls tight. The arrow is between my fingers. The target is twenty paces ahead.

Deep breath. Eyes on the target. Release.

The arrow sails and hits the building's wall, two feet high.

"You shot straight," Baron says, matter of fact. "You're getting the feel. Now let's try real range."

Baron leads Tom and me around the firepit, back another twenty paces, where a line is drawn in the dirt. "You have to arc the shot from here. Play the wind, too."

He sticks his thumb in his mouth then holds it up in the air. He nods like this tells him everything he needs to know. "We're lucky. Only a gentle breeze. Do it like this."

He draws and shoots. Another bullseye.

Tom fires next. It comes up ten feet short.

It's my turn again. The wind has picked up. This shot will be impossible. I lick my thumb and hold it up, like Baron did. As the wind blows I see its strands in the air, glistening like morning dew. I steady my feet, keeping my knees bent, then draw the bow. I feel my heart beating as I pull the string back. Then release.

The shot misses badly. It's right and high, hitting the building's thatch roof.

"Why so tense?" Baron asks, jostling the open collar in his hand. "We must learn to perform under pressure."

Tom shoots and misses again.

I notch the next arrow. The breeze blows harder, messing my hair. I draw and fire. This time, as the arrow sails, my thoughts go with the arrow, focusing on the air around it. Not knowing how I'm doing it, I weave the air around the arrow, nudging it right, then down slightly.

The arrow hits the target dead center, exactly where Baron's did.

"Bravo," Baron says.

In a flash he swings toward Tom, clasping the collar around his neck. Tom's face goes pale.

"I hereby name you T," Baron says. "T, be a good lad and bring some water. Cipher here will want to wash up before his first hunt."

# 25

BARON ACTS LIKE a god in this place, and apparently things go better when he's pleased with you. After putting the collar on Tom—or T—and issuing orders to the other servants, he leads me to his wooden building. It's the largest in the village, with a domed roof made of thatch. Inside there's a single room with a bed of straw, a wash basin made of wood, and a makeshift table with two chairs. The floor is covered with large animal hides. Baron tells me to clean up, then leaves me in the room. I notice both guards, B and D, stay by the door.

It's been many days since I've washed, and it feels better than I could have imagined to rub away all the dirt and grime. My wounds have healed into small scabs, thanks to Seneca. She's probably just "S" to Baron. I head out to look for her.

B and D don't try to stop me, but they stay close on my heels. They don't answer a single question I ask, other than to tell me, "Baron says to watch you."

He must be able to issue orders through the collars without saying a word. That's the only way to explain why one of the guards punched Tom in the gut. What was Tom going to tell me? I wonder if he recognized me. I haven't thought of a better explanation than what Seneca and Baron have said: I was in other towers before coming here.

Seneca is washing clothes in a small creek by the village when I find her. I tell her about what happened with the archery contest, and Baron putting the collar on Tom instead of me.

"I'm not surprised," she says.

"Why's that?" I ask.

She doesn't look up from the vest she's scrubbing. "Baron loves power. He knows all about what you did in Blue, how you led the tower to capture so many. He'll want you to do that here."

"Beats beings a servant," I say. "No offense."

Seneca smiles. "I'm not so sure. Life's more peaceful for me. You'll still have to do whatever Baron wants." She looks past me, to B and D standing guard.

"Can Baron give orders through the collars without saying a word?" I ask.

"Yes."

"How does it work?"

She shrugs. "You should ask Daniel."

"Who's that?"

"Our leader, in the Green Tower. He knows more than anyone. You just have to ask the right questions."

"When will we get to see him?"

"At the Jubilee." Seneca stands, holding the newly cleaned clothes over her arm. "I can't wait. Now, want to help me hang these?"

She does not wait for an answer. I watch her move toward a tree with low branches extending over the ground. Surely there's something more important we could do…but she was the one who healed me. I owe her. As many once owed me, when I was a doctor. I join her and help drape the wet clothes that she has cleaned.

We're almost finished when I hear a blood-curdling scream. It comes from the dark forest ahead of us. Seneca charges straight into the thick trees, toward the noise, before I can even react.

The screaming comes louder, closer.

Moments later a group races toward me through the forest. One of them—Baron—holds someone over his shoulder. He doesn't slow down. Seneca and another girl run at his side as they charge past me. The boy over Baron's shoulder screams and leaves a trail of blood on the forest floor.

Soon after them comes another group, moving more slowly. There are four boys and two girls dragging a huge, hairy shape. At first the dark brown fur looks like a bear. As they pass me I see the tusks, long as my leg. It's a boar.

I follow after them, avoiding the trails of blood. Everyone gathers around the firepit at the center of the village. The flames have already been lit. It takes six kids to hoist the boar on a spit above the fire.

Seneca kneels by the injured boy. I go to her side. The boy is pale, breathing steady but shallow. He doesn't wear a collar. Somehow I know he's in shock, like I was. His shorts have been ripped along the side. There's still a mess of blood, but his thigh shows only a long, wide scar.

"You healed him," I say, amazed. It would have taken hundreds of stitches to sew a wound that size. There could be internal bleeding. There could be…

Seneca looks up, noticing me for the first time, with exhaustion in her eyes. "Yes. He'll be fine."

As darkness falls, more of the tribe filters into the village from the forest. The fire burns brightly in the night. Fat drips from the roasting meat, smelling delicious. The group sits around the fire—those with collars and those without alike eyeing the feast. I sit by Seneca.

Baron steps onto a large stump near the fire. For a moment he silently observes the tribe, with arms clasped behind his back and a sort of repressed power that compels attention.

"Well done, Wolves," he says. "A good hunt!"

The crowd howls back like a wild pack of angry dogs.

"Hoo! Hoo!"

Baron quiets them. "We were near the waterfall," he says. "We saw the biggest hoof prints you've ever seen. I told them all, *it's the stag!* Now Pete here says to me, *it's a boar, Baron, a boar.* I didn't believe him. We're going to get that stag, you know. So we followed the footprints past the falls and deeper and deeper into the heart of the jungle. Into Lion territory."

The crowd responds with another howl.

"But no Lions came at us. M and F and T were our scouts. You three, stand."

The three of them rise to their feet, all wearing collars. The crowd cheers. T is Tom, keeping his eyes on the ground. His hair looks orange in the fire's light. F has wild hair, stern eyes, and a lion mark on his hand. M has an eagle mark on her hand. She is taller than both of the boys. She has curly brown hair and holds her chin up proudly.

"They had the wings," Baron continues. "And I had the point. Pete had the rear guard. M saw it first, charging like an elephant through the underbrush. She sees where it's heading and yells out, *Pete!* But it's too late. I double back and fire an arrow. Hit the boar right in the back. Didn't slow it an inch. So it charges straight at Pete. Think Pete ran?"

"No!" the crowd shouts.

Baron beams down at the injured boy. "Pete stood his ground. He drew an arrow like a sword. It was wolf against boar. The pack against the predator. Who wins, my friends? Who can defeat my pack?"

"No one! Hoo! Hoo!"

Baron holds up a huge tusk. "The beast impaled Pete with this. It went clean through the leg, maybe shattered a bone. But Pete returned the favor. He jabbed an arrow right into the beast's throat. F and I were on it in an instant. We spilled its blood and pulled Pete off the tusk. I brought him back, while the rest of the pack brought the boar and kept the Lions away. Not a bad day, eh?"

"Hoo! Hoo!"

"Now the feast!" Baron leaps off the stump and hands the massive tusk to Pete, who smiles weakly at the crowd.

Servants begin dishing out the sizzling meat. One of them hands me a large chunk on a bone. It tastes amazing, filling my empty stomach. The crowd is quiet now, eating. My second helping goes down almost as easy as the first. By the end, there's only a huge, dissected skeleton left on the spit.

F leans over the skeleton, pulling off the remaining bones, one by one. He holds each bone up in the fire light, inspecting it. Some bones he tosses into a large pile. Others he lays carefully in a row.

"Weapons," Baron says, sitting beside me.

"What do you mean?" I ask.

"The bones," he says. "F used to be a very rich man. Jakob Fugger was his name. Lived in Germany in the 1500s. He was almost as rich as I was, running mines and banks and more. Some say he was the world's greatest businessman, until I came along. He still knows a lot about raw materials, so I put him in charge of our weapons. A skeleton like that can make enough bone daggers for all of us. It's how the game goes. Whoever gets first keeps getting. Whoever wins first can't lose, as long he builds and grows and conquers. You see?"

"I think so," I say.

He takes my hands and studies the scars on them. He holds up his own. The criss-cross shapes are a perfect match. "You should know something, Cipher."

"What's that?"

"It's no coincidence you hit that target. You have powers, very strong powers. That's why you have these scars. Like me."

"Why us?"

"We're different, Cipher. We're the marked ones, cut from the same stone. Everyone here is connected, somehow, and their movements bend and flow around ours. Only we can bring the towers to equilibrium. Daniel says there will be five of us. I got my scar here, after I saw something in the sap. I bet you got yours from other towers. You're the only other marked one I've found."

I gaze at the fire, feeling lost. "I don't understand."

"Let me tell you a story. It might help. My name used to be John Davison Rockefeller." He pauses, as if expecting me to react.

I don't. The name means nothing to me.

"Was this on Earth?" I ask.

He smiles. "Yes, I became the richest man in the world. It took hard work and steady progress and a few good breaks. Bit by bit I built an empire. I had power beyond your wildest imagination. Nothing was impossible for me."

"How did you get here?"

"I died. Daniel says we all did. I don't know how. It hardly seems to matter. What matters is the competition. After every Jubilee I have fifty days to build an empire. I lead our tribe to capture the most, to build the most, and so, to survive. Then I choose my tribe again."

"But then it's wiped away at the Jubilee?"

Baron sighs. "Everything but my memories. I remember every step of how I built Standard Oil, every competitor I bought, every employee I hired. No one had run an operation like that before me. These lessons make leading the Wolves easy, though there are more…challenges. Some know the forest better. Some have more powers. Some are faster, more vicious, more reckless. But I am steady. The forest and the tribes bend to my will, more and more with each Jubilee. Soon I will conquer the tribes within a day, putting their struggles to an end. I will bring peace to the Green Tower. And we can do it together, Cipher."

He studies me as I process all this. It sounds…okay, but something seems off.

"If your name was John, why do you go by Baron?"

"People can call me whatever they want," he says. "I have been called Rock, Jones, Davison, John D., and a dozen other things. Some not so polite. It does not change who I am. I am John Davison Rockefeller. Lately people call me Baron. It stuck."

He says all this with such calm, as if all of it is beneath him, as if he has maintained complete control. It makes his interest in me more confusing.

"Why do you want my help?" I ask.

"It is destiny." He points to my scars again. "Besides, life is more fun when you have comrades by your side. Don't worry. It will be good sport."

I glance to the boy who was impaled by the hog. "I'm not sure if I'm ready for that."

"Oh, you are," Baron says, tracing a finger over his faint mustache. "You will use your wind, and we will hunt the stag."

"What's that?"

"The noblest creature in the forest. People claim to have seen it. Not me. But I figure if you see it, you can shoot it. Trouble is, you cannot simply find the stag. It has to find you. That is why I am taking you with me tomorrow. Maybe two scarred ones will lure it."

"What happens if it find us?"

Baron winks. "You'll get a bow. Maybe a bone dagger, if you want. Will you be ready?"

*Ready?* Right now I'm stuffed and confused. But he does not seem like the type to accept "no" as an answer. He controls the servants. He chooses who wears the collars. It will be better to be on his side.

"I guess so," I say.

He slaps me on the back and hops up, ready to rejoin the celebration. "First thing tomorrow, Cipher. We will hunt the stag."

# 26

THE NEXT MORNING Baron sends out hunting groups like before. He leads three of us: Fugger, Tom, and me. We're armed with bows and arrows and bone knives tucked into our shorts. Baron tells us to be silent, with eyes on the shadows.

We follow the creek that runs by the village and winds through the trees. It narrows upstream to a dribble of water, only a foot wide. The underbrush is so thick that I wouldn't notice the creek unless I stepped right over it.

"Look!" Baron whispers ahead. He kneels down and points to marks in the dirt. "Hooves. Going that way."

"Could be a deer," Fugger says.

"Or the stag," Baron says, smiling.

Fugger shrugs. "We can eat either one."

"So we hunt both!" Baron rises and leads us further into the trees.

We pass through a stretch of pines standing like sentinels around us. The forest is eerily dark and quiet, with pine needles softening our footsteps. The underbrush fades to nothing. Mist hangs at the edges of our sight, obscuring the forest beyond.

Baron doesn't slow. I don't see another track or sign of life. Eventually the pines give way to leafy oaks and maples, with underbrush growing thick again. We weave steadily through the forest as shadows lengthen.

A solid shape appears ahead of us. As we approach I realize it's an immense stone wall, stretching in a straight line as far as I can see. The trees grow almost to the edge of the wall and reach to its top, but the branches come to a stop a dozen feet from the stone. It's like there's an invisible barrier preventing the forest from getting too close.

Baron pauses at the edge of the trees. "It's the Yellow Tower's wall," he says.

"What's on the other side of it?" I ask.

"Other than the Yellow Tower? Don't know. Don't care." Baron eyes the wall like it's an enemy. "Not worth trying. Yellow archers patrol along the top. They'll shoot anyone who approaches."

There are no archers in sight. Something about the wall fascinates me. What could it be hiding, protecting? It looks like we could make it over. With all the resources of the forest, we could make a rope from vines, or even a ladder.

"Can we try to get past them?" I ask.

"No, trust me. I have tried it. An arrow went clean through my foot. The Wolves dragged me back to camp. We didn't have a healer then. I had to sit around or hobble through the woods until the next Jubilee. Couldn't hunt. Couldn't fight. It was terrible."

Curiosity about the wall tugs me forward.

"Hey, wait," Baron says.

"I'll be right back."

I step out of the forest. The ground goes from leafy decay to a smooth carpet of grass. Nothing tries to stop me as I approach the wall. I reach the base and press my hands against the stone. It is warm to the touch. The light feels good on my face, lifting my gaze upward to the blue sky.

Someone yanks my arm, pulling me away from the wall and into the shadows beneath the trees.

"That's enough," Baron snaps. "Quit staring at the sky. Didn't you hear me?" He looks excited but confused.

"No," I say. "What happened?"

"The stag!" he whispers. "Look!"

Sure enough, at the base of the wall in the distance a giant stag stands in the light, calmly munching the grass. Its antlers look bigger than I am.

"F and T are moving into position," Baron says. "They should be there soon. We'll distract it. They'll shoot. Follow me."

Baron hurries along the edge of the forest, where the grass gives way to shadowy underbrush. The stag has not budged. Still it munches the grass calmly.

Crouching, Baron motions for me to be silent. He draws his bow and advances slowly, silently. There's no sign of Tom or Fugger.

Baron stops. He notches an arrow.

The stag looks up and sees us. It remains still.

Baron looses, the string twangs, and the arrow soars.

It's an impossible distance for me, but maybe Baron could hit from here. One second the arrow reaches its zenith, then it's arcing down, zooming like at the stag like a missile.

It's going to hit. It's going to hit. It's…

There's a shout. Then a scream.

The arrow plunges into the grassy ground where the stag had stood. The feathered arrow shaft quivers. The stag…disappeared.

"What!" Baron gasps under his breath.

A sound behind me makes me turn. Heavy breaths. Rustling leaves. The stag is there. Its head moves, like it's bowing, saying hello. Then it turns and bounds off. A moment later it's gone.

The forest is silent. Too silent. No birds. No insects. Nothing.

Baron looks into the forest with terror on his face. He doesn't speak. He rushes toward his arrow. Our footsteps stampede over the silence.

But then there's another sound. Crying. Moaning.

Baron veers toward the forest and moments later we find Tom laying on the floor of leaves. He's curled like a fetus, sobbing. Beside him there's a dark puddle. Fugger is nowhere in sight.

Baron pauses for only a moment. His face turns from horror to grim resolution. He walks off toward his arrow, no longer crouching.

"Tom," I say. "What happened?"

He stays curled on the ground as he looks at me. His eyes are red. Tears streak down his cheek. He breathes out,

"The Hunter came."

"Who's that?" I ask.

"Fugger's gone," Baron says, returning to us. He has put the arrow back in the quiver. His face is hard, unreadable. "The Hunter took him. We have to get back to camp. It'll be dark soon."

"What are you talking about?" I demand.

"Sometimes the Hunter takes a person. There's no use crying about it. Fugger will be back at the Jubilee."

"But—" Tom manages to rise to his knees. "He just appeared. He…there was…blood."

"Did he say anything?" Baron asks.

"No," Tom says. "It happened so fast. He threw Fugger over his shoulder and…vanished."

"When did it happen?"

"We were watching the stag, like you said." Tom glances to the gap before the wall. "It wasn't going anywhere. I don't think it had seen us. We were just here, quiet like you told us. Then the stag disappeared and the Hunter was here."

"Must be connected…" Baron mutters, holding out a hand to Tom. "Come, we have to get back."

Tom looks down at the dark puddle and shudders. "Okay," he says, taking Baron's hand.

We don't stop on the way back. I try to ask Baron more about what happened, but he will not talk. The forest is still eerily quiet. The shadows grow darker. The air grows colder. The day's last light has faded by the time we reach the village, empty-handed and one person down.

# 27

THE DARK, STARLESS night is somber in the village. None of the Wolves' hunters caught anything. No fire is built. There's only a little leftover meat for each of us. "The Hunter took him," is all Baron says about Fugger. The village whispers. Fear lays heavier than darkness as we sleep.

A cool mist shrouds the village the next morning. Baron sends out teams to hunt. This time he sends me off with B, D, and Tom.

I try to ask B and D about their names, but they just tell me, "Baron says to focus on the hunt."

I try talking to Tom, who still looks shaken from what happened to Fugger. "You recognized me from before, didn't you?" I ask.

"Yes," he says.

"How did you know me?"

"Can't tell you," he says.

I pry a dozen different ways, but the only thing I gather is that Baron has commanded him not to reveal anything to me. Eventually I give up asking.

We spend the day moving slowly, silently, through the dense forest. Birds sing in the distance, but there's no other sign of life except two squirrels. We shoot arrows at them but miss. They chatter and scurry away, high and safe in the branches above. We return at dusk. Again there's no fresh food, no fire, no celebration. We eat only mushrooms and a few nuts. The village's food stock is low.

The next day goes the same. And the following day. The mist doesn't relent. After three days we've eaten through the last of our food. No more berries or mushrooms grow. We'll have to get by on whatever nuts we can gather. One boy's trap catches a rabbit. Baron decides we should have a fire. The rabbit won't feed all of us. Baron splits it with our four best hunters. None for me. My stomach groans. Others grumble.

A few of the tribe sing around the campfire, trying to cheer each other up. But the energy is gone. The tribe has gone flat. A boy beside me mutters, "no giving to set us free here...," and I wonder if we would somehow get more food if Baron shared more.

Countless days pass like this. The bits and pieces of food we get are barely enough to stave off the hunger. I begin to accept the constant pangs, to preserve my energy, to live numbly. Leaves begin to turn yellow and orange, some with no green left at all. In the rare places where sunlight shines through gaps in the canopy, it makes the leaves look fluorescent.

One day Baron spots me gazing up at the trees. "Changing colors," he says. "Not much longer until the

Jubilee."

"How long?" I ask.

"It all moves fast," he says. "We have ten more days until the Jubilee. Not that I am worried, but one of my scouts says the Lions have wiped out the Snakes again. Maybe caught a few Eagles, too. They have a stronghold in the jungle. Tough to beat. Wolves do not last long in the jungle."

"What do you plan to do?"

"We hunt, and we wait. Sometimes another tower sends people here to try to capture us. But it is very rare. They know what I am capable of."

The next day Baron brings back a turkey. It is a rare feast, but not as much as it should be for a famished group of our size. The tribe feeds desperately, without celebration, without song or dance. When only the bones are left, we boil them and subsist on broth and roots for three more days.

The next evening, without another catch by the hunters, some of them try to convince Baron to move to a different area of the forest, where there might be more animals. Baron refuses to leave.

"Five more days," he says. "We only have to make it five more days. We can survive that long without food. We have water. We have the most captives. Double our watch at night. Double our defenses. Everyone else hunts. We will win again."

After spending a night on watch, shivering and starving and alone, I can't stand another day in the somber, misty village. I approach Baron that evening as the fire burns low Tonight's feast is a squirrel.

"Hey Baron, can I go out hunting tomorrow?"

His shoulders are slumped. He doesn't meet my eyes. He gnaws the last of the meat off a small leg. "Where will you go?"

"Back to the wall," I say. "Other animals might be there, where they can eat the grass. I know the way."

He looks up. His granite eyes are still resolute. "You want to end up like Fugger?"

"I've been thinking about that," I say. "I think the Hunter didn't want us to get the stag. I won't try it. I'll just look for food and I'll bring back whatever I find. I promise."

He waves the bone dismissively. "Pick two servants to go with you."

I say thanks and walk away before he can change his mind. Who to take? Maybe the servants will do Baron's bidding, but some are different than others—more defiant. I ask Seneca first. She says yes calmly, but my request brings new energy to her eyes. Then I try Tom. He doesn't look happy about it, but he gives in. I'm not sure he has any choice.

The next morning we head out, following the same creek as before. But this time Seneca has us turn away from the creek earlier. She says she knows a faster way to the wall. We reach it by midday.

"Stay in the shadows," Seneca says, moving along the edge of the forest and staying out of the sunlight that shines on the grass between us and the wall. Tom and I follow her.

"Why the shadows?" I ask. The sun would feel good on my skin after so many days in the forest gloom.

"So Yellow's archers don't shoot us," she says.

I look up at the wall. No one is in sight. "Where?"

"They patrol the wall. If they see anyone from Green approach the wall, they shoot them. But we're safe in the shadows."

Maybe I got lucky last time.

Seneca keeps up a brisk pace. There's little change around us. The forest looms darkly to our right. The wall looms brightly to our left. Only once does a person pass on top of the wall above. He stops, bow in hand, as he looks down at us. Then he continues on his way, going the opposite direction. No other life stirs. No animals. No stag.

Eventually we come to a cliff. A dense jungle spreads out below us, leading to the sea at the horizon. The wall turns at a sharp angle and runs along the edge of the cliff to our left. In the distance the vast jungle narrows until the cliff and the wall meet the sea. It looks like a border between Yellow and Green. To the other side, the sun is setting. But…I blink twice. There are *three* suns.

"What are those?" I ask, pointing at them.

"The suns," Seneca shrugs. "We don't know why there are three."

"Who cares, makes more light." Tom sits on the edge of the cliff, with his legs dangling over. "What now?"

"We climb down," Seneca says. She tugs at a long vine

that hangs over the cliff. It's a very long drop.

"Why?" I ask.

Seneca looks to me, her copper face radiant in the light of the three setting suns. "Why not?" she asks.

"Baron says the jungle is Lions' territory," I say.

"I'll make sure we avoid them." There's no doubt in Seneca's voice. "But if you'd rather sleep here and start in the morning, that's alright. It'll be safer to climb down with better light. I could use the time to gather more vines and tie them together, to make sure it holds."

"What about Baron?" Tom asks Seneca. "He could order us to come back."

"Doubtful." Seneca shrugs, looking out over the jungle. "He's like this every time near the Jubilee. He's won the game. He's just trying to win by as much as he can. Besides, even if he loses us, he'll still be number one again. I think he's just amused by Cipher—wants to see what he'll do, like a wolf toying with a mouse."

"I'm no mouse," I say, but my voice betrays me with a squeak.

Seneca laughs. Even Tom smiles.

"Mice aren't so bad," Seneca says. "They know how to hide, how to survive."

We find a place to sleep under a large tree by the cliff. Each of us makes a bed of leaves on the ground between the massive roots. Crickets serenade me to sleep.

The next morning Seneca twists more vines together until she's confident it will be safe. Tom volunteers to go first. He slides down slowly, without incident. Seneca goes next, rappelling off the wall like she's done this before. I go last. I don't look down. I keep my eyes up and my grip tight, staying as close as I can to the cliff wall. It feels like forever before my feet touch the ground.

Seneca waits for me at the bottom. "Tom's keeping watch," she says. "All's clear toward the sea. We should be there by nightfall. We'll catch crabs and dine like kings."

She leads me into the jungle. Tom joins us and the three of us forge ahead together. It is much hotter than the forest above. The jungle floor is also much denser. Vines and leaves and roots grab at our legs and slow our progress. Bugs swarm around our heads. I flap my arms to keep them away, but it's not enough. They are like kamikazes, crashing into my ears and my eyes and any other opening they can find.

*Kamikaze.* The word surprises me. It is from the odd vision I saw before a boy named O woke me up in the giant tree, before the Lions attacked the Wolves, before Seneca healed me. There was a book on the nightstand in Paul Fitzroy's home. It was my home, my book—about planes crashing wildly into ships and sea, exploding in violent flames. Why were the planes crashing? Why was my son, Benjamin, so sick?

I swat again at the bugs, almost relieved at the distraction from my thoughts. I know I've been avoiding them. The isolated fragments in my mind are too small, too sharp, to comprehend. The only thing to do is press forward and survive.

Seneca was right. By nightfall we have reached the

water. We manage to catch three crabs. Seneca builds a small fire to cook them. It makes the hunting expedition seem worth it. We sleep under the mangroves.

The next morning I'm the first one awake, before the suns have risen. The sea breeze, keeping the bugs at bay, fills me with unexpected energy. As I look out over the water, I see something approaching us.

It's a boat with broad, blue sails.

<h1 style="text-align:center">28</h1>

I QUICKLY ROUSE Seneca and Tom. We watch the boat approach the shore, dreamlike, with its blue sails stretched taut and soaring. It's a few hundred feet away when the sails fall. People onboard rush into action. There are at least a dozen of them.

A girl climbs down from the boat to the water. From this distance we can't make out much, but she has long, brown hair hanging over her blue robe. Her foot touches the water, but does not go under. She does not sink. She does not swim. *She walks.*

A dozen others—about half of those on the boat—follow her onto the water. I can see the air underneath them, countless blue threads weaving and forging into a path two feet wide and a hundred feet long. The path leads to the shore, close to us.

"What on Earth?" Tom gasps.

"Not Earth," Seneca whispers. "They're from the Blue Tower."

We slip back into the jungle of mangroves and huddle together. The water walkers will reach us in a minute, maybe two.

"We have to run!" Tom says softly.

Seneca ignores him and looks to me. "Cipher, this is our chance. If we catch some of them, we could be tribe leaders. You have to use your power."

"What are you talking about?" I ask, even as I think of the blue threads, of weaving them to make an arrow hit a target. But that was an arrow, not a person. "I can't…"

Seneca takes my face between her hands. "I felt the power when I healed you," she says, her eyes intense. "I've heard about what you did in Blue. You led them. Your wind blew people like dry leaves. You captured more than anyone in the Scouring. You must do that now. I can help."

"You're crazy!" Tom says. "There are *twelve* of them. Walking on bloody water. I don't care how strong he is. He can't stop them alone. I'm leaving."

"No, it's too late," Seneca says. "They're too close. They'll hear you moving, Tom, and you know it. Do you want to be taken to the Blue Tower and turned into a servant?"

Tom considers it. "I already am a servant. Is that all they'll do?"

"I know very little about Blue," Seneca says. "Ask Cipher."

They both look to me, but I can only shrug.

"I don't remember much either," Tom says, "but Blue can't be any worse than Green, and Baron, and the Hunter. I don't care about Green's stupid game. I'm tired of this forest, the hunger—all of it!"

Seneca points toward the group from Blue. "So why don't you go introduce yourself?"

"Maybe I will!" Tom says, standing.

"We won't stop you," Seneca says.

Tom looks to me. "Want to come, Cipher? Maybe they could help you with your power over the wind. You could get your memories back."

I turn to Seneca, whose hawkish eyes are still intense. She has no fear. It doesn't feel right to leave Green and her, not after she healed me.

I shake my head. "Sorry, Tom."

"Suit yourself, I'm going," Tom says.

He turns toward the shore, scrambling through the mangroves. It doesn't take long for the group from Blue to spot him. Now there are twelve of them against two of us.

"Don't worry," Seneca whispers. "We still have an advantage."

"What's that?"

"Surprise. But there's a problem." She points to the collar at her neck. "As long as I'm wearing this, Baron can feel what I feel. He can command me to do anything. The last thing we want is to capture someone, and then for Baron to order me to return. You'd have no chance in the jungle alone."

"What's your plan?"

"I've been thinking about this," she says. "Usually only the master can remove it, but you have this power, and the scars. Will you try?"

"Won't Baron know?" He's not going to like this…if it's even possible.

"Yes, but he can't do anything about it now." She glances toward the water and the group from Blue. "We could use the link to capture one of them. Try it, quickly now. There's something like a button at the back center. Send your power into that spot."

She leans her head toward me, pulling aside her black hair and exposing her neck and the collar. I hesitate. I don't know what Baron will do. But the group from Blue is an immediate threat, and we could use the collar. I'm also curious. Could I really remove it?

I touch the metal band and summon the wind. It blows but nothing happens other than rustling Seneca's hair.

"More, more," she whispers urgently. "You told me your name was Paul Fitzroy. Remember! More!"

Taking a deep breath, I close my eyes and think of Dr. Fitzroy and the book cover with the crashing planes and my son shaking uncontrollably on the floor. I lived in a mansion. I was rich. But I didn't know how to heal him. My medicines were not enough.

The memories bring anger. My fists shake.

"Yes," Seneca whispers. "Now use it!"

I focus on the blue threads. They strain at my mind, like trying to weave a thousand chaotic strings through a pinhole of light. But each memory widens the hole, and more threads enter. One by one I master them, weaving and coiling until the collar clicks.

It falls to the ground. The cold, lifeless metal looks

unnatural against the mangrove roots.

Seneca snatches the collar up. A huge smile spreads over her face. She looks out over the water. The smile fades to a concentrated grimace. When she looks back to me, her eyes are steely.

"Thank you, Cipher," she whispers. "Now we have to move fast. Just try to grab one or two of them with the wind. If we can get them into the forest, I'll get us away." She clasps my shoulder. "Trust me. If we bring someone from Blue into the Jubilee, this will all be worth it."

I nod, trusting her. She's the one who healed me. And now she has helped me recover this…power.

We move closer to the edge of the mangroves, silently following the path that Tom took. He has made it out of the thick trees and into the shallow water. He wades forward through the crystal clear sea. The group from Blue walks above the water toward him, only a stone's throw away.

The same girl is at the front. Now I see that her hair is long, wavy, and auburn. Her robe has four stripes on the sleeves and sways back and forth as she saunters ahead. She looks like she could be walking down a palace hall, rather than along a path over water into the jungle. Behind her is a boy with a silver collar around his neck.

The girl reaches Tom and says something to him. It's not loud enough to hear. She's smiling. The rest of the Blue group is catching up to her.

"Now," Seneca whispers. "Grab them with much as you can hold."

I summon the threads of air again. Strands weave together at the surface of the water, beneath the feet of the girl from Blue and the boy with the collar. I take a deep breath and yank the air up and toward me, drawing it into a tight net that holds them just above the water. The path of air over the water suddenly vanishes. The others from Blue fall and splash, frantically starting to swim.

Momentum pulls the net closer to shore, but the effort is immense. I fall to my knees, arms extended, doing everything I can to concentrate.

The girl spots me. There's fury in her eyes. Wind hits me like an uppercut, flinging me backwards into a tree, head thudding against the trunk.

Stars flash across my vision. Wind batters at me, then tightens and constricts my movements. The power slips.

The girl and the collared boy from Blue charge toward me through the shallows. I'm held by her air, fixed in place. As the girl comes within a few feet, she stops and stares at me as if frozen in shock.

I grab again for the power, but she shakes her head and hits me with another blast. The wind gusts around me, too wild to control. The girl is too strong. She glares down at me.

"*You…*" she growls.

A blur of motion springs at her from the side. It's Seneca, with the collar. She clasps it around the girl's neck. The wind suddenly stops.

Seneca rushes to me and pulls me to my feet. "Follow me! Don't look back!"

She dashes away from the water, deeper into the mangrove jungle. I scramble after her. The boy and girl from Blue are just ahead of me, trying to keep up with Seneca. The sounds of shouting from the rest of the Blue group become more distant. The mangroves give way to thick jungle. Bugs swarm and birds sing.

Seneca does not slow down. Her pace is relentless. I trip a dozen times against roots and vines. Scrapes and bruises and bug bites multiply over me, itching and burning.

Seneca finally comes to a stop by a small, gurgling creek. Darkness has begun to fall over the jungle. Lush green trees and plants take on ominous shapes in the shadows, crowding us like unwelcome guests.

"We'll rest here," Seneca says. "Let's build a fire."

# 29

SENECA ORDERS THE collared boy and girl from Blue to search the jungle for a certain kind of root. She tells me we will cook the roots, and that there's no need to worry about the new servants running away. "I've given them clear orders," she says. "Let's gather sticks to burn."

She leads me into the jungle, and I stay close, fumbling through the dense leaves and vines. The shadows seem closer, darker, than in the forest above. It would be easy to hide in this place. An ambush could come any moment.

"What if the Lions capture them?" I ask.

"They'll warn us before that happens. I'm not worried about the Lions. Got enough wood yet?"

She sounds so casual, too confident. Even Baron had a healthy fear of the Lions and the jungle.

"Almost." I continue groping around for sticks. The bundle in my arms is moist and decaying. "Are you expecting me to dry the wood?"

Seneca laughs lightly. "You sound tired. I'll have our Blue captive do it."

"Won't a fire attract attention?"

"Are you always so worried?" she asks. "Trust me, the Lions are no threat to us."

"What about Baron?"

She sighs. "It feels so good to be free of him."

"So I guess we're not going back to the Wolves?"

"Oh no, we can't do that. Baron knows his mistake now, letting us leave. He felt it the moment you took my collar off. We'll see him at the Jubilee. It's only three days away. Here, carry some of these leaves back too."

She hands me the leaves. I can barely see them in my own hands, but they feel thick and heavy, like elephant ears. She continues gathering wood and leaves and layering them in my outstretched arms. The chirping of insects fills every nook and cranny with life. It keeps me on edge. There's no way I'd hear someone sneaking up on us.

Seneca leads the way back along the gurgling stream. Once we reach the small clearing, the servants from Blue are waiting. The girl uses the wind to dry the wood, just as Seneca said, and she makes it look easy. I marvel at her robe, her power. She uses the wind as I do, but she is stronger. She would have taken me if not for the collar. I wonder what they teach them in the Blue Tower.

Seneca strikes at something and makes sparks. Each flash of light reveals her concentrated face, a dull gray stone in her hands, and a carefully arranged stack of wood. Eventually the sparks light twigs, and soon flames are licking up into the dark night.

We can see each other. So others can see us, and maybe the smoke from our fire too. A handful of stars peer down through the small gap in the canopy above.

Seneca wraps the roots that the servants found in the thick leaves and lays them on the hot coals. The four of us sit silently, close around the small fire as the food cooks. It smells good. My stomach growls. The girl from Blue stares intently at me, with firelight reflecting off her collar. There's a knowing look in her almond eyes, but she doesn't say a word. I have so many questions, but I follow Seneca's lead and keep quiet. I have no idea what we're supposed to do with captives.

Seneca serves us equal portions, even though we do not have much. Baron would have kept the roots for himself. I'm glad she shared. The roots taste nutty. It's almost comforting. They go down easily.

"Now," Seneca says to the girl, "tell us what you remember from Earth. Quietly."

The girl nods. "My name was Helena. I was born with nothing except my looks," she says. "A powerful thing, they were. I used them to win over an emperor. We had a son together. I traveled the whole empire, raising the heir. But others started to want the throne. They didn't think my son deserved to be emperor because of me, his mother. So the emperor, my husband, left me. We were not poor. But we were not as rich as we once were. We waited. And waited. Year after year. They could have been sad days. They were my happiest memories. It didn't matter how much money I had, because I had my son, my precious Constantine."

"What happened to him?" Seneca asks.

"He became the Roman Emperor. He named me Imperatrix. We had more power and wealth than anyone in the world. We did amazing things. We built palaces and gardens. We traveled to the Holy Land searching for the cross, the true cross. There were fragments, mere splinters of wood. It was a good life."

"Tell me more," Seneca says. "I want to hear all of it."

As the girl, Helena, continues to speak—of life in Rome, of ruling an empire with her son—something tickles at the edges of my mind. It is like a light barely bright enough to reach the walls of a room. The shadows still cover the walls, but the light grows. It penetrates and small spots of the walls are revealed. And there, in those spots, is something that I remember.

*Helena has told me this before.*

With that flash of recognition comes more light, connecting pieces of the past. Helena told me this in the Blue Tower. It's true. Seneca was right. I was in the Blue Tower. But when? And how did I get here? What's happening to me? All I know is the fragments of light, and I'm desperate for more. I delve into the memories, searching. Helena told a group of us this story. We sat in an underwater room. We ate squid soup. I didn't remember who I was then, either. But then I looked into the Sieve. I saw myself…before I died. I was a doctor. Dr. Fitzroy, chief neurosurgeon. *Respect the mind.*

"Hey." Seneca's hand is on my shoulder. "Are you listening?"

"Sorry, no," I say. "I remembered something."

"What is it?" Seneca asks.

I turn to Helena. When our eyes meet, she leans back as if afraid of what she sees. She knows. She sees now that I recognize her. But the memory is dim. There's still so much I don't understand.

"You told me this before," I say. "Some of it."

"Yes," Helena says. "And I learned more after you left. This is what I have told you."

"I believe we were meant to capture you," Seneca says.

"Why's that?" Helena asks.

Seneca takes my hand, then Helena's. She holds them both in front of her, so that the fire lights up the backs of our hands. They bear matching scars with two perpendicular lines crossing each other in the center. "You are both marked," Seneca says.

"Did you have this before?" I ask Helena.

She shakes her head. "Not when you were in Blue."

"What does it mean?" I ask.

"Two gatekeepers together..." Seneca whispers. "And now three of you in Green!"

"Baron is the third," I say, remembering his scar.

"Yes," Seneca answers. "Daniel says there will be five of you." She sits back and gazes up into the dark canopy above. "I don't know what it means, but it's no coincidence. I'm certain of that. Helena, when did you get your scar?"

"Only recently," Helena says. "It happened as I reached into a bowl in Blue that is used to assign groups. It was just before this Hunting."

Seneca looks to the boy from Blue, who has been silent this whole time. She checks the backs of his hands, but there are no scars.

"What about you?" Seneca asks him. "What do you remember?"

"My name was Frank Rockefeller," he says, with surprising confidence. "Helena captured me. I told her my name was Jack, so that's what they called me. Cipher here dragged me back to this forest as a slave. They tried to make me steal my friends from here. Too bad for them my brother stood in the way."

"Is this true?" I ask Helena.

She nods. "You and I came to Green together. If Frank's brother hadn't grabbed your little princess and held a knife to her throat, we might have captured a host of them. But you offered to trade me. We barely got away."

"And still you took me," Frank says. The light from the fire makes his wild eyes and sandy hair look alive with energy. "If you'll take my collar off, I'll tell you all you want to know."

"Helena, make him—" Seneca goes still, her eyes alert.

The jungle has fallen completely silent. The insects have stopped chirping. The howls start distant and soft, muffled by the jungle, but they're approaching.

"Baron…" Seneca's face is pale. She springs to her feet. "Quick, follow me!"

# 30

SENECA WIELDS A burning stick from the fire like a torch as she takes off into the jungle. Helena, Frank, and I race after her, but she's too fast, moving like a ghost through the dense undergrowth. Limbs and leaves and vines batter and grab at us. Only the light of Seneca's torch draws us forward, flashing in and out of the foliage ahead.

The howling comes from ahead of us, louder and louder, as if Seneca is leading straight toward them. But then she stops, hiding by an enormous tree. She studies the jungle as we approach.

"Come," she whispers. "Be still, be silent."

We huddle close and listen as the howling passes us, sounding no more than a stone's throw away. It makes my spine tingle with the fear of being prey. But why hunt us? Because I took off Seneca's collar? Surely she'd put it back on rather than die. I expect to see Baron and the Wolves charge out of the jungle and attack, but the howling continues on, growing fainter.

"They missed us," Seneca says. "They will go to the fire, but they will be back on our path soon."

"Why run?" I pant out. "Baron will be pleased...we caught others..."

Seneca grabs my arm tightly. The back of her hand shows a lion. Her copper face is savage in the torchlight. "I'm not a Wolf anymore."

*Oh. She's a Lion again.*

I shake my arm free. "But I am a Wolf."

"Please, do it for me," she says. "You know what Baron will do to me..."

Her panicked tone eliminates any doubt. She will be made a servant again, or worse. And she has done so much for me. "Okay," I say. "But why did you risk a fire? Baron must have seen the smoke."

She shakes her head, confused. "He was too far away, and he never comes to Lion territory this close to the Jubilee. I do not know how he found us—maybe a spy— but it does not matter now. We must hurry."

She turns and ducks into the verdant tangle again. We move as fast as we can but the jungle slows every step. The servants from Blue trip and fall in their heavy robes, leaving a clear trail. It's only a matter of time until the Wolves track us down.

Again Seneca pauses, her torch down to faint embers that barely keep the shadows away. We rush to her, but a vine snags my ankle and trips me to the ground. The smell of humid earth fills my nostrils. Seneca helps me up. Helena bends over, hands on her knees, breathing heavily. Frank looks back toward the forest, excitement in his eyes. The howls have turned back. The Wolves are coming.

"Off with the robes," Seneca demands. As the servants strip down to their undergarments, Seneca looks from Helena to me. "The wind. You must use it. Both of you. Make a path."

Helena begins to weave the air in front of us, making the dense jungle ahead blow in the wind. I add my weaves to Helena's, and our combined powers somehow multiply the force, blasting the leaves and branches back. Everything bends and gives way except tree trunks, opening a tunnel large enough for us to pass single-file.

"Yes!" Seneca says. "Keep it up. Hurry!"

She rushes ahead through the tunnel, with us racing after her. I look from the ground to the trees, and back, over and over, dodging roots and holding the jungle's entanglements at bay as we race through, and then letting all the leaves and vines fall back into place once we've passed.

The howling of the Wolves still comes. My power weakens. Helena stops weaving entirely, her power sapped from using so much more. Only my wind forms the tunnel now, and it is not nearly as wide as it was. Seneca comes back to me and takes my hand to guide me forward. My vision blurs. My knees threaten to give out.

Finally Seneca stops. She looks up at a massive gray wall looming above us. We've reached the cliff.

"What now?" Helena pants.

The howling approaches, closer and closer. I glimpse a distant torch behind us, flashing in the gaps where our tunnel had opened.

"There's a cave halfway up," Seneca says, pointing at the cliff wall. "We hide there."

High above us, and above the top of the jungle's canopy, the moonlight reveals a dark spot on the grey rock wall. No vines lead up to it. No tree branches are close enough to even consider leaping into it. How did she know about this?

"We can't get there," Helena says.

Seneca puts both arms on my shoulders and looks into my eyes. "Cipher, you need to give us one last push. Back at the sea, you lifted Helena and Frank. Can't you lift us?"

I shake my head. "Sorry, I'm drained."

Seneca sucks in a deep breath, then looks to Helena. "Order Frank not to move."

Helena nods. Frank eyes Seneca angrily, his feet fixed in place.

"Good," Seneca says. "Now, Cipher, take her collar off and put it on me."

"*What?*" Helena and I say together. She sounds more surprised than I am.

"Just do it," Seneca says. "We don't have time. Once I'm your servant, it will be easier to pull on my power. Weave your power through me. Take whatever you can. Then lift us to the cave."

"But—"

"Do it," Seneca demands. "Now."

*Hoo! Hoo! Hoo!* The Wolves howl.

I rush to Helena. My hands feel around the back of the collar around her neck. Our faces are close. She looks hopeful. I press my fingers into the back, at the center, and summon every ounce of wind I can into that spot. Like before, the band unclasps. It feels cold.

"Quick, on me." Seneca bows her head.

I fit the collar around her neck. Each hand grips the edges of it tightly.

"Close it!" Seneca says.

The collar snaps shut. Her emotions flood through me, forcing me to my knees. Seneca is a maelstrom inside.

"Do it now," she says.

Leaves and branches rustle so close that we can hear it past the howling. Torches light up the jungle around us.

Through the emotion and the fatigue, I summon the air again. It is only a narrow thread, hardly enough to lift us. But I do as Seneca says. I weave my threads *through* her. Into her, and out. As the air moves it picks up thick, golden threads. They coil around each other, blue and yellow, blurring into faint green. The feeling is familiar, like I've done this before. The weave takes shape as a small platform, hovering at our knees.

"Get on," I say.

Seneca goes first. Then me. As I step onto the platform it shimmers, but holds.

Helena watches us, unmoving. "You can't lift all of us," she says. "Maybe not even you two."

"We have to try," I say.

She shakes her head, feeling at her bare neck, no doubt sensing her freedom. She doesn't have to obey any longer.

A boy crashes out of the jungle. Then another, and

another. Four collared servants, including B and D, along with Baron. The five of them surround us, trapping us with our backs against the cliff. Their faces are fierce in the torchlight.

Baron steps forward. "Seneca," he greets formally. "Nice to see you back in a collar." He looks to Frank. "Who's your master?"

Frank rubs at his collar as he glares at Helena. "That's her."

"I see." Baron reaches with his scarred hand to the back of Frank's neck and presses the collar firmly. Just as I think that he can't do it, that he's not the master, the collar falls off and Baron snatches it. *But how? Do we have the same kind of power?*

"Ah, at last!" Frank says, arcing his head back.

"Was she so bad a master?" Baron asks. "You didn't tell me she was beautiful."

"She's terrible," Frank replies, glaring at Helena. "How'd you get out of your collar?"

Helena takes a step back from them, toward us. "Cipher took it off. He put it on Seneca."

"Cipher," Baron says with disappointment. "Did you let Seneca fool you? Now you want to take some revenge by making her your servant? That is fine by me. But it is time to come back to our village. No one has to get hurt. You may even keep Seneca, if you like."

Seneca whispers by my side, "Don't trust him."

"Don't trust *me*?" Baron says. "You're the one who ran away. What happened to T? Let him be taken by Blue, I suppose? And now here you are, back in the jungle, trying to find the Lions, yes? I already saved you once from this humid, bug-infested place."

"You made me your slave," Seneca says. Her voice is steady and controlled, but the link tells me what's inside her: raging anger and desperate hunger for freedom.

"Ah, but you made my little brother *your* slave," Baron says. "I believe that makes us even." Baron smiles at Frank, by his side. They have the same bushy eyebrows and faint mustaches, but Frank has a wilder, fiercer edge. Baron remains solid as granite.

"*Was* your little brother," Frank says. "I'm my own man. Always will be." He glares at Helena. "I'll never be your slave again. You'll pay for what you did."

"Steady now, both of you," Baron says. "We might still find a mutually beneficial arrangement." He holds out his hand to me. "Cipher, trust me, you will be safe. We will be stronger together."

Time slows. Everyone looks at me. Waiting for me to decide.

I study Baron's outstretched hand, with the criss-cross scar. Seneca's emotions scream at me through the link. She's terrified, uncertain, angry. But she'll have to do whatever I command. She said the Jubilee is soon, and that it will bring freedom. I still remember so little, but Helena has shone light into my past. I was the leader of the Blue Tower. We captured from the Green Tower. Baron wants me to join him. Maybe he knows that I'm a threat. I have two scars. Baron has one. Helena has one. She knows about me. She can help me remember more. And with Seneca on my side, I don't need Baron to survive. I'd rather be free than share in his power.

"Helena," I say softly. "You coming?"

She glances back at me, then nods. She steps onto the edge of the platform. The Wolves move closer, almost within reach.

I draw as much of Seneca's power as I can, coiling it in and through mine beneath our feet. Helena begins to weave her own faint threads of air around ours, strengthening the platform. Only we can see it. Our threads work together, uniting and, in an instant, lifting.

The Wolves shout and dash forward. Only Baron stands his ground, eyeing me calmly as we soar up, out of reach. The platform rises and rises, even as my power fades to almost nothing. With a final surge we reach the cave halfway up the cliff and leap inside, leaving the Wolves and the jungle below.

# 31

THE CAVE IS hardly more than a crevice that opens a few feet deep in the cliff wall. Seneca, Helena, and I wedge into it as best we can. The Wolves howl furiously below us for a while. But they do not try to climb up in the dark. Maybe they will in daylight. For now we are safe. It's not comfortable. It doesn't matter. I could sleep anywhere. My eyelids feel like iron curtains.

"Can you take this off?" Seneca asks, motioning to her neck. In the moonlight, the silver band around her neck has soft, yellow luster.

I try to weave my power into the link, but there's no force to it. I shake my head. "I'm sorry. Too tired."

"You drained my power, too," Seneca sighs. "As soon as you can then. I'll keep watch. You two sleep."

She sits at the cave opening, looking out. Through the link she feels alert, but surprisingly hopeful. Maybe she's used to being a servant, and now she's glad it's me instead of Baron as the master.

Helena is no longer under our control, but there's nowhere she could run. She must be as tired as I am. She curls up in the back of the cave, with the walls pressed tight around her, and sleeps. I lay on the hard surface between her and Seneca. Sleep comes over me like a sudden fog.

Rain wakes me up. It patters loudly against the cave walls and floor. It blows almost straight into the cave and the water collects in a pool on the floor.

Yawning, sitting up, I see Seneca in the same spot as before. "How long did I sleep?" I ask her.

"All night, and almost all day," she says. "This is the second storm. You slept through the first one."

"And you?"

"I caught a few winks," she says. "But someone had to stay on guard."

I glance back at Helena, still curled up. At the back of the cave there's a ledge just above the water. She's still dry. "Has she woken up?" I ask Seneca softly.

"No." Seneca's hand goes to the collar as she looks past me, to Helena. "Can you put this back on her? Now, please."

"Who will be the master?" I ask.

"You will," she says. "Whoever puts it on gets control."

Helena might have helped us get away from Baron, but she's still our captive from Blue. She might try to run if she has a chance. I move closer to Seneca. The rain pours, dripping into my eyes, as I summon enough wind to take the collar off.

I take it quietly to Helena. Her breathing is slow and steady. Trying not to stir her, I reach behind her neck and close the collar.

She snaps awake immediately, sitting upright. She glares at me with her lips pressed into a tight line. Her feelings rush into my mind through the link. Mostly there's hunger and fatigue. But under that, there's confidence, curiosity…and desire. I can't tell what the desire is for. She's restless. Maybe for freedom. No surprise there. She's my servant now.

"Stay still and silent," I say to her.

"You don't have to say it out loud," Seneca says behind me. "You can issue orders as a thought. But be careful what you think. The link requires obedience only to the precise thing you have commanded."

"Okay." I back away from Helena. The rain still blows horizontally with the wind into the cave. Seneca's hair is soaked, hanging wet down the sides of her face.

*Helena*, I think, as if I'm saying to her, *use your power to keep the rain from coming in here.*

She concentrates, looking past me. The weaves form into a thin wall of air. It covers the opening to the cave. No more rain gets inside. And none of my power is drained. I could get used to this.

*Keep that up*, I order Helena, *and don't do anything else but breathe.*

Seneca, now shielded from the rain, smiles as I approach. We sit beside each other, looking out over the jungle below. The green canopy extends like a lush carpet below our feet, until it is obscured by the layers of rain and clouds, like a grey-green wall in the distance.

"What now?" I ask.

"We wait," Seneca says. "The Jubilee is tomorrow."

"How will we get to the tower?"

She shrugs. "Last time I went back with a tribe. This time maybe the Hunter will come for us. Daniel requires everyone at the Jubilee."

"The Hunter that killed Fugger?" I ask.

"Yes, and Fugger will be fine. The Scouring tribe probably lost someone and needed more to keep their group at twelve, so the Hunter took him. Either that, or Baron wanted him gone."

"That doesn't make sense," I say. "Baron *wanted* us to get the stag. Fugger was helping."

"Fugger was a threat. You don't know Baron yet."

I'm unsure whether to believer her or not, but I'm not excited about the idea of the Hunter coming to get us. "Can't we just get back to the tower ourselves?"

"We shouldn't risk it," Seneca says. "Even if you and Helena got us out of this cave safely, it's Wolf territory through the forest above. Baron will have his scouts in the forest."

"Why are you so worried about Baron?" I ask, looking at Seneca's lion-marked hands in her lap. "Just because he'd make you a servant again—for one day?"

She shakes her head somberly. "I plotted against him, hoping to rejoin the Lions and help them beat Baron and his Wolves. I'll admit, that's why I built the fire. I wanted the Lions to see the smoke and come to us. Baron knows that now. And you helped me. He'll kill us, then we'd be wiped."

"Why would he do that?"

"For spite. He doesn't need us for the Wolves to win. The pack had over forty members. That's almost half of the entire Green Tower. Baron can't stand for anyone to resist him. I've heard he was like this on Earth, too. He would never stop until the universe conformed to his will."

"Stop what?" I ask.

"Chasing money."

"But there's no money here."

"Of course there is," she says. "Anything can be money if it can be traded and hoarded. The collars are the Green Tower's currency. The tribe leader with the most collars has the most wealth, and so the most power. That's Baron."

"But doesn't this reset at every Jubilee?"

"Yes, except the winners are the next round's leaders. And the leader gets the collars." She turns to me. Her eyes match the grey-green curtain outside the cave. "I want to be free from him, Cipher. And I don't want to start all over again. I don't want to forget everything. I've come too far."

Seneca goes quiet, gazing out at the sheets of rain blowing over the forest. We sit together for a while. Then I move back into the cave. It's drier now. Helena has the same look of concentration in her eyes. She doesn't flinch as I approach. She still feels confidence and desire, which makes me uneasy.

"What do you know about me?" I ask.

"You were in the Blue Tower," she says.

"What else?"

"Your name is Cipher."

"Yes, I know. Tell me everything."

"Everything." Her lips return to their expressionless straight line, but her eyes are amused. Surprisingly, she feels…playful, flirtatious. Like this is a game.

"Seneca told me I became Blue's leader," I say. "Did I tell you about my past?"

"You didn't say much. How did you get wiped?"

"I…don't know." Helena's question somehow makes me smile. How could I remember? "Maybe I jumped off a cliff," I say. "All I know is I woke up in a giant tree and got a tiny glimpse of my past as a doctor. Then I woke up with the Wolf tribe, the Lions attacked, broke my neck, and Seneca healed me. But hearing your story brought a few things back, I think because you'd told me it before. What else do you remember about me?"

"You were an American. A successful doctor who did brain surgery. After you left for the Red Tower, word got around the Blue Tower that you'd learned something about your past that unsettled you. Whatever it was, it weighed on Emma."

"Emma?" I ask.

"Your former servant," Helena says softly. "I'm surprised you're not with her." An emotion flashes through the link and even colors Helena's cheeks. Jealousy.

"Why do you feel that way toward Emma?" I ask.

"It's not about Emma," Helena says. "It's about you."

"What do you mean?"

Helena looks down at my hands, at the scars that match

the one on her hand. "It's nothing special," Helena says dismissively, even as the jealousy and desire burn through the link. "I felt the same way about Emperor Constantius. I've always had a thing for power."

It's the truth. A complicated truth—pulsing with emotion through the link.

I ask Helena for more details of what she remembers. The more she says, the more my memories return. They spread from point to point, one leading to another, like a web that grows in light. Yet vast sections of my past remain dark. Helena tells me that Abram said the point of these towers is for us to be scoured, for our dark spots from the past to be scrubbed away. Only when we are light can we enter the White Tower. Seneca told me something similar, that the towers are like locks to a doorway. The truth settles heavily in my mind. The White Tower is the only way out. Not even death is an escape. We'll wake up in young bodies again, with our minds cleared again. As many times as it takes.

Eventually the rain slows and stops. The clouds begin to break and reveal the setting sun. The light beams through the last of the mist rising from the hot, wet jungle, making a rainbow stretch from one end of the horizon to the other. Red fades to yellow. Green fades to blue. All the colors are there, except black and white.

# 32

WHEN DARKNESS FALLS, with nothing to eat, Seneca says she needs sleep. We've drunk most of the water that pooled at the bottom of the little cave. My body is still weak and tired from using so much power, and having no food, so I tell Helena to take the next watch. I make sure the orders are clear: stay quiet, stay awake, and do nothing but watch and alert us of any danger.

Thoughts of the Jubilee and Baron fill my mind as I fall asleep. It's dawn when I wake up, alone.

Helena and Seneca are gone.

I rush to the mouth of the cave. There's no one in sight above or below. And everything is silent. The jungle, with all its bugs and birds, makes no peep.

"Time to go," says a deep voice behind me.

I jump in surprise. I almost fall off the ledge. But a large hand grabs my sleeve, holding me steady. It's a hooded man—the Hunter, the one who woke me up in the Green Tower, the one who apparently killed Fugger. He was not here a moment before, when I woke up. He couldn't have come inside without me noticing. He just…*appeared.*

Before I can react, he places his hands on both sides of my face. His wild eyes look into mine.

Then he blinks, and in a blurred flash, we…shift.

We're not in the cave anymore. We're standing on grass, in the middle of a crowd, beneath an enormous tree. The Green Tower. Familiar faces surround me. Seneca and Helena. Baron and Frank and all the other Wolves. Their bodies are thin, their faces gaunt. No one looks like they've eaten a crumb in days.

"That's everyone," the Hunter says, looming like a giant over the rest of us. "The Jubilee begins! No more fighting. No more tribes. You enter the Green Tower as guests of the Provider."

He turns to the door of the great tree, draws his knife, and stabs it into the wood. The door swings open and the crowd funnels through.

As I wait to enter, a girl taps me on the shoulder. Matted hair hangs down by her sad, tired eyes. Her pale cheeks are hollow.

"Hey Cipher," she smiles faintly. "I survived, thanks to you."

"What do you mean?" I ask.

"Before the last Jubilee, you distracted that other tribe," she says. "Min and I did what you said and made it to the Eagle's nest. We lost Min later to the Wolves, but I never got caught. We hid in the cave. We managed to get by."

I shake my head. "I'm sorry. I woke up with the Wolves. I don't remember much before that."

"Oh no," she says, looking down. "Well, I'm Shelley. We know, or knew, each other from the Blue Tower. This is…rough, but hey, we'll get more memories back now. Maybe I can help you remember some things."

"Thanks. I'd like that."

We make our way through the door. Inside, stairs rise as steep as a ladder, carved directly into the tree's trunk. It's a long way up. Shelley stumbles several times. I help her up. We keep going.

When we finally reach the top, my legs are weak and my head spins from the climb, but the smell overwhelms me. There's more food than I could dream of. Tables are scattered around a vast platform. Others have begun filling their plates. No one wears a collar now. Groups cluster tightly together. Baron stands with dozens around him.

I go with Shelley to the table where Seneca and Helena wait. About ten others gather around, taking food. No one talks. It seems understood that there is a primary goal here: filling our famished bodies.

Shelley grabs a turkey leg. I go straight for the grapes. After that I eat roasted meat that falls apart in tender little strips and is drenched in a savory brown sauce. I'm smiling by the time I move to a dessert of pecan pie. We sit peacefully on the ground, bellies full. Seneca tells the group around us how we managed to escape the Wolves.

It grows dark and thousands of small, moving lights appear among the branches and leaves above us. They drift lazily down, together lighting the entire platform. One lands on Helena's shoulder. She takes it delicately on her hand and gazes down at the silent fairy, marveling at the light its wings produce.

An old man appears on a wide set of stairs leading down to the platform. Seneca tells me he is the leader, Daniel. He taps his staff, and the crowd falls silent and gathers closer. He gazes out over us, pausing with a penetrating stare on me. His expression is inscrutable behind his thick beard.

"Come, Scouring tribe!" Daniel says, his staff held high. A murmur spreads through the crowd behind me as others begin to descend the stairs behind the old man. They stop at the stair beneath him, facing the crowd. It is a large group, and one of them is Fugger, looking like he was never hurt.

"You have fought well for Green," Daniel says. "No one has been lost, and one has been captured. A girl from Red. This brings us to ninety-four."

The crowd cheers. Fugger puffs his chest out proudly.

Daniel taps his staff for attention. "It is time to announce the leaders. Baron wins, again, with the most captives. When will you trust the Provider?"

"I provide for myself," Baron says as he joins Daniel and looks over us like a proud, victorious tyrant.

Daniel shakes his head. "All must learn…giving sets you free. Our second leader is Polo, from the Lions. Jade is third. And the fourth leader will be someone new."

As the three named leaders move toward Daniel, whispers spread through the crowd with nervous energy. Seneca looks back at me with a smile.

"This person has done something special," Daniel continues. "For the first time in many Jubilees, there has been a capture from another tower—outside the Scouring, right here in our very own territory. Cipher, come."

All eyes swing to me. Most faces are surprised, some show awe. Seneca nudges me forward. "Go on."

The crowd parts as I move forward and step up to the platform, joining the other three leaders. A tall, sandy-haired boy in the Scouring tribe gives me a wink, like he knows me.

"Welcome your leaders!" Daniel announces. "For the rest of you, come and drink deep of the Provider's bounty."

The crowd moves toward the trough of sap. The line of boys and girls from the Scouring tribe steps down to do the same, but two of them turn toward me. One is the tall boy who winked at me. The other is a girl with blonde hair and eyes so blue that they send a chill down my spine as she approaches.

"Cipher!" the boy greets.

Before I can answer, Daniel steps between us, with his back to me and a bright red fruit in his hand. "I am afraid Cipher is not ready to speak with you."

"But you will give him the fruit?" the girl says, with her hands folded neatly in front of her. "I have earned it."

Daniel bows his head, the grey beard silently touching the wood beneath our feet. "Your gift will be given."

"And then?" the girl asks.

"After he eats, he will be free to choose you for his

tribe, if he is able. Now, both of you, to the sap."

The boy turns to go, but the girl stays and takes my hand. "I am Emma."

*Emma.* That's the name of the girl Helena spoke about. She's the one who spoke to me in my mind, the one who said she would give me the fruit that gives me my memories back.

"You spoke to me," I say.

She nods and holds up a hand between us. It bears a scar that matches mine and Baron's and Helena's—criss-crossed and deeply grooved in her delicate skin.

"Yes, Cipher. I am now marked like you. My power has grown. I use every color but Black, which is no color at all." She sighs, as if letting her precise voice relax. "Yet still I have not found Oliver. After you eat the fruit, please remember him. Perhaps, this time, we can search for him together."

"Of course," I say, not understanding, but grateful that she has helped me. "Thank you."

Daniel taps his staff to the ground beside us, fixing his eyes on Emma. "It is time."

The girl's icy blue eyes are moist as she turns away graciously, toward the crowd huddled around the sap.

Daniel watches her go. "You are most fortunate to have such a friend," he says.

He's right. But it's not just her. Emma's words gave me hope, Seneca took care of me, and Helena helped me remember. "I'm not sure I deserve it," I say.

His wrinkled eyes and bearded lips turn up in a broad

smile. "Wise words, Cipher. I too have had friends I did not deserve…seeing this lets some light through, eh? So it goes with the wiping and the remembering. Here now…" He holds out the small, red fruit. "This is for you."

# 33

EVERYTHING FLASHES INTO my mind at once. Neurons fire and synapses connect like long-lost friends. Dr. Paul Fitzroy. My wife, Susan, and the mansion. My son, Benjamin, and the seizure. The Blue Tower, the Scouring, and Emma. Red, passion, Samantha. Green, wealth, Rockefeller. Fugger killing me. Baron killing me—his face over mine, hanging over the edge of the cliff, falling, dying. The whole time with the Wolves...*Baron knew*...but I realize now that I know something he doesn't: he was the rich patriarch of Susan's family, my own son's ancestor. And we have the same scars on our hands...

Something taps me on the back. "It's time."

My eyes blink open. I'm curled up on a broad wooden stairway in an enormous tree. Daniel, the bent old man with the mossy beard, stands with his staff raised. Three others are behind him. I shudder and curl tighter, not wanting this reality, wishing I could sleep instead.

Another tap, now to the head, and harder. "It's time."

I rise reluctantly, pressing my temples. "That hurt."

"The past or the knock to the head?" Daniel asks.

"Both…"

"Eh, you won't feel it in the morning," Daniel says. "Come now, the other leaders are waiting."

"Yeah, hurry up, wind boy," Polo says.

He stands beside Baron and Jade. The three of them could not look more different. Jade stands the tallest. Her skin is dark brown, her hair cut very short. She's all predatory muscle and sinew. Polo is rotund, with a red face, a widow's peak, and his chest puffed out. Baron is smaller but looks a thousand times stronger, from his granite eyes to his calm, composed stance. I'm not sure whether I detest or respect him more after what I've learned.

Beneath us, the crowd lies still on the platform. Most are flat on their back, their closed eyes not seeing the thousands of glowing fairies floating above them. The sap put them to sleep, remembering. Emma and Hank and Seneca and Helena and all the others must be among them.

Daniel assigns our tribes—Wolves to Baron, Lions to Polo, Eagles to Jade, and Snakes to me—then he tells Baron to make the first pick.

"Fugger," Baron says.

My hands go to my throat, where Fugger's arrow had hit, where my life had ended, temporarily. The lack of a physical scar does not change the dread I still feel at the boy's name.

"Not your brother, eh?" Daniel asks.

Baron only shrugs, no emotion in his eyes.

"So your little feud will continue," Daniel says. "Very

well. Reap what you sow. Polo?"

"Frank," Polo says, glaring at Baron.

"A poor choice," Baron responds dryly. "Franklin is like our pathetic father. He may change his name, pretend to be something he's not, but in the end he'll produce nothing and burn through everything you give him."

"Not before he takes you out," Polo says. "I will tell him what you've said."

"He knows." Baron's lips, shadowed under a faint mustache, hardly move as he speaks. "It will end as it always does—with me on top."

"Enough," Daniel commands. "Jade?"

"Seneca," she says.

"Very well." Daniel turns to me. "Cipher?"

It's an easy choice. My recovered memories point directly and unwaveringly to the same person.

"Emma."

No one reacts to my pick. Daniel continues the process, going through multiple rounds. In the next round Baron takes Helena, I take Hank. I pick Shelley in the third round, Lily in the fourth. Baron picks B and D, his large servants from before. Polo picks three of the strongest looking boys. Jade picks Violet and two other girls I don't recognize.

As several rounds pass, each pick takes longer to make. We parse through the sleeping bodies that lay on the platform, oblivious to our presence and our influence over their fates. I don't know even half of them. I try to choose based on how they look, but it feels like guessing.

Daniel accompanies us, ensuring the process is orderly. He kneels down beside each choice, taking the person's hand in his. When he releases, there is a new mark—showing a wolf, a lion, a snake, or an eagle. No one wakes.

By the time we finish, we have formed four new tribes with about two dozen members each. Ninety-four total.

"Now the Scouring tribe will be chosen," Daniel says. "Baron, three from each tribe."

"Wait, no." I panic as I suddenly remember. The first leader of the tribes picks the Scouring group, but how could I know it would happen like this? I've never been a leader before. I look to Daniel. "You can't let—"

"Her, him, and her," Baron says, cutting me off and pointing to three of the sleeping figures I had picked—Emma, Hank, and Shelley. Baron grins at me, showing as much emotion as I've seen from him since the Wolves' bonfire. "Oh, you didn't know? Such a shame. But you had your chance to join me. Maybe you will choose more wisely after you are captured and wiped and scoured."

I turn to Daniel again, frantically seeking a way out of this. "Please, we both have the scars. You wanted us to talk, but look at what he…"

Daniel holds up his hand. "This is the way of the Green Tower. The process works as it must."

"But it's not fair!"

"Do not speak of fairness," Daniel says. "Whoever has will be given more. Whoever does not have, even what they have will be taken from them."

"More, more, and more," Baron taunts. "Good luck

with your Snakes, Cipher."

Baron quickly picks the rest of the Scouring tribe. He chooses the strongest looking boys and girls from the Eagles and the Lions, then he picks the three weakest from his own tribe, the Wolves. He will start with an advantage. And he will be my enemy, no matter who he was on Earth.

"As always, the games begin at dawn," Daniel says. "You will each have your allotment of collars. Use them wisely. Now it is time to drink deep and sleep."

He points his staff past us to the amber liquid. The other three leaders move forward. I'm suddenly unable to look away. I shuffle to the trough, kneel, and dip my hand. The sap slides stickily down my throat.

The casket's gloss has such luster that I can see my pale face in it. There are crowfeet wrinkles at the corners of my eyes, peppered gray at my temples. The casket's silver hinges dazzle under the sun. The body inside has no dazzle left. It should have rained. Clouds should have swept in with wind and storm and blasted us with hail until we had to flee the cemetery and the six-foot hole and the little boy who should never had died, not like this.

Nothing went right. My son is gone.

Some priest with a collar says some words. Some people try to look in my eyes and tell me, sincerely, that they are sorry. But my eyes are a world away. I can't see the people. I see only the hospital room with the tubes and the heartbeat and, finally, the flat line. I hate the flat line more than I hate myself.

They lower the coffin. The luster will not shine anymore. The dirt and the worms can enjoy the company. The brain has stopped. Life has stopped.

But I go on. First to home. Susan and I do not talk. She serves casseroles that people brought. The next day the servants return to work. We still do not talk. It is easy to hide from each other in a home this size.

I take shelter in my study, underneath an old poster showing a lightbulb and a quotation. The poster has followed me from a college dorm at Chamberlain Hall to medical school to the chief neurosurgeon's mahogany desk. Pinholes dot the poster's corners. Before, it was a reminder of how I got here. Now its message is haunting:

*Genius is one percent inspiration; ninety-nine percent perspiration. - Thomas Edison*

The words loom over my desk like a divine finger pointing at my failure. Have I not sweated? Was there an hour I'd slept soundly while my son suffered? Every waking second was perspiration. One hundred percent. Which meant Genius must have been lacking. No inspiration. No cure for this tumor, this cancer of the brain that entered the world with only a thirst for pure, innocent cells to invade and conquer and kill.

I will sweat more. I will sweat until it comes out of my skin as blood, as if that could bring him back. Benjamin. Ironic how much I care after he's gone, when I'd taken his life for granted while he was here. I will make it up to him. After what he had said to me—what he said...

*What had he said?*

It's missing, even now, sitting under the Edison poster and the lightbulb. I can't remember what Benjamin said. We'd had a conversation. I know it. He was in the hospital bed. I stood by his side, doctor and father in a white coat. We both knew he had only days to live. He'd said something to me.

What was it?

It will come back to me. But for now, there can only be sweat. Edison tested thousands of materials and did thousands of experiments, all to find the right filament and flow of electricity to make the lightbulb burn. That's what I will do for the brain. It could be transplanted, I feel sure of it. Take the healthy brain, cut off the tumor, and put it in a healthy body, where the cancer had not spread. I can do it. I will do it. I will perspire until my dying breath to fight back. We could be gods, if only our brains could survive. Edison invented the lightbulb. Dr. Paul Fitzroy will invent eternal life.

"Are you hungry?" Susan asks, peeking her head into my office, eying the papers strewn around the floor.

"No, thanks."

"It's been two days, Paul. You have to eat. It's your favorite, broccoli cheddar."

"Maybe later," I say. "I think I'm onto something."

# 34

THE HUNTER WAKES ME. He kneels by my side as I sit up, trying to remember where I am. Soft light touches the scars on my hands, with a sinuous snake shape imprinted over them. The small wooden room looks golden. About twenty others lay on the floor, sleeping. This is not the mansion where I hid and worked after my son died. This is not Earth. This is the Green Tower. This is the tribe I picked, the Snakes, except Emma, Hank, and Shelley aren't here. Baron, my own son's ancestor, chose them for the Scouring. I feel hollow inside.

"Take these." The Hunter holds out a plain, brown sack. As I take it, whatever's inside rattles around like it's alive.

"What is it?"

"Links," the Hunter says. "You're going to want them."

*Right, the collars.* "How many?" I ask.

"Enough to capture another tribe, or maybe make some of your own into servants." He glances past me to the sleeping bodies. "Better do that soon, if you want. You only get a few minutes head start."

"Why would I do that to my own tribe?"

The Hunter shrugs. "There are no rules, except that once they're all awake, you have to leave the tree. See you in fifty days, Cipher."

He stands and turns, his head almost grazing the low wooden ceiling.

"Wait. What should I do now?"

"Trust the Provider," he says, "and don't get collared."

He leaves the room through a ladder in the floor. I kneel to open the bag. Inside are the chrome metal bands, unclasped, ready to close around necks. Now I know Green's game. Put a band around someone's neck to make them a servant. Whoever has the most servants after fifty days will pick the Scouring tribe, and the four with the most servants will each lead a tribe. I can't let Baron win again.

I pull one of the collars out of the bag. Its smooth surface gleams in the morning light. The boy closest to me rolls over, starting to stir. His eyes are still closed.

*There are no rules.*

I could start with a host of servants—taking everyone in this room before they wake up. Or maybe just half of them. If we captured servants from another tribe, I could remove their bands and take command.

No, I picked this tribe. What would I want my tribe leader to do? I can't make them start as servants. I put the collar back in the bag.

"What's that?" asks a sleepy voice. It's a familiar, white-haired girl on the far side of the room, watching me. More of the others are stirring, as if some invisible force rouses them awake all at the same time.

"Collars," I say. "It's good to see you, Lily."

"I've heard all about you." She yawns widely. "Thanks for picking me. What tribe are we?"

She doesn't remember how, many Jubilees ago, she helped me, but Baron collared her. I will tell her, when the time is right.

"Snakes." I rise to my feet, holding the bag of collars at my side. Everyone is awake, staring at me. Whispers spread around the group.

"What shall we do now?" a boy asks formally.

"Stay alive. And free."

The boy stands and approaches me. We're about the same size—smaller than most here. He has flaxen hair and bright blue eyes. He's the one who called himself O and led me out of the tower with the Wolves last time. That's why I picked him. But now, with my memories back, I immediately see his striking resemblance to Emma. The hair, the eyes, the elegant formality.

"What's your name?" I ask.

"Call me O," he says. "Do you not remember me?"

"You were a Wolf. One of Baron's servants, before the Lions attacked us. But what's your real name?"

He tenses, looking startled by the question. "No time for that," he says. "We must leave quickly."

I can barely keep down the excitement that I might have finally found Emma's son, but he's right. This can wait. It'll be fifty days before I see Emma again.

"Okay, where should we go?" I ask.

"I have survived with the Snakes before," O says. "There is a place we can hide, if we hurry."

"Any other ideas?" I ask the tribe gathered around us, but no one responds. Many of them stare at me blankly. I know little about the Snakes, except that they get the worst start and once hid in a cave behind a waterfall and got wiped out by the Lions.

"Is the hiding place a cave?" I ask O.

"No," he says, "a swamp."

That's new. "Alright, lead on."

He rushes out without another word, dropping down the ladder out of the room. We hurry after him, trotting along the trunk of a wide branch to the open space where we had the Jubilee feast the night before. There's no sign of the other tribes.

I hesitate by the stairs at the center of the platform. "What if the Wolves are waiting for us?" I ask O.

He shakes his head. "It is not Baron's way. He usually goes straight to where the Wolves build their base. That is where we were headed last time when the Lions attacked."

"How do you know so much?" Lily looks at O like she's measuring him.

"Yeah, how we gonna defend ourselves?" asks another boy. "We ain't got no weapons."

The group looks skittish. I need to calm them. "O is right," I say. "The Wolves should be gone. But if they are not, or another tribe attacks, I'll make a way."

I summon the air and coil it softly around Lily, lifting

her until she floats several feet above us. It is easier than ever, with my old memories restored and new memories gained. I reluctantly release the air and set Lily down gently. Part of me *wants* Baron to try trapping me.

"Amazing!" Lily says with a laugh, looking around at the startled faces.

"We have heard about you," O says, studying me. "You are the one who led Blue, then Red." He takes my hands and holds them up to the others. "Look."

"Just like Baron's," a boy says.

"Except Cipher has two." O lets my hands drop. "He will take care of us."

"Other tribes are powerful too," Lily says.

"We shall slip away and hide, like snakes," O replies.

Lily rolls her eyes, but she doesn't argue. The others nod with varying degrees of confidence. I lead them down the steep stairs through the trunk of the tree. The door is open at the bottom. No one is in sight outside.

O turns to me and gives a slight bow. "As I said, Baron and the Wolves are gone."

I still don't like it. The grassy glade surrounding the tree looks peaceful, but it's about fifty feet to the dark forest. Anyone could be hiding behind the trees, ready to attack us once we're out in the open or, worse, once we're within the woods. I tell the group to stay close and warn me if they see something. Then I summon the wind, holding it ready, and lead our tribe out at a jog. The clattering collars in my bag are the only disruption of the glade's serenity.

"Wait, look," Lily says softly beside me, pointing to the

forest just ahead and to our right.

"What is it?" I ask.

"I saw something move," she says.

The forest seems the same everywhere around us. Thick trees with dark trunks and dense underbrush. The air is thick with humidity, as if the dew has only levitated a few feet from the carpet of grass. It's so quiet I can hear myself breathe.

"Stay close," I say, moving warily away from where Lily pointed. I make it five steps.

Baron charges out from the forest. Wolves come from the right and the left. Ten. Twenty. All of them closing around us, collars gleaming.

I thread the weaves of air and swipe at the attackers, scooping them up like ants and hurling them to the right. They crash into the trees at the edge of the forest. I forge a wall between them and us.

"Run!" I yell to my tribe, pointing away from the Wolves. "That way!"

They stare at me in shock, but then do as I say. Except for O, who stands by my side.

"Look," he says. "Baron."

I turn back to the wall of air. Baron has somehow gotten through it. The collared servants behind him—and behind my invisible barrier—vanish, then reappear on the other side. They can pass through it when they disappear.

I reforge the air and blast it into them. Many of the Wolves are hurled back, but Baron vanishes and reappears, unaffected. He marches forward, with his granite eyes studying me calmly. He points at me and the Wolves behind him charge again.

As much as I want to take Baron out here and now, I'm not sure I can. And I have to stay with my tribe, which has gone into the forest.

"Let's go," I say to O.

We turn together and I thread the air into a rushing wind at our backs. We bound like gazelles toward the trees, with Baron and the Wolves chasing.

As we enter the forest, there's shouting ahead of us.

"Stop!" O yells. "Lions!"

Just as I freeze, a figure lunges from behind a tree and swings something into the side of my head. O slams into the attacker as I collapse. The bag of collars drops and falls open. Metal links spill out onto the forest floor.

Sitting up, stars flicker in my vision. Two, no three, boys surround O and me. O stands defensively, with bare fists raised. The other boys are taller, wielding staffs in their lion-marked hands. One of them is Frank. Another is Polo, the Lions' leader.

Polo snarls and dashes at me, as Frank swings viciously at O. The air erupts from me. Polo soars back, grunting as he slams into a tree. I weave a shield inches from O's head, just in time. Frank's staff thuds into the invisible wall and rebounds. He stares at his staff in shock. Rising to my feet, I channel the air into a rope and coil it around Frank, squeezing. The third lion boy turns and runs.

"Hoo! Hoo! Hoo!"

The howls are behind me. Spinning, I see Baron and

the Wolves charging into the forest, closing on us. The open bag of collars lays on the ground between us. I can't let Baron get them. I lunge for them.

O grabs my arm, stopping me. "Come on! Run!"

I shake my head, turning back. I have to stop Baron.

But then a collar snaps around my neck.

# 35



O sprints into the woods. There's no room for thought, there's only obedience. I run as fast I can, barely keeping up. It takes everything I have to stay with him. He dodges trees, leaps over roots. I stay right on his heels. Branches fling back. One hits me in the face, almost knocks me off my feet. Doesn't matter.

I must follow him. Closely.

By the time he stops, in a thicket of briars, I'm covered in scrapes and gasping for breath. My chest can barely contain my pounding heart.

"I think we lost them," O pants, bent over with his hands on his knees. "But we need…more distance…between us."

My fingers feel around the metal band at my neck. I know what happened before, but I can't help trying again. I reach around to the back and try to summon the wind. The moment the power touches the link, I double over and retch. My stomach empties on the thorny ground.

"You may not do that," O says. "It is for…your own

good. Silence now…follow me."

He walks briskly ahead through the forest. I try to stand still, to resist. I try to speak. My mouth opens, ready to say, *No, no, no! How could you do this to me?*

But I can't. The effort makes me feel sick to my stomach again. He's only a few steps ahead. I have to follow. An invisible force weaves through my mind and my body, making my muscles move, making me walk without saying a word. I stay close behind him as we move out of the briars and through a stretch of pine trees with soft needles that brush lightly against my wounded skin.

At least O has not prohibited thought. He made me his servant. He could command me to do anything.

*Anything.* My heart sinks in terror.

We eventually reach a steep drop. To the right, across a chasm, rust-colored mountains rise steeply to sharp, rocky peaks.

"That way is the Red Tower," O says. "No food there. But this is the cliff's lowest point. The forest turns to jungle below. There is a swamp where we can hide. Let me get to the ground before you follow. Jump where I do."

He doesn't wait for me to respond. His command to stay silent still holds. While my tongue stays firmly planted in my mouth, my thoughts twist and jerk like a man in chains, chafing his wrists raw in futility.

O takes a few steps back, then charges forward and leaps off. In mid-air he grabs a tree branch that hangs near the cliff's edge. He scrambles along it and climbs down. As soon as his feet touch the ground, I start moving. I don't have a choice. I follow his movements as precisely as I can.

Take a few steps back. Race forward. Leap.

My hands grab at the branch but lose their grip. I swing and slip. My arms and legs flail as I fall. It's a long drop.

*Follow closely.* I must follow closely.

I seize the wind and weave it into a net by the ground. It catches my fall gently. I land on my back beside O. I spring to my feet.

O smiles at me. "See, I left you some discretion. But no more powers, now. It is not much farther."

I don't respond. I can't.

We press forward through the jungle. It grows much denser than the forest above, with roots and vines and thick-leafed bushes along the ground. It's louder, too, with the sounds of a million insects around us. I remember this. The jungle. Violet once led me through it. Seneca did the same, and she wore a collar then, under Baron's control. He must have made a serious mistake with his commands to have let her get away. But he had so many servants. He still does. How does he control them all?

As we walk, my mind continues to race through the implications. My thoughts are still free. Could O command them, too? Could he tell me not to think? Could he tell *what* to think? It's terrifying all over again.

But this is O—it could be Emma's son! I have to find a way to tell him. It could be leverage. I consider the ways to convey this, to do whatever it takes to get this cursed metal off my neck.

The ground becomes soggy beneath our feet, eventually

turning to mud. We reach the edge of a swamp where trees are submerged in still black water, stretching into the distance ahead of us.

"No one likes the swamp," O says. "Many ways to die here. It can be an advantage. I know of a dry spot where we can hide."

He starts to wade forward.

I follow. Closely. Silently.

The water is up to our bare knees when O pauses. "Hey, could you use your power to clear a path through the water?"

His question unlocks something inside me. It feels like I've come up from the depths of the ocean for a gulp of fresh air. I have to answer him, so now I can speak.

"I know your mother!" I blurt out.

O shakes his head, confused. "Answer only my question."

*Only his question.*

My will battles for margin, for some freedom within the command. He asked me, *Could you use your power to clear a path?*

"Maybe," I say. "I have used a lot already. I don't know how far I could make it."

He rubs his chin. "Interesting. What happens if you use up everything you have?"

The question forces a memory from the Red Tower into my mind. I had less power then. It took everything I had to save Marcus and Seymour when they went over the waterfall. I caught them, then I collapsed.

"I usually lose consciousness," I say.

"Very well, that seems worth a go." O points ahead. "At least this way we will see the crocs before they strike. Blow them away if you can. Do whatever it takes to keep us safe. But keep following."

"Okay. I'll do my best," I say cautiously. He didn't command me to stay silent. His questions and this new command seem to have dissolved the earlier command. But maybe part of it still holds. I don't test it, yet. *Do whatever it takes to keep us safe.*

Whatever it takes. Yes, I can use that. I'm stronger when I'm free. That will keep us safe. I've taken collars off before. I can keep us safe by taking mine off. I have to try it again. The possibility makes me ecstatic.

O turns to me. I suddenly remember that he knows what I feel. He looks confused again.

I pretend to yawn. I reach behind my neck and press my fingers to the back of the collar. I summon every ounce of power and funnel it into the collar.

The collar blasts back. It makes my whole body shake violently, doubling over and retching again. I vomit up everything left inside, bile and all.

The band feels tighter than ever around my neck.

"You may *not* take it off," O says, shaking his head. "Oh, I suppose I share the blame, being too loose with my commands. You, dear chap, must be keen in finding gaps. I shall be more clear, even telling you aloud. You will not even *try* to escape. You will stay close to me, and you will protect me above all else. Now, stand up."

I stand up.

"Apologize," he says.

"I'm sorry."

"Good. You will again stay silent and create a path through the water for us. Focus all of your attention on it."

I focus all of my attention on it. I ignore my empty stomach and pale, clammy skin. I summon the wind and weave it into a wedge that presses forward and parts the water for several feet ahead. I seal the area around us, creating a tight wall. The ground is dark, odorous mud beneath our feet.

"Impressive," O says, as he starts to move forward into the dry space between the walls of water.

I move the wedge ahead of him, and then follow. Closely. Silently.

The black water becomes deeper in places, sapping more of my energy. I'm exhausted but it doesn't matter. There's no limit to the command. My attention is on the weaves, pushing back the water, and following O.

He finally stops at a small, dry island.

"This is it," he says. "Get some rest."

I lay down and curl into a ball and fall immediately to sleep.

# 36

WE SPEND THE next day digging down into the little round island—surrounded by swamp. O says we cannot assume we are safe, unless we are hidden. "Every inch of this place will be searched before the Jubilee," he tells me. "Especially when the food runs out."

He gives me specific commands and works almost as hard as I do. We dig with our hands, burrowing into the soggy dirt, making a primitive ditch that we cover with swampy sticks and moss. It's impossible to see from a distance. I think it's good enough. O doesn't. We spend the next day gathering better branches and patches of moss. O wants it just right. He wants it to look perfectly natural. We do not travel far from the island. As we hunt better camouflage, we also search for food. There are reeds throughout the swamp that O says we can eat. I gather up large armfuls and carry them with the wind. We eat them raw. He won't risk a fire. The third day we catch a snake as long as I am tall.

"I am terribly sorry," O says. He can feel how badly I want to cook it, how disgusted I am at the idea of eating it raw. "We cannot have a fire. Others would see the smoke."

So we eat the snake raw. My empty stomach revolts but keeps the food down. The survival instinct is strong.

We sleep until morning, then we hunt for more food but find nothing but reeds. A few times I spot floating logs that suddenly blink open an eye and reveal a crocodile. O has ordered me to stay away from these larger predators. He says we should save fighting them for when we're desperate.

We stick with whatever reeds we can find. We pick the area around the island clean. The reeds don't regrow. There won't be enough to last us fifty days.

O sends me further out, commanding me to keep my wind ready. If I see anyone, I must blast them away and retreat without them seeing where I go. "No one can track you in the swamp," O says.

It happens two days later. I'm the furthest away I've been from our island when I spot a girl.

She's hard to see, disguised by a layer of brown-grey mud on her skin. She carries a stick carved into a harpoon, and she looks like she knows how to use it. She balances on the roots of a tree, peering into the black water, hunting. I try to stay silent and back away, but she sees me.

"Hey!" she shouts.

I follow my orders. The wind blasts her off the roots and into the black water. I turn and flee without looking back. When I reach the island, there's no sign of anyone following.

O commands me to stay silent in the burrow the rest of

the day. He does the same. We sit together in quiet. It's too hot and humid to sleep. O won't let me leave, but I've learned he can't control my thoughts, not completely. He can command me to be silent, to think only of how to get food. But once I get the food, the orders lift. I continually prod at the gaps in the commands.

My thoughts go to the girl in the swamp. I wish I hadn't hit her with the wind. A crocodile could have pounced on her. She might have been able to help us. She was hunting for food just like me. It would be better to join with others, not to stay isolated and hidden in this nightmare place. But I don't have a choice. I take a bite of another bitter reed.

A gnat flies into my eye. I stand up and pace in the tiny cave. My feet are pruned. They might never be dry again.

"You are impatient," O says softly, knowing what I feel. "I understand why. I have been a servant, too. It is hard, I know, but you really can trust me. I have survived many times by hiding here. My memories are almost filled to the brim. I cannot risk losing them, you know."

He takes a bite of swamp reed. The white milky inside makes his hands look pale in the dim light. His words only make me more frustrated.

"I see," he says. "Do you feel that it *is* worth risking memories? Perhaps you do not like what you have seen of your past. It is different for me."

I doubt it.

"Come now, Cipher, be charitable. Here, tell me about your past, then I shall tell you mine. We have plenty of time. Start at the beginning."

This isn't a suggestion. It's another command. I begin to speak just as readily as I had kept silent. I tell him all I can remember, about how I was Paul Fitzroy, a wealthy doctor, with a wife and a son who died. I tell him about my mistakes. I tell him about the other two towers—Blue and Red. When I mention Emma Chamberlain, he interrupts.

"Wait, who is she?" he asks.

"She was the daughter of a British Lord," I say. "She lived in the 1800s. She's beautiful and amazing. She has golden hair and bright blue eyes and a warm, gentle spirit." The more I say, the more I want to see her again, to work together, like we did in Blue, and in Red, paired.

"Go on," O says, rubbing at his eyes.

I'm desperate to ask him if he's her son, but I can only do what he has commanded. So I continue. "She's a healer. She was in Yellow before I caught her and took her to Blue. That's when she told me about her past. I saw it with her in the Sieve—the way we saw our memories in Blue. She ran away from her family and had a son. Her husband grew sick and died. She was heartbroken, alone with her baby. She also saw visions of alternative pasts, things that had not really happened, like returning home to her father, Lord Chamberlain, who welcomed her back with open arms. In the Red Tower, she saw what would have happened if she had not run away from home, following her passions. She…"

"Stop, just stop," O says. He buries his head in his pale white hands, sobbing. He cries for a long, long time. The gnats keep their distance, as if out of respect.

He finally looks up with bloodshot eyes. "My name is Oliver." He points to my collar. "Take it off."

It's an order. Hope surges. But will I be sick again? I have no choice but to obey. I reach behind my neck and summon the air and funnel the power into the smooth, silver metal. It unclasps and falls into my lap.

"Why?" I gasp, stunned with my sudden freedom.

"I cannot bear your feelings any longer." Oliver shakes his head, keeping his head bowed. "And I cannot keep a slave who feels that way about my mum."

# 37

OLIVER CHAMBERLAIN IS the son of Emma Chamberlain. It's enough to keep me from running away, even though now I could. It's enough to prevent me from slapping the collar around his neck. It's enough to make me ask him to tell me his story.

Like every person's story, it begins with his mother. He remembers her laughter, her golden hair. He remembers how she would take him out to a pond in London where they would feed the ducklings and she would tell him how he would learn to fly just like them. Even as he should have started to walk, and it became clear that his youthful sickness had forever left its mark in his futile legs, Emma would tell him that he would fly. She sang to him to sleep every night. She loved him with everything she had.

But then she was gone. An illness, they said. Oliver doesn't remember exactly what happened. He was too young. He was sent off to his grandfather's manor, then to boarding school. He was the subject of constant mockery. He couldn't run with the other boys. He couldn't play sports. He could only hobble about with canes under both his arms. That left him plenty of time to study, which he did. In books he could fly. In stories he could hear his mother's songs.

He grew up bitter and fiercely smart. He returned to London as a banker at a time when a Lord's grandson would never do such a thing. Instead of tending the manor or going on fox chases—which he couldn't do anyway—he controlled the finances of expeditions and then empires. He became one of the wealthiest men in London, and then the world. He was forty years old when he met his wife. She was an American, fifteen years younger than he was. She didn't look at his legs or his canes. She looked straight into his mind and his heart and she didn't run away. She loved him like his mother had. He moved to the United States. He founded a university. They built Chamberlain Hall. I tell Oliver it's the same dormitory where I'd lived as a college freshman. He smiles and shakes his head. "This place is quite something," he says. "I do not think it is a coincidence that we found each other."

"No," I say. "It can't be. But why do you think it's happening?"

"In all my memories," Oliver says, "I constantly seek the next big thing. I bought a mansion. It was not enough. I founded a university. It was not enough. In my last memory, I stand before a grand new college dormitory, with my wife and two sons, proud as a man could be. I had everything a man could ever want. But that is not how I felt. Nothing would ever be quite enough. I felt empty, Cipher."

"I know what you mean."

"Do you?" he asks.

I tell him what I've seen in the Green Tower, of my own mansion and wealth. It wasn't enough. Neither was my wife nor my son.

"These towers lay us bare," I say. "The leaders say we all have to be scoured. Something about this place wipes away these things, so that we can be filled up with something else. I wish I could figure out what it is we're supposed to be finding."

"You have any guesses?" Oliver asks.

I smile, looking at his red eyes, dry now after the tears. "Each other," I say. "We definitely have to find each other. Daniel told me that, and it makes sense. Emma has helped me. Finding my own mother helped more than I could imagine. We have to get you to Emma."

"Yes, I want that very much," Oliver says. "And I would prefer to do so with my memories intact."

We start to plan. We put the past—and the collar he snapped around my neck—behind us. But that doesn't mean I ignore what happened. Emma was my servant. Now I've been Oliver's. We may need to make someone else a servant. It could help us and them survive. There's one thing I'm convinced of: we can't just stay alone on this island. Maybe Oliver eked out survival here, but there's not enough food for both of us. We're already thinner than we were, and filthy. I hardly recognize Oliver as the boy I met in the tree. We need to move on, to look for others. We'll be stronger with more help, even if that means using the collar again. Oliver reluctantly agrees. He tells me he can lead us to the shore, where the swamp turns brackish and meets the sea. He says there are often others in that area.

The next morning we eat the last of our reeds. We don't know when we'll return, if we ever do. Oliver shows me the way to go, and I use the wind to carve a path through water. We trek most of the day. We manage to find a few reeds as darkness falls, but there's no other food. We climb a tree and sleep as best we can, tucked high in the branches. We press on the next day. The sun is high when the dark trees of the forest give way to a webbed maze of mangroves. My wind is no help getting through their dense roots and branches. We navigate slowly. We see so little ahead of us that we're almost on top of a lean-to shelter before we even know it's there.

We peek inside and see no one, but there are still warm coals in the sand. Whoever has camped here can't be far away. They probably heard us coming. I form the air into a shield around us.

"Anyone out there?" I say.

There's no response.

"It's okay," I call out. "We're not hunting for another tribe. We're just looking for food."

Leaves rustle behind us. Something slams into the wall of air before I can see it. A broad-shouldered boy grips a staff. He has straight black hair, tanned brown skin, and a fierce look in his eyes. There are eagle marks on his hands. A collar gleams at his neck.

"Hey," I say, with my hands up peacefully. "Where's

your master?"

The boy rushes at me again, but bounces back. I weave the wall into an invisible rope of air that ties around him. He fights for a moment, then goes still. His head drops to his chest, defeated.

"There must be others," Oliver says, eying the mangroves around us.

"No," the boy grunts, but his eyes glances past us.

There's a faint sound. Like a footstep, very close.

But I see no one.

I weave the wall back into place, still holding the boy. I step closer to him and reach behind his neck. I'll undo the collar and reclasp it to put him under my command. Just as I start to do this, there's a piercing shout.

"No!"

Someone grabs me from behind, with an arm appearing out of nowhere. A blade presses against my throat.

"Don't move," a girl's voice growls.

Without budging, I let go of the air holding the boy and funnel all of it at the girl behind me, yanking her blade away and fixing her in place. I draw the collar tucked into my waist and spin and snap it around her neck before she can react.

Then I see her dark hair, almost purple. The familiar face shocks me so much that I let the power slip.

"Violet?"

Her feelings surge into my mind. Fear. Anger. Hunger. But there's a whole other set of sensations. She senses someone else's feelings. The boy. He's on high alert. He must be her servant.

"Is there anyone else?" I ask.

"No," Violet says.

*Tell your servant to be still,* I command.

She looks to the boy. "Be still."

I don't need the wind. They both have to obey. This could be how Baron does it. He doesn't just make everyone in his tribe his own servant. He has layers of order.

"Do you have any food?" Oliver asks.

Violet shakes her head. She doesn't trust us.

I meet her eyes. "Don't you remember me?"

She feels doubt, but then tilts her head as if seeing me for the first time. A sudden, warm awareness settles over her.

"Cipher?"

I smile. "It's me."

"You look…rough."

"You don't look so good either. What happened?"

"We're the last Eagles," she says. "The Wolves were too strong. We had to flee the nest."

"I'm sorry," I say. "Who's your servant?"

"He's Alika."

The boy glowers at me. He tried to attack before. I can't leave any gaps in my commands.

*Order him to sit, stay silent, and do nothing else.*

"I have done it," Violet says darkly. She may be my old friend, but the storm of emotions raging through her convinces me to keep the collar on her, for now.

"Do you have any food?" I ask.

She moves past me and kneels beside a pool of water, by the root of a mangrove. She retrieves a small wooden structure, almost like a net. A fish flops around inside. She feels protective of it. She caught it. She wants to eat it. Her feelings scream that it won't be fair for me to take it. She's been saving it, even though her stomach is empty.

I understand how she feels. I didn't share with Polo when he was my servant, and Baron didn't share with me. But Seneca did share, then Helena helped us and I became a leader. *Giving sets you free*, Daniel says. It's time to try.

"Don't worry," I say. "We'll share the fish evenly. And we'll catch more. We're going to work together now."

# 38

WE COOK THE FISH over the coals, wrapped in thick mangrove leaves. The four of us share the meal. Oliver lays back and dozes off. The link around Violet's neck tells me she feels more at ease. She knows me, though she's not happy about being my servant. I don't blame her, but I can't free her yet. She might run and take the boy with her. We need to stick together if we're going to have any chance against Baron and the Wolves.

I ask Violet more about what happened. She tells us that she and the boy, Alika, are the last of the Eagles. The Wolves captured all but five of them before they made it away from the Green Tower. They even caught the leader, Jade, and took almost all the collars. Violet led the five who escaped to the nest—the cave high in the cliff—but they ran out of food and had no choice but to send out hunting parties for more. They mostly went to the jungle below, in hopes that the Wolves would not have that area under control. Violet thinks the other Eagles were captured. She had no choice but to flee.

"Why did you put the collar on Alika?" I ask.

Violet looks to her servant, who has been listening quietly. "I needed to be sure he wouldn't run off on his own." She glances back to me, with a finger running along the metal band at her own neck. She senses the implication of her answer: this is why I can't let her go, either.

"Alika, tell me about your past," I say, testing the command through our indirect link, from my servant, Violet, to him.

At first he stays silent, but Violet says to him, "Go on."

It seems the commands can't be given directly, but only through my own servant. I also can't feel what he feels, not like I can with Violet. This would make managing a large group of servants difficult. But Baron does it. He must have mastered the types of commands to give, requiring obedience but allowing enough freedom for his servants to command their own servants. I don't like the idea. I'd rather have a tribe that *wants* to stay with me.

Alika tells us that he lived in the South Pacific in the seventeenth century, in a small fishing village. Tribes were always battling there. Men with white skin came in ships and tried to tell them things about a man who rose from the dead. Some tribes did not like it. They attacked, and sometimes ate, the men with the white skin. But not Alika. He argued in his village to protect the visitors. He learned much from them. He also taught them many things. If there's one thing he knows, it's how to find food in the sea. That's why he has survived many times by hiding in these mangroves, a lot like Oliver in his swamp. They find a place with just enough food and cover to survive.

As the sky grows dark, we take turns sleeping and keeping watch. The next morning, with empty stomachs and no food, I order Violet to order Alika to show us everything he knows about this area. We go to the shore, where Alika tells us how to gather snails and catch mud crabs. We each make long wooden staffs with a trident of sharpened points at the end. Among the mangroves, there are small, muddy pools of brackish water.

Moving quietly, Alika inspects each pool for life. He stops by one of the pools and slams his trident down. He lifts a crab the size of my head.

"Better than lobster," he says.

Violet builds a fire on the sandy coast and cooks the crab in its shell. The steady sea breeze blows the smoke of our fire away. We eat in quiet as the three suns drop like marbles into the vast sea.

The next day we discover that we've emptied the last of the gourds that Alika and Violet had filled with fresh water.

"This is a hard thing," Alika says.

"What do you mean?" Oliver asks. "Water's everywhere."

"It's all salty. Can't drink it." Alika sweeps his arms around. "The sea pushes inland here. The closest sweet water is almost a full day's trek."

We decide that Alika, Violet, and I will search for water. Oliver agrees to stay at our camp and keep an eye on things.

The trek is long and uneventful, other than bug bites and parched throats. Deep in the jungle we find a fresh spring and fill up new gourds that Alika plucked out of one of the trees. We drink until our stomachs are ready to burst, then make the return trip slowly, hauling the heavy containers.

When we get back, Oliver is not alone. He sits by the fire, cooking a mud crab, with a scrawny girl resting calmly beside him. She has plain brown hair, brown eyes, and a Lion mark on her hands. I immediately recognize her face, but she looks so unlike when I last saw her—in a red dress, wielding fire—that it takes a moment for it to hit me.

"Apple!" I say. "How did you get here?"

She smiles. "It's good to see you too, Cipher. I snuck up on your friend when I smelled the food. Lucky for him he mentioned your name."

"But you were in the Red Tower…"

"Emma captured me in the Scouring. She's quite something now, weaving all those colors together. Maybe she learned it from you. I won't hold it against her. I don't mind Green. The leader gave me fruit that restored my memories."

"All of them?" I ask uncertainly, remembering how much she had hated me when we first paired, and how hard her past was.

She suddenly laughs. "What, are you still scared of me? I suppose I gave you some reason to be, but I've seen a lot since then. We were on good terms in the end, weren't we? And I've grown softer still. Would you believe that I got married? He was a retired general, a good man. We had a beautiful family and a beautiful estate on the Danube."

"I'm glad," I say. "Very glad."

"So why are you so…" She eyes me up and down, no doubt seeing the filth and scrapes. "You were the Alpha."

"Things have not gone so well in Green," I admit. "The tribes battle. Food is scarce. It's hard to survive."

"I've seen that," she says. "Reminds me of Earth, trying to hide in the middle of a war. But don't you still have your power?"

"I do now, but I lost it—and my memories—for a time. Emma helped me get them back."

"I see. Well, I still have my flames."

"You do…?" My mind races at the possibilities.

She holds out her hand. A thin rope of fire extends up into the air. "That's how I escaped the Lions."

"What happened?"

Apple tells us the whole story. The Wolves and the Lions clashed early, apparently smashing the Snakes between them. The Wolves took seven Lions, but couldn't win outright. Polo led the rest of the Lions to build a fort deep in the jungle, like usual. But they began to run out of food, like everyone else. A few days ago the Wolves attacked with everything they had. All of them but Baron wore a collar. They were too strong, too organized. Apple was almost caught, but managed to keep away three boys with the fire, then set part of the jungle ablaze. In the confusion she made it away. She doesn't know if any other Lions made it.

When she finishes, she proposes that we attack the Wolves. "Cipher can win," she says. "I have no doubt."

"Not a good idea," Oliver says.

"Why not?" Apple asks. "I have the fire. Cipher has the wind. Surely he's more powerful than they are."

"I'll fight with you," Alika says.

"Thank you, both," I say. "But Baron and his Wolves can evade my power when they disappear."

"So can I," Violet says. "But it only lasts a short time. Maybe we could outlast them. How many are with the Wolves?"

"Lots. I couldn't count them," Apple says. "There was only one other servant who could summon flames."

"This is nonsense," Oliver says. "The Wolves are too strong. And even if we could face them, it is not worth the risk. Do you all want your memories wiped? It is not long at all until the Jubilee. We can survive here. The way things stand, Cipher, you will likely be in second place."

*But I could be first.* Or is that Dr. Fitzroy speaking? No, this is different. It's not just about me. It's about stopping Baron. He collared me. He killed me. He took Emma from my tribe and sent her to the Scouring. On top of that, he was the richest man on Earth. Knocking him off his pedestal might do him some good. So…how?

"Baron relies entirely on the collars," I say. "We could hunt down his servants in the forest. If I remove their collars, they would freely join me."

"True, but we are too weak now," Violet says. "Look at us. It takes more than this to fight the Wolves. I think Oliver is right. We should wait. Maybe next time you can try this idea and take on Baron before he becomes so strong."

In the end Oliver and Violet convince me. Apple may be thinking of how I defeated Max in Red, but I have never faced someone like Baron. After all the times I've been wiped here, maybe I've learned some patience.

We sleep soundly under the mangroves. There's no disturbance. The next day Violet, Alika, and Oliver hunt for food and guard the camp while Apple and I go for more water. We bring back a dozen empty gourds. Alika uses thick, waxy leaves to make funnels for catching rain water. When it pours that afternoon, it fills the gourds. We won't need to forage in the jungle again.

Days pass like this. Catching mud crabs. Swimming the shallows. Talking around the campfire. We scratch off the days and nights on a tree by our camp. Our tally reaches forty when the food starts to run low. By day forty-three, there are only a few scattered snails and crabs. On day forty-four Alika manages to spear a large fish. He carefully salts half of it, making small strips that we can store. We share the rest of it evenly and go to sleep less hungry. The next day there's no food, only water. And the same the day after that. We venture further from the camp, going a half-day's journey inland. The trees that formerly had fruit now have none. We ration the last strips of salted fish. We finish them on the forty-seventh night.

Violet urges us to stay put and preserve our energy. "There won't be more food," she says. "But we have had just enough. We can make it to the Jubilee."

We agree to wait. We subsist on rainwater, filling up the

remaining gourds and keeping us alive. On day forty-nine, my stomach twists in pain. I stay by the campfire. If a mud crab slinked by, I doubt I'd have the energy to get up and catch it. But no crabs come. No snails or fish either.

It's the dawn of day fifty when the Hunter appears in our camp, out of nowhere. "Time to go," he says.

# 39

INSIDE THE GREEN TOWER, on the wide platform high in the tree, we feast. I try to take it slow, to not stuff myself all at once, but I can't help it. After days without food, I gorge on meat and fruit and pie and more. Some of the others look almost as rough as our group. Apple was right about the Lions. Other than her, only two of them survived without being caught—Polo and Frank. One Eagle, Seneca, managed to hide alone in the jungle with one captive Lion serving her. Everyone else was caught by Baron and his Wolves.

Baron stays to one corner of the platform. A crowd gathers around him, no doubt trying to convince him to pick them for the next competition. It hurts to see some of them—Helena, Min, Lily. They'd rather be picked as a Wolf than caught by the Wolves. They'd rather be slaves than risk getting wiped.

Not me. I'm finally going to get Emma in my tribe, and we will unite the tribes to fight the Wolves. Then *I* will decide who goes to the Scouring. This is the last time Baron is going to win.

Darkness falls and the glowing fairies light up the great tree. The wisened old leader, Daniel, descends toward the crowd as usual. He announces that the Scouring tribe has had tremendous success, capturing twenty and bringing our numbers to one hundred sixteen. When the Scouring tribe emerges, the others make way for Emma like she's the leader. I point her out to Oliver.

Daniel releases the Scouring tribe and calls forward the tribal winners in order: Baron, me, Polo, Seneca. We join him on the stairs, and after introducing us, with more somber warnings given to Baron, he tells everyone else to drink the sap.

I rush back into the crowd and find Emma moving toward the trough. "Emma, wait!" I say.

"Cipher, you are…thin." Her initial look of concern gives way to a smile. "But you made it, memories intact. This is better. You should have seen us in the Scouring. Hank and I used some tricks we learned from you."

"Well done!" I scan the crowd and spot Oliver. "But hey, you really need to meet someone."

"Who?" she asks.

I only smile in response as I take her hand. We hurry together to Oliver. They're the same age, with the same ageless dignity, flaxen hair, and sapphire eyes.

"This is Oliver," I say.

Emma's scarred hand covers her mouth in disbelief.

"Mum?" Oliver says.

"Can it truly be…?" Emma chokes up.

Oliver smiles, his eyes moist. "I remember your

voice…how you sang to me…"

"I hoped you would, oh how I hoped." Emma wipes at her eyes. "You are bigger than I remember."

"And you are just as beautiful."

They embrace, crying or laughing or both. Emma looks up and smiles at me through the tears. "Thank you, Cipher," she says. "Thank you."

A while later Daniel approaches and says it's time to pick tribes. He whispers something to Emma. She nods, waves goodbye to me, and leads Oliver toward the sap.

"What did you say to them?" I ask Daniel.

"That they could share a vision, if they liked. And they liked that idea very much. Come."

We join the other three leaders. Baron greets me calmly, his face unreadable granite. Polo says a tense hello. Seneca smiles. Maybe Polo will not join me, but Seneca and I can join forces.

Daniel assigns our tribes—Wolves to Baron, of course, Lions to me, Eagles to Polo, and Snakes to Seneca. Then we start choosing our tribes.

Baron picks Fugger first again. The boy who killed me.

Daniel looks to me. "Your turn."

"Hank," I say. It's not an easy pick, but I've learned since last time. I can't pick Emma first, because then Baron will just assign her to the Scouring. I'll pick her fourth or fifth. But Baron's smart, so I still had to pick someone I wanted, to try to hide my strategy. Hank would understand.

As Polo and Seneca name their picks—Frank and Violet—Baron studies me with all the emotion of a rock studying an ant crawling over its surface.

Next I pick Apple. My third choice is Oliver. Polo and Seneca make their picks. I barely notice who they choose. I'm thinking about Emma. I can't wait any longer. I will take her next.

It's Baron's turn again. Fourth round.

He turns to me and says, "Emma."

My vision narrows. The reality of what he's done slams into me. "No!" I shout.

A slight grin appears under his faint mustache. "As I thought."

*No, no, no.* He can't have Emma. He can't! Fury swells in me. I don't think. I rage and summon the wind. I forge it into a fist and blast—

*Boom.*

I'm flat on my back, dazed.

Daniel stands over me, gripping his staff. "No powers here. This is the Jubilee," he says. "It's your turn to pick."

I stand slowly. The others are staring at me. Baron hasn't moved. The grin is a slender crack across his granite face. It takes me a while to think straight again. The anger doesn't fade. It boils viciously in a closed pot. Daniel is able to shut me down as easily as Rahab did in the Red Tower.

So I must make a pick. And it can't be Emma. I'll have to find her and free her from Baron. I need more power to defeat him.

"Helena," I say.

The picks roll on, round after round. In the end we have named tribes with twenty-nine members each.

Last it's Baron's turn to choose the Scouring tribe. He picks my top three, just like last time, but he picks others from Polo and Seneca. He must know something about them I don't. Then he names his last three picks as his final choices for the Scouring.

This means I've lost Hank, Apple, and Oliver. And Baron will have Emma. He will put a collar around her neck. But I still have my power, and Helena. We will use the wind. We will join with the Snakes and hunt the Wolves. I glare at Baron—Rockefeller—as Daniel leads us to the sap.

"Are you sure you want to do this?"

Susan sits beside me in the cold, motionless car. The ground is white. The sky is grey. The mansion is dark, without a single light on inside. The old stone had once lured me in, warmed me, delighted me. Now it feels like a weight that I have to shed.

"Yes. I want to live lighter."

"I understand about the house," Susan says. We both look out the windshield, at the dark stone rising out of the snowy lawn. "But Chicago? Your position? You have done so much to get here. You really want to leave all of it?"

"Yes."

We sit in quiet for a minute, maybe two.

"Okay," she says, "but I have to ask: are you going to blame me for this?"

I turn to her. The once soft and innocent eyes are harder now, as if pressed by time and pain.

"No," I say. "It's not your fault."

"I know. It's not yours, either."

The steam of breath drifts between Susan and me.

"God gave us Benjamin," she says. "He took him home. We have to accept that."

"I could have saved him."

"Paul, please." She reaches out to me, then pulls back. It's still very cold. "You can't keep doing this to yourself. And you can't just run away from it."

"I'm not running away. But this place has too much…"

"I know," she says. "You don't have to say it."

"But I do. I'm leaving it all behind. The mansion. The family fortune. Benjamin. Samantha."

"Please, don't…"

There are tears in her eyes. It feels cold enough to turn them to ice. I start the car. The engine clinks and rumbles to life.

"I'm going to sell the car, too. We won't need it in Washington. Life is going to be simpler."

"With only work?" Susan asks, her voice feeling a million miles away. "You know what this new title will mean…"

"There will be work. But it's not for me anymore. It's for children like Benjamin."

"Benjamin said God has a plan for you. Maybe it's waiting at the National Institute of Health."

"I don't know about that."

"You don't have to." Susan puts her hand on mine. "I do. And I'll be with you."

The warmth of her touch, after all I've done. The cold outside. The engine running.

I swallow back tears. I put the car in reverse.

"Thank you," I say. "I don't deserve your loyalty."

"We don't deserve anything." She squeezes my hand. "It's a gift. It's grace."

She can call it whatever she likes. I'm past that. I can admit that I'm glad to have her by my side. I won't be able to do this alone. But with her in the passenger seat, we pull out of the long driveway and rumble coldly away from the mansion, from Samantha's visits, from Benjamin's seizures, and from everything else that once mattered to me.

<h1 style="text-align:center">40</h1>

THE HUNTER WAKES ME and drops a sack beside me on the wooden floor. Metal rattles inside.

"Twenty-eight," he says, then vanishes.

The little room is packed full. The Lions. My tribe. I start moving from person to person, prodding them to wake up. "Up, up. Come on. We must go. Let's get out before the Wolves. Up!"

They yawn and rise slowly. Most of the faces are unfamiliar. I picked them in a daze after losing Emma. I'm tempted to collar a few of the stragglers, but no, I won't win like that. They are probably dealing with whatever memories the sap showed them, like a cold mansion and a spouse's touch. But there's no time for that now. Baron will be enslaving his tribe. He'll be ready. I have my power, and Helena's. It should be enough to protect us. Then we can join the Snakes and hunt the Wolves and take Emma and defeat Baron.

"So you picked me, huh?" Helena has a hand on her hip, a sly grin on her lips. She looks just like she did in the Blue Tower, with long auburn curls, except now she wears

273

a sleeveless shirt and shorts instead of a heavy robe with stripes at the sleeve. "Who was your first pick?"

"Doesn't matter," I say.

"Oh it does," she says. "Why'd you pick me?"

"I may draw on your power, so stay close."

She takes my hand in hers. "This close?"

I look down at our interlocked fingers. The backs of our hands show matching scars. If I don't collar her, then the touch will help me draw on her power—as it did with Emma.

"Yes, that's fine."

I instruct the rest of the Lions to form into two lines behind us, and to follow as closely as they can and shout if they see any trouble. I tell them that we'll go straight to the Lions base in the jungle. They obey, moving into formation. The lines aren't perfect, not like they would be if the boys and girls wore collars, but we'll be stronger with each person thinking on their own. We have to be.

Leading the tribe out of the room, I immediately see why the leader in second place gets the Lions. We are just above the platform. It will be very quick to get out.

Only the Wolves are closer. They're already climbing down through the trunk. Baron must be at the lead, out of sight. The final two Wolves, with bright bands on their necks, move down the ladder.

I sprint after them. We can't let the Wolves get in position for a surprise attack. The Lions hurry after me.

We climb through the opening at the center of the platform, into the dark path through the trunk. Scattered fairies provide only faint light for the steep stairs and hanging ladders. But I've done this before. It feels almost natural.

When we reach the bottom, the Wolves have already gone out. We need to be ready. I take Helena's hand again and summon the air. In the open doorway, the blue threads weave together and swirl into a dense net. Reaching into Helena, I pull her power and weave more and more threads. The air pulses with energy. It will be enough to block any attack, or to propel us away if it comes to that.

I turn back to the Lions. "Don't stop. Don't wait. Don't look around. I will protect you if you stay right with me, all the way to the jungle. Got it?"

Heads nod in the dim light.

"You've still got it," Helena says, eyeing the dense network of blue threads. "So. Much. Power."

"Even more with your help. Now hold on."

I lead the charge out. The Wolves are waiting outside. They didn't bother to hide in the forest, to try another sneak attack. They're right by the doorway, springing at us the moment we emerge.

The wind blasts them back before they can vanish. Bodies fly ten, twenty feet, rolling away on the grass. Among the chaos, as I'm running away, I spot Baron in the distance. His granite eyes watch me calmly. Emma suddenly appears beside him, with his arm draped over her shoulder. There's a gleaming collar at her neck.

All the anger releases, blasting in a furious, focused gale straight at Baron. He vanishes an instant before it hits.

Moments later he reappears further from me, still with Emma by his side. I blast again. They vanish and reappear again, untouched.

I draw as much as I can from Helena, straining to hold it and swelling with power until it bursts like a tornado over Baron. But it's blocked. All of it. A wall deflects the power such force that I fall to my knees. Baron and Emma still stand there, calm, with a bubble like molten gold protecting them. It's Emma's power, drawing on Baron. They're as strong as we are, maybe stronger.

Helena pulls me up. "Come on. They're coming."

The other Wolves charge again, closing on us. Another tribe has exited the tree behind them. Baron is manipulating me, taunting me with Emma. This isn't the time and place to fight.

"Run!" I shout, propelling our tribe with the wind.

We sprint toward the forest and quickly reach the trees at the edge of the glade. I glance back. Counting heads, I get to twenty-eight. No one was lost.

We move into the darkness of the woods. The air is still. Birds sing in the distance, but all is quiet around us. Pine needles muffle our steps. As the adrenalin wears away, fatigue comes in its place. I release the power except for a small ribbon around our group, just enough to warn us if someone attacks.

The pine forest grows thicker, interspersed with broad, leafy trees. The underbrush snags and slows us. Bushes are full of berries. We stop to catch our breath. The tribe eats, mowing through clusters of berries.

A red-haired boy, about my size, approaches. "Hey, nice work back there. Remember me?"

He's Stephen, the boy who Daniel introduced at my first Jubilee—the boy who Baron left to die at the bottom of a trap pit, and who caught a snake for the Eagles. That's why I picked him. He'll be glad to fight Baron.

"Of course," I say. "Still going by Stephen?"

A smile spreads over his freckled face. "Yes, and I've been a Lion twice since we were Eagles together, so I know where the path is down the cliff, and where the Lions usually build their base. Want me to show you?"

Minutes later we are on the move again, with Stephen at the lead and Helena by my side. Nothing interrupts our steady march through the forest. By the time we reach the cliff, the suns are low on the horizon.

Stephen points to a waterfall. "The path is there."

Jade told me about this long ago. She said the Wolves and the Lions usually battle over it—the one place where you can pass the cliff without a lethal rock climb. This path looks dangerous enough. It's steep as a ladder, crossing back and forth down the cliff. No one else is in sight.

"Lead on," I say to Stephen.

He moves carefully down the path, as if considering each step and hold. The path looks like it has been worn into the cliff face by a million mountain goats. In many places the ledge is hardly wide enough for my foot. It's slow going, but we make it before darkness has fallen.

"Want to camp here?" Stephen asks at the bottom. "Or should we press on to the normal base? It's another hour."

"Press on," I say.

The jungle at night is miserable. Insect chirping reverberates torturously in my mind. The creepers and branches grab and snatch like thieves' hands. My feet ache, my mind grows weary. Still, I preserve the last of my power rather than clearing a way. Baron can't possibly be ahead of us, but I no longer underestimate the threats of this place. I want to be ready.

Stephen stops when we reach a small clearing in the jungle, where tall grasses reach to our waists.

"This is it!" he says triumphantly.

"This is it?" Helena groans.

"You'll see in the morning," Stephen says. "We're elevated slightly here. Good for defense. We can build shelter and a wall. There's a fresh spring and fruit trees, so we can survive a long time without even needing to leave."

"Thanks, Stephen," I say, looking back over our tribe, feeling proud of them. We stuck together and we're all here. "Everyone get some sleep. I'll take the first watch."

They find places to sleep, curled up in the tall grasses. I pace around the clearing, counting the bodies. I come up with twenty-nine. It's one too many.

I count again and get the same number. The only way to know who's new is to check hands. I search until I find one that's not a Lion. It's an Eagle. The boy looks familiar, but it's hard to make out his face in the dark. He's from Polo's tribe. Polo betrayed me, led me into a trap. I can understand why someone would want to flee from him. But I can't just let the newcomer sleep here as if he's one of us, not until we've confirmed he's loyal. I go to the sack of metal bands. I don't want to do it, but I'm responsible for the Lions, not the Eagles. The metal feels like ice in the jungle's heat. The boy sleeps soundly. The band clasps easily around his neck.

He jerks awake. The feelings surge into me, but they are not threatening. He's shocked, but calm, confident, and controlled.

*Stay there*, I command. *Sleep.*

He does as ordered. He's no threat with the collar on.

I continue pacing, trying to measure out the space, and to keep awake. Maybe Stephen's right. If we can secure this area, it could become a place to welcome other tribes. And to bring back anyone we capture from the Wolves.

A small circle of stars shines through the clearing in the canopy above. Emma was with Baron, collared and dangerous. Could we still talk to each other? Would Baron know? I gaze up at the stars a long time, hoping and waiting for her. No voice comes. The only sounds are the clicks, zips, and chirps of bugs, like a faint war in the night.

When my eyelids refuse to stay open, I wake Helena. She agrees to take the next watch. She says she'll keep an eye on the Eagle, too. I lay where she had laid, holding the sack of collars close to my chest, in a warm spot among the tall grasses.

# 41

IT ALL HAPPENS at once.

The collar. The command.

Waking up, fingers yanking at the metal band, mind hearing the order: *Bow down. No power. Bow down.*

My mouth opens.

*No words.*

My mouth closes. I'm on my knees.

We're in the jungle. There's grey light. A shadow above me. A person. There's a shout behind me. Are they Wolves? No, please not Baron. But Helena was keeping watch. My fingers go to my throat again. The metal is so tight. *Helena…*

"Must you feel so disappointed?" It's her voice, behind me. "I told you I have a thing for power."

*She betrayed me.* I want to scream it, the anger blazes, the power… But I can't touch the threads, can't move. *No power. No words. Bow down.* Only my thoughts and feelings can rage. Let Helena know. Let her suffer my feelings.

"One might think you never even went to Red!" Helena says. "Aren't they supposed to teach you to control your passions? Oh, what anger, what fury! This is going to be such fun, Cipher."

"Enough," says a boy, the shadow above me. "Tell him to take it off."

"Very well." Helena's voice whispers into my ear. "Be a good pet and take Frank's collar off. Do nothing more than that."

The boy leans forward. The morning light reveals him clearly: Frank. Baron's brother. Polo picked him as an Eagle. He must be the one I collared the night before.

These thoughts swirl as I do what Helena commanded. I can summon the power for this purpose now, her later command overriding the former one. I close my eyes and take a deep breath, focusing and envisioning the seal buried within the silver metal. I funnel the tiniest tendril of air and blow into the spot, pressing my fingers hard against it at the same time.

The collar snaps open and falls to the ground.

Frank rubs at his throat. "Ah, much better."

"The deal is done," says a familiar voice.

Polo steps forward and scoops up the open collar. He turns to Frank, running a finger along the metal. "A fine deal indeed. Helena has Cipher. Frank has the Lions. And I lead the alliance. It is time for Baron to lose."

"We'll build up the defenses here," Frank says.

Polo nods. "No spies. No leaks. It all fails if Baron learns what has happened."

"I'm not so sure," Frank says, looking down at me. He has the same wide brow as Baron, but with wilder hair and eyes. More like a burning coal than granite. "My brother might hate me more than he hates this boy."

"You both make fine lures," Helena says, her olive eyes gleaming in the day's first light. "But I think Baron will come for me. He knows about my power. He *wants* my power. Tell me now, don't you all?"

Polo and Frank laugh. I take a deep breath. It's a command. I can speak.

"No," I growl from my knees. "I don't want you. You know nothing—"

*Silence.*

My lips freeze. My tongue drops to the base of my mouth like it was injected with a million pounds of lead.

Helena smiles as she kneels down and rubs my hair like she's petting a dog. "Cipher, Cipher, it's a shame to see you like this."

The boys laugh again, walking away and talking together. This might be my only chance. There's still an opening from Helena's earlier command. I summon the wind again and—

*Stop*, she commands. *You will never use your power without my express permission.*

I would collapse to the ground in despair, but I have no choice except to stay on my knees, head even with the tall grasses. I will bow down until she commands me otherwise. Tears of frustration moisten my eyes.

"Oh, stop crying," Helena says. "You'll get used to it. Let's start again, shall we?"

*Stand.*

I try to stay still but my muscles move despite myself. I'm on my feet before I can help it.

*Bow.*

I bow.

*Tell me your favorite thing about me.*

"You are…interesting."

Helena smiles. "It's a start. What else? Now, now, no need to say any feelings like that! Only something good!"

"You are…pretty."

"There, was that so hard?" She smiles as she holds out her hand.

*Kneel. Kiss my hand.*

I do as she says.

"Much better!" Her smile stretches even wider, like this is the happiest moment in her life. "Remember, it is a high honor to serve Helena Augusta Imperatrix."

Helena taunts me on and off, but mostly she puts me to work. Backbreaking, all-day work. It's what Polo and Frank want. Polo brings his enslaved tribe of Eagles. Frank collars every single Lion except Helena and me. I'm the only one she controls. Frank seems to trust her. He's wrong, but I'm not going to tell him that.

The first job is the wall. I spend the entire first day on hands and knees, pulling away fistfuls of wet, dark, jungle soil. Dozens of others do the same work as I do, in a line, commanded to silence. Some are strong, like one boy who looks like a boulder with hairy arms. Others are small, like Stephen and Lily, my white-haired friend who came with the Eagles, under Polo's control. Seeing her is salt in the wound after what Baron did to us when I first arrived in Green. He still reigns while I am in the muck.

Once we have the trench dug out, the next day we search the jungle for sticks. We sharpen them and bury them in the ground, one by one, until we have a complete barricade along one side of the little clearing in the jungle.

By the end of the second day, my muscles start to cramp. Helena commands me to keep working. On the third day two more servants join the effort. They have Snakes imprinted on their hands.

We dig. We bury sticks. We obey and build the wall.


Several nights later, I lay on my back, body exhausted, within the wall but outside any building. Helena and Frank both have their own shelters now. First thing tomorrow, we have been ordered to build a barracks for us servants to share. Our leaders are so kind.

The trees above sway gently in the wind. The strands of air glisten like ribbons, taunting me. The leaves part and reveal stars above.

There must be some gap in Helena's commands. She's told me to not use my power over the air, to stay silent, to stay in the base, to not even *try* to escape. What else can I do? Eat and sleep. Work and work.

*Think.*

*I can still think. Respect the mind.*

That's the one thing Helena can't take away from me. My mind is still free. So how can I use that?

A gust of wind parts the trees again. This time a half-moon peeks through. It has a pale orange glow. It reminds me of when I slept outside and gazed up at the moon without trees blocking the view—in the Red Tower. Seymour and Marcus were with me. We camped under the stars. That was before I'd learned anything about Samantha or what I'd done. That was before I'd lost my mom and reunited with Emma.

*Emma.*

I miss her. Is she still with Baron?

*Cipher.*

The voice drifts into my mind like a feather's touch.

I imagine her face, her golden hair. The word forms in my mind like I'm saying it to her.

*Emma? You can hear me?*

*Yes, I am here. With the Wolves.*

*You found me…* I try to calm my quickening pulse. I can't let Helena feel my excitement.

*I am sorry it took so long,* Emma says. *It has been hard to venture away from Baron.*

*Are you free?*

*A little. More than at first. I wear his collar, but I have earned his trust. He was a good man, on Earth.*

*What?* My heart sinks. Baron must have lied to her, just as he did to me. *You can't trust him.*

*He had good intentions.* Emma's words are patient as ever. *He did amazing things, but struggled as we all did. He got more and more wealth, so much that it began to suffocate him. He tried to use it for good. But still he had the desire to build, to ever build. He is doing the same here. He is planning an attack.*

I feel numb. I send back a single word: *Good.*

*What?*

*Helena betrayed me. She joined forces with Baron's brother and the Eagles' leader, Polo. They're planning to fight the Wolves.*

*How can that be* good?

*Maybe if Baron attacks, he'll win. And then I can be free.*

*What do you mean?*

*I'm wearing a collar. I'm Helena's servant.*

*Oh no.*

*It's terrible. I don't think I'll survive until the Jubilee…*

*When we attack, I will come for you.*

*There's a wall around our base now. But there's a gate. I can help you and the Wolves get in.*

*Tell me when and where.*

*Tomorrow night, and—*

A figure appears above me, blocking the moon and stars from view. Helena gazes down at me, her ringlets cascading like a dark waterfall. She wears her usual smile, but underneath there's curiosity, maybe even concern.

"What are you so excited about?" she asks.

My heart thumps loudly in my chest. I couldn't hide all my feelings. Of course she's suspicious.

*Are you okay?* Emma asks.

*Wait,* I tell Emma. Then I say to Helena, "I was thinking about someone."

"Who?" she demands. "Tell me the truth."

"Emma."

"Still her?" Helena sounds angry. She kneels down and

studies my face. Then she looks up at the moon and stars, then at me again. There's something like fear or confusion in her eyes.

"You were looking up there," she says. "What made you so excited?"

"The stars."

"Come, you'll sleep in my hut from now on."

I have no choice but to stand and follow her. But as I do I glance up to the sky and send thoughts racing to Emma. *Helena might know something. You can't wait. Come tomorrow. Convince Baron. Two hours after dark. Come to the tall beams along the wall. I'll make sure the gate is open.*

*Okay,* Emma replies. *Be careful.*

"Go in," Helena demands, stopping in front of her shelter. "And stop feeling so happy about it."

# 42

THE NEXT DAY Helena pelts me with questions and demands. She knows something has changed. She feels what I feel. I can't feel her emotions, but it's clear she's annoyed that she can't ferret out what's going on. She asks me a dozen ways, but I dance around it. She can't control my thoughts, only my actions. She has no way to know that I spoke to Emma through the stars.

In the afternoon Polo brings a new group to the base—twenty or more Snakes, but not Seneca. They all wear collars at their throats. I've never seen so many gathered outside the Green Tower. There are seventy or more of us. The strongest and fastest are sent out hunting, while the rest continue building and serving the leaders.

As dusk falls, a group returns with a huge boar. Helena orders me to help build a bonfire. We go in and out of the fort, gathering more and more wood with our bare arms and no trace of power.

The boar begins to roast on a spit over the fire. The decadent smell fills the jungle.

*One last load of wood,* Helena commands. *Then join me.*

I do as she says, and on the way back, I make sure I'm the last one. I calmly leave the gate ajar.

I lay the wood onto the pile. The others have started the feast. Boys and girls bang makeshift drums with sticks. They dance. It almost reminds me of the Red Tower. The two aren't always so different—chaos underlies both passion and freedom. Neither one is like Blue at all. I miss the control, the calm.

Helena spots me. She commands: *Dance.*

Anger and embarrassment flush my cheeks. But it doesn't matter. I move to the beat, dancing with Helena and the rest of them, hips swaying, arms swinging.

*Cipher?*

It's Emma. I glance to Helena, who dances beside Frank and pays no attention to me. Still moving, obeying, I look up to the stars. *Are you here?*

*Yes, I see the smoke.*

*Is Baron with you?*

*All the Wolves. We have arrows. Find shelter.*

*I'll try. The gate is loose. West side of the wall.*

*See you soon. Into the trees now.*

Emma's voice is gone. The dancing goes on.

Helena finds me. She takes my hands and sways. "Quit being so serious!" Laughing, swinging, her long hair brushes against me. "Try to be free! Laugh!"

I try and I laugh, as I must. The drums thump steadily. My body settles into the motion. I lose track of time. The fire burns low.

Then comes the shout. Not outside the walls. Inside. A

boy is screaming, on his knees. An arrow protrudes from his shoulder.

"Attack!" Frank shouts.

An arrow thuds into the stack of wood beside him.

"To the walls! Defend the walls!"

He's not my master. I dance though the others run, though the drums have stopped. Arrows rain down around me.

Helena grabs my hand. Panic in her eyes. "Make a wall!" she shouts. "Use your power, and mine!"

The command, the urgency, overrides everything else. She wills me to weave the air, and so I do. Blue through blue, in and out, in and out, like linear bruises through the night, until the whole fort is covered in an impenetrable, invisible shield.

Arrows slam into my wall, cracking it. I weave and mend each spot, drawing heavily from Helena. We are motionless, every ounce of focus and energy funneled into the shield, the arrows. Another hits. Fix the crack. Another. Faster and faster, more and more, until there are no more. The arrows have stopped.

Shouts and clashes erupt around us. Dark figures rush through the base. The Wolves.

*Make a wall.* That was the command Helena gave me.

In an instant I unwind the threads of air above us and condense them, shrinking the shield down, condensing it, until it is like a fortress around Helena and me. The two of us cannot be touched.

*Find Baron,* Helena commands. *Stop him.*

For the first time in days, I smile. Teeth bared, shield in place, Helena's hand in mine, I spring into motion. Not my body, but my mind. Our powers merge like raging rivers, and I am the only force that matters. I sweep up everyone at once, grabbing bodies I cannot see but can feel. I lock them in place. Lift them. Move them to me.

A mass of boys and girls hovers by the fire. I hold them in place and laugh as I use more power to throw more wood onto the fire. It blazes into light, casting faces in a red glow. Picking through them I find the one I seek.

Baron. I move him toward us, floating parallel to the ground. Granite eyes meet mine. Now, at last, I have him.

"Let him go," Helena commands. "Gently. And keep the others where they are."

*No, no.* Desperate but hopeless to resist, I lower Baron to the ground. I cling to the power coursing through me, the effort still immense, as I focus on holding the others now, against my will.

"Shall we be civilized?" Baron brushes something off his shoulder, then faces Helena. "You *were* right, Empress. You have the gift. And here I thought I was the only one. It will be a pleasure sharing the tribe with you."

"Likewise," Helena says. "We make a good team."

"You have my brother?" Baron asks.

Helena nods and looks to me. *Find Frank and Polo. Bring them here.*

I do as she says, but I try something else. To find the two boys, it would be helpful to release some of those held by my power. Otherwise I won't be able to sustain it much longer. And if the power failed before I find the ones Helena commanded me to find, then I would not be obeying her fully.

I move the mass of bodies, rotating them as I look at their faces in the firelight. I see Violet. She's not Frank. I move her to the back of the group and release the wind around her. I see Emma. She's not Frank. I do the same. Then I see Polo. Then Frank.

I draw them toward us, parallel to the ground as I did with Baron.

"Release them," Baron says.

"Release them," Helena commands.

I let the two boys fall to the ground with a heavy thud. They grunt and slowly rise.

Polo has his hands up, inching forward. "I can explain. I can—"

Baron slaps a collar around his neck before he can get out another word. The motion looks as natural as walking for the Wolves' leader. He doesn't say a word or lift a finger, but Polo immediately cowers back and retreats, like a dog with its tail between its legs.

My grip over the wind begins to slip. I feel the strain of it, pulling through Helena and me. It's too much.

"Let go of the rest," Helena says to me. She studies me closely. She knows how I feel. Weak, but also hopeful and sly. "Don't let anyone leave. Protect Baron and me at all costs. And don't do anything else."

She turns away, to where Frank now stands face to face with Baron.

"John!" Frank says cheerfully, moving forward with his arms spread wide.

I stop him with the wind, inches from Baron. Frank hits the invisible wall and staggers back, looking confused.

"Let him come," Baron says.

*Let him come*, Helena orders. *But still protect.*

I release the air.

Frank approaches Baron more cautiously. "It's so good to see you again," he says.

"Are you ready to repay your debts?" Baron asks.

"Really John? Won't you let all that go? It hardly matters anymore, now that we're here."

"It will always matter, Franklin. Debts must be repaid."

Frank shrugs his shoulders. "But how can I pay?"

"How many servants can you give me?" Baron asks.

Frank looks to the crowd of boys and girls. Most of them wear collars. They are not trying to run. They are watching us. I don't see Violet or Emma.

"I will give you half of them," Frank says.

"Have you still not learned?" Baron asks.

"Three-fourths."

"Your debt to me is everything you have."

"But…but John, I became the Lions' leader! Doesn't that mean anything to you? Aren't you proud of me?"

"You played the cards that I dealt," Baron says. "Now you will pay me your winnings."

"You never played cards!"

Baron grins. "I learned enough of their evil influence from you. Now, the payment."

"Fine, take them." Frank hangs his head, looking more sad than angry. "Take all of them. Just like you always did."

"Yes, and you," Baron says, as he suddenly clasps another collar onto Frank, who curls up on the ground at his brother's feet. Baron looks to Helena. "Have Cipher remove everyone else's collars and give them to me. It must be methodical. There can be no slip ups."

"Of course," Helena says, casually twirling a curl of hair in her finger.

*Do exactly what he said*, she commands. *Free them, hold them, give the collars to Baron.*

Drawing my power and hers, I gather the many servants into a perfect line, held still within two currents of wind. The first in line is Stephen. His silver collar gleams in the firelight. Everyone watches us and there's a sudden, heavy silence.

I step forward and funnel air into the link. It falls open. I catch it with the air before it touches the ground, floating it a few feet to Baron's outstretched hand. As he moves to snap it around Stephen's neck again, a breeze ruffles my hair. It's not my power.

There's a metallic flash.

The collar jerks out of Baron's hand. A golden figure appears out of nowhere, directly between Baron and me. It's Emma, radiant with the light of her power. She snaps the metal around Baron's neck. He immediately removes her collar—master turned servant—then falls to his knees.

*Help him!* Helena orders, as Emma turns to us.

I try to resist but can't. Just as I form the wind to

attack, Emma reaches behind my neck and unclasps the collar. I gulp as she holds up the metal link in her scarred hand. She's marked now. She can remove collars.

"Come out, it is safe," Emma says softly.

Violet suddenly appears beside us. She takes my old collar her white-knuckled fist, turns, and clasps it around Helena's neck.

"Remember me?" Violet asks her. "I was the servant you ordered to be crucified."

Helena's face is ashen. "Valentina?"

Violet smiles. "You may call me master."

"Yes, master," Helena says.

"You've done it!" I say, looking from Violet to Emma.

"No, you did," Emma says. "You let us in and then freed us. Violet made us invisible."

"We have them," I say in disbelief. "Baron, Helena, Frank, and—"

Something sharp presses into the back of my neck. A voice hisses almost imperceptibly by my ear. "Silence. Release Baron. Or die."

"What's wrong?" Emma asks, staring at me.

She can't see him. The voice—it's Polo, invisible. He must still wear the collar, doing what Baron commands. I open my mouth to warn Emma, but the point stabs into my skin, making me gasp.

Emma steps toward me, and Polo pulls me back, holding the point painfully steady.

"Release Baron," he hisses. "Tell her to do it!"

My eyes catch Baron's, watching me with his perpetual,

commanding calm. I'm free now. There's no collar around my neck. I'd rather die than serve him again. I left my mansion behind to be free of its weight. I left the Rockefeller name and took only Susan with me. Even after everything I'd done, she put her hand over mine.

*The warmth of her touch. The cold outside. The engine running.*

The memory of that content moment wraps me in light. I lift my hand slowly, glancing down at it. It's completely invisible. I have vanished.

"What?" Polo hisses. The prick at my neck shifts.

It's all the opening that I need. I grab him with the wind, holding him motionless, squeezing until the blade drops from his hands. I move him in front of me and open his collar, then snap it shut again. He's Baron's servant no longer. None of us will be.

# 43

WE CAN'T CHANGE the forest overnight. But we try.

With all of us gathered, I draw on everyone's power—Helena, Emma, Violet, and a dozen others who have traces of it—to remake the entire fort. There are more threads than ever, with every color but Black, weaving and coiling into a magnificent tapestry. It lays over me like a boundless energy that could do anything if I truly knew how to control it. But what I can do amazes even me. I blast away the wall and use the wood to build a prison of individual cells and bars. We clear away more of the jungle, snapping trees like toothpicks with the air. It won't be the Lion's base anymore. It will be everyone's village.

We free those who agree to join us. Some say they agree but will have to earn our trust. Others go straight into the prison, but once they are locked inside, I remove their collars. Even Polo's, Fugger's, and Baron's. Being invisible might get them past my power, but it won't help them slip through thick wooden bars.

That night, as a bonfire burns, Violet and Helena approach Emma and me. Helena keeps her eyes down.

Violet greets us with an open collar in her hand. I suddenly go tense, realizing Helena wears no collar. Did Violet set her free?

"She's not safe," I say.

"Go on," Violet says to Helena, "Tell him."

"I'm…I'm sorry…" Helena glances at the collar. "I know I deserve to wear this."

This doesn't sound like Helena. I look to Violet. "What did you do to her?"

"I helped her remember some things about our time in ancient Rome," Violet says. "I know now what Helena feels about it. She couldn't fake that kind of sorrow. And she told me that, after I died, she convinced her son, Emperor Constantine, to outlaw crucifixion throughout the entire Roman empire. No one else would have to suffer what I did."

"Is this true?" I ask Helena.

She meets my gaze. Her eyes are tinged with red, as if she's been crying. "I've made a lot of mistakes," she says, "but I'm not all bad."

"It's true," Violet says. "If everyone else is going free, Helena doesn't deserve a collar either. I'll keep an eye on her, if you'd like."

I hesitate. Helena looks contrite now, but only a day ago she tormented me with the collar. She was on Baron's side. I turn to Emma. "What do you think?"

"I agree with Violet," Emma says. "But, to be safe, we should get rid of the collars. All of them. No more surprises."

I agree to the plan. Violet and Helena walk away together. Emma and I use the air to send a sack full of metal bands soaring all the way back to the tree. Maybe Hank, Oliver, Shelley, Apple, and the rest of the Scouring tribe can lock the links away. I would be okay never seeing one in the forest again.

The next day, once the village is in place, I project my voice through the whole forest to make an announcement: *The tribes are defeated. We are uniting. We will work together. Come to the base that once was the Lion's, but now is Green's.*

They begin to come. Seneca and a few Snakes at first. Then the Wolves who fled during the battle. As we gather more and more food, building a stockpile, more come. We build shelters in a day. Emma and Seneca heal wounds. Violet and Alika teach them how to hunt. Within ten days, we have over a hundred in our village.

I try many times to talk with Baron. I do not taunt him. The battle is over now. I only want answers. Daniel told me that some secret lies hidden in our matching scars, no doubt from the connection of our pasts. I tell Baron about the visions I've seen of my family from before, how my wife was his descendent. I even admit that I sought his wealth by marrying her and used it to buy a mansion. He sits behind the wooden bars and listens, silent as a boulder. Only once, when I tell him about my son, do I detect any reaction—he rubs at his eyes, and they almost look moist.

On day thirty, we release his brother Frank from his cell. When I ask him if he thinks Baron will repent and join us, Frank shakes his head. "He won't accept any reality in which he is not in command. He grew too accustomed to it on Earth."

So Baron stays behind the bars.

Food supplies run low, but we manage it as well as we can. Once the jungle empties, we search the forest. Once the forest empties, we search the coast. Alika and others catch fish and preserve the meat with salt.

Polo and Fugger plead to be released, and Emma convinces me to give it a try. They tell me they're sorry about what happened. They say they appreciate what I've done in the village. Then they prove it, catching a stag so large that Helena has to use her wind to bring it back. It's enough to feed everyone for a night.

We ration what we have. The final days before the Jubilee bring hunger, but not starvation.

We talk, we rest, we wait.

One night Emma and I watch the suns set by the coast. Soft white sand underneath us, palm trees above, picked clean of their coconuts. We flew to the place together, soaring on an invisible carpet of Blue and Green and Yellow powers. It took most of what we had, woven together, but it was worth it, seeing the jungle from above. There's so little that we can't do now.

I wonder if we could even fly ourselves over the Scouring wall and drop down onto the flat gray surface. We could escape the Green Tower and run…where? Back to Red? Back to Blue? To Yellow? As far as I can tell, no tower is much better than the others. Except for Black, which still seems like the worst. Kiyo and Max and

Samantha could still be there. Maybe each tower holds its own allure, and its own torture, for those who find their way inside.

"How did we get here?" I ask Emma. I've asked her this over and over in recent days. I've asked myself and Helena and Baron the same thing. We are the marked ones. Daniel told me that if we learn this, we will be close to finding the way out.

"I still do not know," Emma says. "But I doubt the answer is here. I have been thinking a lot about this. I want to leave."

"Where would you go?" I ask.

"Yellow, perhaps."

"I thought you were finished with Yellow."

"Me too. But I have seen new things at the Jubilee, including with Oliver. You know what these visions left me with…." She holds out her hand to me, the one bearing the scar of crossed lines—exactly like mine.

"Daniel said there will be five of us. Maybe if we can find the fifth person, we'll get some answers."

"The person may not be marked yet. Mine came only in my fourth tower. There was something here that built on everything before, but revealed something new. You have seen the common thread. It is money, wealth, greed. It is why Daniel tells us that giving sets us free."

"Yes, but…" This doesn't fit with what I know of her past. She ran away from her family estate with the guy she loved. She was in a hovel with the dirt floors, with a baby—Oliver—and her husband, dying. "I don't understand," I say gently. "Didn't you leave your wealth, when you left your family?"

She nods. "I became poor for a time."

"You make that sound ominous."

"It was. It is, just as the hunger is here. Before I ran away, I took my family's wealth for granted. The manor, the servants, the dresses, the toys—they were all I knew. But once I was gone, I missed it terribly. I grew…bitter."

"But you must have gone back. Oliver remembered growing up on your family estate."

"He did not know all of it. I had to tell him." She falls quiet and looks toward the horizon where the suns dip into the sea. "The sap showed me a missing piece," she continues. "After my husband died, I took Oliver—only an infant then—to London. We had nothing. I had to beg. I found work with a wealthy family. But they were not kind. It was not easy. I earned barely enough to live on. I grew angrier and angrier, at myself, at everyone. One night while the family was gone, I snuck into their home and took something. A necklace made of diamonds. I planned to sell it and use the money to leave and go home and beg my father to forgive me. But I got caught."

"How?"

"They came home early. The mistress never liked me. She saw the necklace in my hand and summoned the police. They put me in jail."

"You…in jail?" This is hard to imagine. No one so elegant and dignified could be held behind bars.

"Yes. For months."

"But your son, Oliver, he did very well. We saw it in the Red Tower, in the fire at the top. He gave all that money to my college."

"My father found out. He paid my bail. That's what I saw when I returned home. What I did not know then was that I was under a death sentence. My father took in Oliver. He tried to help me get out of the punishment, but even he could not. The law was the law, penalizing betrayed trust more severely. They came one night, after Oliver was asleep. The carriage had bars on the windows. We rode through the night and arrived in London on a bitter cold morning. That is the last thing I saw. I believe that day was likely my last."

"I'm so sorry."

"Now do you see? Money was a curse both ways. Too much made me think I could do anything when I was a little girl. Too little made me steal when I was grown."

"Yes, I know what you mean. It was the opposite for me. Too little when young, too much when old. But I think I got away from it. In my last memory, I was giving it all up. I was moving on."

"What happened after that?"

I shake my head. "I wish I knew."

"Let's go to Yellow together. You will see more there."

The idea leaves me speechless. *Me, in Yellow?*

"You haven't been there," Emma continues. "You will see. It will add to your perspective, and your power."

She could be right. She told me Yellow serves the Healer. Blue has the Genius. Red, Passion. Green,

Provider. And Black something else. Each one has its mirror—its darkness to be scoured.

"What is it that Yellow shows from the past?" I ask.

"Fear and courage. It could be anything, and everything. Only the brave learn to heal."

The longing in her voice reminds me of when we were in Blue and sailed to Yellow's land together. Part of her had wanted to return to Yellow then. But so much has happened since that time.

"Why do *you* want to go back?"

She takes a deep breath. "I need to talk to my father."

"Why? Haven't you already?"

"At the last Jubilee Oliver told me something surprising about him. Very surprising. The sap showed Oliver a memory of his grandfather—my father—telling him that he had known all along that I planned to run away and marry in secret. Daddy had even given my husband his blessing before we went. I'd thought that Daddy would never approve. I need to know what really happened."

"I see." She sounds like she has already made up her mind. She must feel as I did about going to Red, to find my Mom. I should have let her come with me then. I should not let her go alone now. "Even if we wanted to go, how would we do it?"

"We will be leaders at the Jubilee, so we can volunteer for the Scouring. Then we can let Yellow take us."

It's so bold it makes me smile. "Daniel won't like it."

"He will accept it, as long as we capture enough to put Green in equilibrium. He says the end approaches, and I think he yearns for it."

"He also told me he saw signs of darkness here," I say. "I don't know what he means, but I think it has something to do with the pit. And he said—"

I swallow, my mouth suddenly unable to speak. I turn but Daniel has not appeared. Still I cannot say the words that he once let slip. The thought alone makes me feel cold. *The Colorless One.*

"Are you okay?" Emma asks, studying me.

"Yes, I just…" I choose my words carefully. "What Daniel has told me makes me worried."

"He is very cryptic. It troubles me, too. Whatever it is, Daniel knows that Green cannot scour all our stains, and the Scouring will continue as long the stains remain."

"So there's nothing to stop us…"

Emma gazes at the darkening sea. "Only ourselves."

# 44

ON DAY FIFTY, the Hunter comes. He takes us back to the tower, one by one. We feast at the Jubilee, under the light of the fairies. Unlike before, the crowd does not separate into tribes. We are together. We are one. All of us except Baron. He eats alone at opposite edge of the platform. It pains me to think that he could be unleashed in the forest again. At least this time he won't be a leader.

Daniel comes with his usual Jubilee welcome. He invites the Scouring tribe to line up. It is good to see the familiar faces—Hank, Oliver, Shelley, and Apple. Daniel announces that they did well, but apparently not as well without Emma. They caught five and lost one. The Green Tower now has one hundred twenty members.

Next Daniel proclaims the winners of the tribal competition: Emma, Violet, Alika, and me. He is pleased with how we shared with each other—with more peace than struggle. "Giving sets you free," he says. He invites the leaders forward and the others to drink the sap.

We greet Daniel on the stairs. Emma says to him, "You should have put Cipher first. He was the leader."

"Perhaps," Daniel says, rubbing his long beard. "But who is stronger, Emma?"

"We are strongest together," she says.

Daniel smiles. "It is only a taste of what's to come. You will have far greater powers than these once time is gone. You must learn to use them."

"Time will be *gone*?" I say. "You told me that after this place will come a place full of love."

Daniel raises a finger. "I believe you said that."

"Yes, and you agreed."

"So I did."

"Then why do we fight each other here to prepare for a place without fighting?"

"You do not battle against other souls," Daniel says, "but against the stains that cover them. If there were no stained past, there would be no scouring and no fighting. There would be peace."

I consider his words. The Green Tower has been like a scouring unto itself, taking my memories and giving them back. I lost Benjamin and left the mansion. I gave up the money, the wealth, the power. But for what?

Emma takes my hand. "We brought peace."

"Ah, yes," Daniel says. "And now the Provider will give you new visions, perhaps even powerful ones."

"Through the sap?" I ask.

"Yes, and more memories may mean more powers," Daniel says. "Already you talk through the light, as all will in the place to come, for you both peeked into the White Tower. Once time is no more, talking to each other through space and time will be as natural as breathing."

"Why does it only work with the stars?" Emma asks.

A smile spreads under Daniel's beard. "It is good to wonder about the suns and the stars." He taps his staff. "But now you must pick your tribes."

"We choose the Scouring," Emma says.

Daniel looks surprised. "Cipher, you as well?"

"Yes."

"Hm, you sacrifice much. You may no longer pick the tribes, for you give up your place as leaders. Your opponents may rise to power again. You understand?"

"That's okay," I say.

"Yes." Emma nods. "Others can lead."

The old leader sighs. "This has not been done in some time, but you may choose freely. It is the Green Tower, after all. So be it. I will call the new leaders."

He turns away from us and points his staff toward the crowd gathered by the trough of sap. Two figures emerge from the crowd toward us, as if entranced.

Helena and Frank.

My feet feel planted into place, watching the two of them step up beside us. I knew Emma and I were giving up some control when we chose the Scouring, but that doesn't make it easier to see the two who betrayed me become leaders, even if they have changed.

A hand grips my shoulder. "You are almost ready." Daniel looks from Emma to me. "Both of you."

"What do you mean?" I ask.

"You brought the tribes together. How did it feel?"

"Better," Emma says.

"Hm, giving, sharing, often turns out that way, yes?"

"Is that the whole point?" I ask. "You send us into the forest without enough food and expect us to share?"

Daniel shakes his head, his long beard swaying. "There is enough food, if you work together. But so many rely on their own power, instead of trusting the Provider."

"Like Baron?"

"All will learn," Daniel says. "How did you?"

"I didn't want to be like Baron. I wanted to be like Violet and Seneca."

"They have learned much from their pasts. What have you learned from yours?"

It was learning to disappear that saved me, and that came from my visions. "My wife, Susan. She stuck with me, and helped, even though I didn't deserve it."

"A most graceful example." Daniel taps me in the chest. "Yes, giving is the solution. Sharing is the answer. Go now and drink deep of the Provider's bounty. You will awake with the Scouring tribe."

We've made our choice. We can hope that the example we've left in the forest will be followed. We kneel over the sap and drink.

The sun shines in the bright blue sky, with the pinnacle of the Washington Monument in the distance. Birds sing and lazy spring warmth drifts through the open window. As I gaze out, a half-eaten bowl of Lucky Charms rests in my hands. The city's wealthy patrons stroll the leafy sidewalk below, lined with brownstone mansions. We didn't buy one of those. Susan said she'd support me if I wanted a proper home. She understood—or maybe even she herself felt—that moving from a lakeside estate in Chicago to a little apartment in Washington would not be without difficulty.

"It'll be okay," I'd told her. "We'll keep things simple. I'll put the money into my research. No distractions."

We picked a nice neighborhood called Kalorama. There was only so much change one could handle at once. The penthouse apartment was a tenth the size of our Chicago home. The chandeliers were much smaller. But there was this view, looking out over the more expensive homes that we could have bought instead. Maybe we should have.

*No distractions.* But there they are: the brownstone mansions. I look away, down at my feet. I wear loafers. Like the loafers Thaxton wore at his place in the Hamptons so many years ago. I kick off the shoes. My feet are pale against the parquet floor.

Focus, Paul. Focus on the research.

I take another bite of the playful marshmallow cereal and remember a vow I'd once made to myself. *If I ever have a kid I'll buy him all the Lucky Charms he could ever eat.*

It brings back the pain. Tears blur the mansions and millionaires outside. I'd done that, and more. Benjamin had everything. But now Benjamin was gone.

I should never have made the vow. It came from my own mother not being able to buy me cereal that cost an extra buck. She'd worked and worked to enable me to…to what? To work and work and helplessly watch my son die before his time? Her life was too short. Benjamin's was too short. And now mine drags on.

No more vows. No more mansions. No more Lucky Charms. This will be a new start. I'm going to work for something outside myself, leading the National Institute of Health. I will give what matters most to me: my time and my mind. I leave the cereal bowl unfinished on the window ledge and walk barefoot to my study, where research awaits.

# 45

LYING ON MY back, unmoving, my eyes open. Light filters through the leaves above, making them glisten and dance in a gentle breeze. My fingers begin to wiggle, then my toes. I slowly roll over and sit up, hugging my knees, thinking of Lucky Charms.

Eleven other boys and girls are on the small wooden platform, beginning to rouse. The Scouring tribe. I recognize several of them: Emma, Hank, Jade, Seneca…and Baron. He watches me with his granite eyes, but there's something unusual about him. He looks too happy. It's unsettling.

Daniel sits cross-legged in front of us, with his eyes closed and his hands resting on his knees. His beard spills down into a neat pile, like moss in his lap. Beyond him, thick branches lead down, down, and down to the trunk. This is the highest I've been in the tree. Even the Jubilee platform looks small from this perch.

A soft whisper comes from beside me, "Cipher."

It's Emma. She sits up, in the same posture as Daniel.

"Hey," I say. "Good vision?"

"Apparently not as good as yours." She points down at my feet with a surprised look. "What happened?"

Then I see it. The scar. On the top of my right foot, in the same criss-cross shape as the ones on my hands.

It wasn't there before the last vision. I'm certain. What caused it? Kicking off the loafers, walking barefoot to my research, renouncing my vows of wealth? Daniel said we might get a powerful vision. Is this what he meant? My third tower, my third scar…

I force myself to look away from the scar, to Emma. "The vision was different," I say. "It was almost…good. I think it left me with this."

Emma puts her hand over mine, her gaze still fixed on my new scar. "It was similar for me," she whispers, "after seeing the hard truth from my past. Perhaps it had to be this way in Green, the struggle here opening our eyes to what truly drove us before, and how we changed."

Her words give me hope. Maybe this third scar means progress. Daniel told me I would get five scars, and that when I learn why there are five towers and five marked ones, then I would know the way out.

I turn to him. "Why did I get this?"

He strokes his beard as he studies the mark on my foot. "That is not for me to say. But you see more light, eh? May it shine forth soon, brighter and brighter. But now…" He takes a deep breath and glances around the group. "We prepare for the Scouring."

He raises both of his hands overhead. The folds of his loose robe fall to his shoulders and reveal thin arms as weathered as driftwood. Beside me, Emma raises her arms in the same way. Most of the others are doing the same. As if under a spell, I feel my arms going up, the muscles stretching.

"Now, breathe deeply," Daniel says. "In. Out."

Daniel leans to his right all the way until his arms touch the floor. We breathe in and out. Then he rises and leans to his left. He continues with these slow motions, and slow breathing, for a long time. My body begins to awaken and heat up as my questions simmer. Eventually we come to our feet. The sky grows brighter.

"This is a new day in the Green Tower," Daniel says. "What the sap has shown you is in the past. Here you will be scoured of your mistakes. All your regrets will pass away, leaving only works that can endure. Some of you may have seen glimmers of hope. But the process is long. It can be slow. Sometimes you must go backward before you go forward. Then you might advance beyond your dreams. Prepare now. The Scouring begins soon."

Daniel presses his hands together in front of his chest, closes his eyes, and—in a blink—disappears.

"Whoa," someone mutters behind me. It's a boy I don't recognize. He must have been wiped.

"He will come again," Emma says, "when it is time for us to enter the Scouring. If it's like before, we have only an hour or so."

"But how did he vanish like that?" the boy asks.

"It is a power of the Green Tower," Emma says patiently. "Some do it easily and go invisible for as long as you hold your breath. You must think of a good memory—from before, on Earth. The better it is, the longer you can stay hidden."

"Does that mean Daniel's still here?" the boy asks.

"I doubt it," Emma says. "We looked for him last time. We rarely see him in the tree. I think he leaves for some reason. He seems tired when he returns to escort us to the Scouring and the Jubilee. The Hunter does most of his bidding."

The boy moves forward to where Daniel was standing and reaches his arms out, as if to touch him. It's only air. He's not there anymore.

"Come, everyone, sit in a circle," Emma says. "You heard Daniel. We need to prepare for the Scouring."

The twelve of us do as Emma says. We each sit cross-legged on the wooden floor. Emma smiles at me as she tells everyone that it's best to start with introductions. "We have to know each other to work together," she says. "But we have little time. Keep it short, for now."

Each person gives a brief introduction around the circle. They lived in many different times and places. One girl was the wife of a silk trader in the middle ages. Another boy captured and sold slaves from Africa in Europe. Jade says she was a judge in Chicago. Emma and I say who we were. Hank tells of his wandering past around the time of the American revolution, which makes Seneca pipe up.

"Did you ever visit New York?" she asks. "The Genesee River?"

"Matter of fact, I did," Hank says, running a hand

through his sandy hair. "Got robbed and hurt pretty bad there. Rough place."

Seneca leans forward, fixing her dark eyes on Hank. "Henry?"

"You knew me?"

"I tended your wounds. My name was Dehgewanus."

Hank smiles, shaking his head. "Unbelievable."

"We must talk more," Seneca says, holding Hank's gaze, then looking to the girl beside her. "But the rest of you, please, go ahead."

We finish going around the group. Baron is the last one to introduce himself. He tells us what he told me before, about how he was John D. Rockefeller, the richest man in the world. He folds his hands in his lap, looking younger and more innocent. Unlike before, there's no shadow of a mustache above his lips. His only blemish is the scar on his right hand, matching mine and Emma's.

"The sap showed me something new," he says calmly. "You all know what Daniel says, *Giving sets you free*? I think I understand it better now. Two women came to me. They told me about a school they'd started. My country had fought a war, you see. My side had won, and slaves had been freed. They needed opportunities. These two women wanted me to help support their school to teach young women who had been slaves, and their daughters. I gave to many causes, and I gave to them. It was very well known. But the sap showed me something peculiar. The women asked me if they could name the school after me. It could be Rockefeller College or the like. But I told these women,

*No, thank you, choose a different name. Don't mention me, but I'll give what you need.* In no other memory have I felt such…peace."

Baron takes a deep breath. Then he disappears, causing a few gasps among the group. The wooden floor creaks faintly, and a few moments later Baron reappears on the other side of the platform. "Easier than ever," he says.

"Not bad," Emma says. "But will you follow our lead?"

A genuine smile cracks the granite of Baron's face. "I told you my story, did I not?"

"It's a start," I say, but I don't trust him.

"What was the name of the school?" Jade asks Baron softly.

"Spelman," he says.

"Oh my…" Jade covers her mouth, her eyes moisten. "I went there," she says. "Years later. Many wonderful women did. Spelman gave us opportunities. It prepared us to advance equality and freedom. One of the students was even the mother of Martin Luther King Jr."

"Who was that?" Baron asks.

Jade laughs and wipes away tears. "A man who changed the world. Like you, Mr. Rockefeller."

"Please, call me John."

# 46

WE PRACTICE DISAPPEARING. Nearly all of us can do it, some for longer than others. Emma says this will be important in the Scouring. She knows how to capture for Green, working together. Only a few of us bring powers from other towers. Seneca and Emma can heal. I can summon wind. Emma can summon fire. We will be cautious and attack by surprise.

"Daniel will give us daggers, and vines like ropes," Emma says. "The blades won't do much on their own. But if we stay in a line, and vanish as someone approaches, we can spring on any attackers and tie them up."

"What about Black?" Hank asks. "They'll stay together."

Emma glances to me. "Best to avoid them, if we can."

As they talk on, tension creeps into my muscles. It has been a long time since I've entered the battleground between the towers. I feel more powerful than ever, with three scars and more memories, even good ones. But I will be rusty. It feels like forever since I led the Red team out and watched my mother soar up into the White Tower.

The competition in the forest is very different from the Scouring. No trees. No shadows. No tribes. And so much more power.

Blue will have the wind. Red's girls will have flames, the boys weapons. Yellow will have healing. Black will have its suffocating smoke. Their phalanx of boys with shields and spears will protect two darkly robed girls who can shut down my power. One of them could be Samantha. I have seen, in the pit beneath the towers, what her life could have been if not for what I'd done. But she doesn't know that. I failed to find her when I visited Black's territory. She will have every reason to hate me, to attack.

By the time Daniel returns, Emma has laid out our strategy. We will link hands and move in a line against Yellow. They are close to us and far from Black. It might draw the team from Blue, which is beyond Yellow, but Emma and I should be able to overpower them. She will take control. And if Black tries to shut us down, we will disappear and scatter, moving back toward Green.

Daniel leads us down through the trunk of the giant tree. It is the same way we would go if leaving the tree for the forest, but Daniel stops before we reach the ground and enters a dark passageway.

"What is this?" I ask Emma in front of me.

"We're going through a root." She glances back. "The door to the Scouring is ahead. Ready?"

"I am if you are."

She grins. "Good."

Fifty paces later Daniel comes to a stop by a wooden

door with an ornate tree carved into its center. A few fairies flit about, making pale light flicker on the brown walls of bark and dirt. The floor beneath us is made of planks, like the platform in the tree above us. It makes a hollow thudding sound as we gather around Daniel.

Beside the door, the wall is solid, grey stone. The Scouring wall. It bears a tally:

*Black 225*

*Red 147*

*Blue 142*

*Green 120*

*Yellow 86*

"We approach equilibrium," Daniel says, looking to Emma, then to me. "Will you reach it now?"

"How many Scourings before the Jubilee?" Emma asks.

"Four or five, as usual."

"We will reach it before then," Emma says, "but perhaps not all at once. It would risk too much to try capturing twenty-four."

"Hmm, it could be done." He looks to me, then Baron. "Three marked ones risking much can accomplish much."

The tally troubles me. I led Blue to the equilibrium number of one hundred forty-four, but now it is two below that number. And Red has three too many.

"If we capture from any tower other than Black," I say, "won't that move the towers *away* from equilibrium?"

"Is your vision still obscured?" Daniel blinks slowly, lowering his canopy of bushy eyebrows. "You are with Green. Do your part. Others will do theirs."

He sounds like the other leaders, treating us like children. I glance down at the scar on my foot. I may have a young body, but I earned it in an old life. "You want 144 in Green," I say, meeting Daniel's eyes, "just as Abram wanted in Blue, and Rahab in Red. You want me to go from tower to tower, like a pawn in your game. Was the competition in the forest your training ground, to make me stronger?"

Daniel's beard bobs up and down as his hand goes to his belly and he laughs.

"What's so funny?" I ask.

It takes him a few moments, but he manages to straighten up. His eyes are moist—from the laughter, not tears—as he looks at me and taps his staff against my chest. "You still think this is about you!"

"No, you're wrong," I snap. "I know it's not about me, it's about all of us. Why else would the towers reveal visions of our past? Why else would we even be here?"

"The light, Cipher. It's about the light. You will see."

With that he turns and taps his staff against the door. He vanishes the same moment that the door swings open, suddenly letting in a blinding light from outside. We emerge from inside the dark root, eyes adjusting as we step onto smooth grey stones. They feel cold and hard beneath my feet. I've gotten used to walking on wood and dirt.

Emma grips my hand firmly and leads along the wall to the right. Hank is behind me, then Seneca and Jade. Baron follows at the back.

"Look, Black and Red," Emma says.

Across the vast Scouring, under the three bright suns, figures clash against each other in the distance. Black and Red. Flames spring into life, only to be smothered by black smoke. The sound of clashing metal rings out, interspersed with shouts.

"Now," Emma says.

I feel her work before I see it. She draws the power through me, weaving a thick ribbon of blue and a faint line of green. It twists around her yellow and red threads and spins and coils in radiant light. The force moves ahead of us along the wall, toward the Yellow team. They stand still, in a triangle formation before their gate, as if clueless of the raging flood of power channeled directly at them.

The power slams into them and crystallizes, locking them in place. Emma weaves so much power that I feel the strain from her. Her grip on my hand is iron as she lifts and pulls the group from Yellow. The twelve of them hover quickly toward us and float overhead, helplessly caught in this river of color. Their faces show shock.

"Hank, take them in." Emma looks past me. Tiny beads of sweat glisten at her temples.

"On it!" Hank says.

He races off immediately, pulling Jade and Seneca with him to help. The line reforms, with a short, brown-haired girl taking my hand.

"Let's go for Blue," Emma says, eyes fixed on mine. "Ready?"

"I am if you are."

She grins and presses ahead, pulling the nine of us from

Green, hands linked, toward the center. The Blue team has reached the white circle. They are not far from us. Red and Black still battle on the opposite side of the Scouring.

Emma glances over her shoulder. Behind us, Hank has tied the team from Yellow in ropes. He rushes them through the gate, then turns back. At his wave, Emma swings the power back, rushing over us and funneling now with full force at the Blue team.

They are ready, with a wall of air, and more. There are strands of yellow and green. But no red, no black. Beyond the invisible wall there are two faces I recognize. Luther and Tom. Luther was the one who bullied me and got wiped. He must have risen to the top again. And Tom is back with them, as he'd wanted.

The forces collide. It is soundless but brilliant. Light explodes like fragments of a shattered rainbow. Emma slams into their wall again. Another silent explosion shakes the colors of the air.

"Take it," Emma says weakly. She staggers to a knee.

Still gripping her hand, I take over the weaves. It is too much at once, like trying to step in for a juggler of a dozen burning torches. Some fall, the red ribbon slips. I thread it back into the channeled force, but then yellow fades.

"Attack or run," Emma demands.

A memory comes. Edison and his lightbulb. *Genius is one percent inspiration; ninety-nine percent perspiration.* Genius. Blue. I have worked harder. I have sweat and bled in the forest. I have been killed and wiped and restored again. I ignore the yellow and red threads. I glance back, down the line of Green, with our hands linked, all the way to Baron in the rear. Feeling through them the pain and suffering of the tribal competition, of the hunger and the hunt, I draw on the Green power pulsing within each of them. None of them resist. They give it. They're with me.

Focusing on the coil of blue and green, I channel everything I have at the Blue wall. It gives. It breaks.

Luther is in my hands. Tom is locked in place. All twelve of them are ours.

I begin to pull, reeling them in, ready to race for the Green Tower.

The moment I turn, I stop.

Black. Smoke.

It's suddenly everywhere, smothering all the light I'd held. The threads dissipate into nothing. The Blue captives slip out of my grip and run.

Emma eyes me with fear. "It's her, isn't it?"

Samantha. It could be. She's the only one who has so completely doused me before. The smoke wraps tighter around me, clouding my thoughts.

"Run!" Emma shouts to our group, then vanishes.

The others behind us begin to disappear.

I search for a happy memory, but can think only of Samantha. I hear the clinking metal before I see them. The boys from Black, shields and spears raised. Right in front of me, ten paces away. Five paces.

A girl's eyes catch mine from behind their square formation. It is her. Samantha.

But then I see something impossible. A blade flashes at

Samantha's neck. An arm and a body blink into vision. It's Baron. He must have snuck behind her.

The smoke is suddenly gone.

"Go!" he shouts to me, dragging her back while looking at me. "Run!"

But I can't leave him. Not now. Everyone else has scattered, no doubt retreating to the gate. Baron has only me. Whatever has happened, we're both Green, and both marked.

In an instant I summon my power again. Only the blue threads of air, but they're enough to blast the boys from Black away, skidding across the flat stone of the Scouring.

"Look!" Baron shouts.

But it's too late. This time the smoke comes from behind me, smothering my power again. I spin and see a dark figure almost within reach. Only her eyes are visible. But their darkness, their flecks of gold, are unmistakable.

"Kiyo?"

She doesn't react. She points toward the Black Tower. "Go."

I step toward her but something slams into my side. I crumple to the ground. A boy from Black looms over me. "Go," he demands, holding his spear at my head. "Or die."

Rising slowly, I spot Samantha moving freely across the Scouring. A group of boys escorts her—and Baron— toward Black.

A soft touch grazes my arm, then an invisible hand grips mine. The boy and Kiyo gasp.

"Now!"

It's Emma's voice. She's pulling me away, running as fast as we can, before I can even make sense of what she's done. She has made me invisible. She used her power to cloak me, right under Kiyo's nose.

We quickly reach the Green Tower's gate, which is empty and quiet. I stop and look back.

"Baron saved me," I mutter. "Black took him."

Emma takes shape beside me, pale-faced in the gateway, pulling me inside. "Giving set him free."

# 47

NIGHT BEGINS TO fall when we reach the tree's uppermost canopy. The Scouring tribe—the eleven of us who made it out—gathers again on the wooden platform where we'd woken up. The light of a dozen glowing fairies drifts lazily overhead, slipping in and out of the branches and leaves between us and the stars. Daniel is nowhere in sight, but the Hunter appears.

"Well done," he says. "As fine a catch as I've seen."

"How many?" Emma asks.

The Hunter uses a large knife to pick at his nails. "You should know. You caught all but two of them."

"So sixteen," Emma says. "Twelve Yellow, two Blue, and…what?"

"Two Red," Jade says proudly. "We snagged them from Black when they attacked you."

The Hunter smiles. "Daniel will be pleased."

"Where is he?" I ask.

"Attending to other matters," the Hunter says.

I remember Daniel saying something like this when he warned of the pit and the Colorless One—that the leaders were *attending* to it. "What other matters?" I ask.

The Hunter shakes his head. "It need not concern you. Daniel will learn of your success when he returns."

Emma looks down. "He wanted twenty-four."

"And I want to be a unicorn," the Hunter says. "Instead I'm a stag. We live with what we get."

A girl behind me laughs. It's Seneca, eyeing the Hunter. "You, a unicorn?"

"Just wait," the Hunter says. "The White Tower will reveal us as we truly are. Daniel taught me many things in Babylon. One is to pay attention to your dreams."

*Babylon?* Is that what he calls Earth?

"Hold on." Seneca laughs again. "You *dream* of being a unicorn."

"And you dream of being an ant. Are we so different?"

Seneca goes silent. "How——?"

The Hunter waves his knife casually. "Doesn't matter. The point is you did well. Only eight more until equilibrium. Now, we've got captives to tend to until the next Scouring. Who wants first duty?"

"I'll take it," Emma says.

"Don't act like it's a punishment," the Hunter says.

"I'm not." She stands and faces the Hunter. "I led our group, so it's my responsibility. I'll take Cipher and teach him how to do it."

"Fine. I'll be watching. And Daniel will be back. I figure the next Scouring will be——" the Hunter holds up his thumb, as if judging the direction of the wind——"about five days from now. So get some rest."

He vanishes, leaving a heavy quiet.

Emma tells everyone else to get some sleep, then leads me through the huge tree, down ladders and branches and across rope bridges. We reach a cluster of small wooden huts perched near the trunk and the platform where we celebrate the Jubilee. Below the huts, near the trough of sap—now dry—there is a small opening in the trunk.

Emma reaches into the opening and pulls out a slab of salted meat and a handful of mushrooms. "This supply never runs out," she says. "It refills every day, with just enough. I think the Hunter does it. He says it's from the Provider. The mushrooms help the captives sleep until they are ready."

"Ready for what?" I ask.

"To meet Daniel and get the fruit. This is how it worked for us, too, except you ran away. Remember?"

I nod. "Feels like a long time ago."

"An eternity!" Emma hands me a tray with a piece of the meat and eight mushrooms on it. "Take this to that hut," she says, pointing to one of the small wooden buildings above us. "Set three strips of meat and four mushrooms on the tables beneath the captives. Take their waste and refill their water. Do it as quietly as you can. We will meet again here."

Emma begins to fill another tray for herself. I go to the hut she assigned to me. Two boys hang in nets above me in the dark room. Neither of them stirs from sleep. As I place the food on the tables beneath them, I can't help but wonder why it happens like this. In Red the captives start in a warm cave—locked away, but not for long, and not tied up. In Blue the newcomers start as servants or swimming in an underground lake. I wonder what Black will do to Baron. At least Blue and Red gave some freedom. But then, Green gives nothing but freedom once captives are out of the nets, and it leads to a brutal fight to survive. Maybe the nets aren't so bad.

Emma is waiting for me when I return. "What took you so long?" she asks.

"Guess I just lost track of time," I say.

"You thought about cutting them free, didn't you?"

I shrug. "Sort of. It seems wrong."

"It's not so different than the other towers. Come, I want to show you something."

She takes my hand and leads me across the Jubilee platform. We walk along a thick branch that narrows and begins to sway up and down with our steps. A clearing through the leaves reveals the flat, grey stone of the Scouring far beneath us.

Emma sits on the branch. It is barely as thick as my thigh this far from the trunk. I sit cautiously beside Emma. The motion makes us sway slightly.

"You sure this is safe?" I ask.

"Not at all," she says, "but there's no better place to talk through the stars, or watch the suns rise. See?"

I follow her gaze to the horizon. The sky is black above us, speckled with stars, but a pale grey light emerges in the distance. As the light grows, it reveals the Yellow Tower and its flat lands. The sun comes up like a golden ball, followed soon by two more suns. The Yellow Tower glistens brightly. The leaves block our view of the Red and Black Towers behind us. Clouds obscure the Blue Tower, except for an occasional glimpse of its top extending above the perpetual fog that surrounds it.

"Beautiful, isn't it?" Emma asks softly.

It is. I put my scarred hand over hers, and we sit together in quiet, watching the suns rise.

Eventually Emma turns to me. Her face glows in the morning light. "I want to thank you again for finding Oliver. Being with him cleared away so much pain and answered so many questions. I never expected to feel such joy here."

"I'm glad I could help," I say. "You know, if we leave, you might not see him for a long time. You were together such a short time."

"As it was on Earth. I no longer think time is the right measure of things. You were with your mother only a short while, but it mattered greatly, did it not?"

"Yes, I see what you mean." My mother showed me so much about my past in our moments together in the Red Tower, and maybe I helped her as Oliver did for Emma. My mother made it out through the White Tower. I wonder what this means for Emma...

"You still want to go to Yellow?" I ask her.

"I must," she says. "I have to see my father again."

"Are you sure he's still there?"

"We're going to find out."

# 48

SIX DAYS PASS, then seven, since the day we captured sixteen in the Scouring. We tend to the captives in the nets, who are apparently "cleansing" with mushrooms and sleep. They will be given the fruit. They will get their memories back and start afresh at the Jubilee. Then they will join tribes. The peace that Emma and I brought could prove short-lived. New leaders will rise, thirsting for more. Food will be scarce. The competition could march relentlessly on—hunting and starving, enslaving and killing. It will take more than a strong leader to calm the wild forest.

One day the Hunter returns with Min. He says she will join our Scouring tribe now, taking Baron's spot and keeping our numbers at twelve. Min tells us that she saw a stag, and next thing she knew, she was in the tower—whole and dressed in fresh clothes. It must be what the Hunter did to Fugger. The puddle of blood in the forest made it seem far worse, and the forest far more frightful. Maybe that was the point.

It's dawn of the eighth day when Daniel appears again. He is there when our Scouring tribe wakes, sitting cross-legged as he did before. He leads us through breathing and stretching exercises. He tells us that it is time for the next Scouring.

"This will be different," he says. "A trade has been arranged."

"*A trade?*" Hank asks. "How is that possible?"

Others echo his question, sounding just as surprised. Daniel sits quietly, studying his wrinkled hands in his lap.

Trading requires compromise, civility. It can't be with Red, or Black. But there was one time—my first in the Scouring—when Abram had assigned me to capture Emma, and Yellow had offered to trade her for Helena. Other towers had attacked, breaking up the deal, but it was possible then. And Emma had come willingly.

"Yellow," Emma says, quieting the others. "The trade will be with Yellow."

"Hm, yes." Daniel sighs so deeply that his old bones sound like they're rattling. "You desire it. I have arranged it. They will give ten for you and Cipher."

Emma nods. "Very well."

There seems to be an understanding between her and Daniel, but it brings a thousand questions to my mind.

"How did you know what Emma wanted?" I ask.

"The trees tell me things." He gives me a playful wink, like a grandfather delighted by his own joke.

I don't smile. "How did you arrange it?"

"Yellow's leader is an old friend."

"Hold on," Hank says. "This ain't right. Cipher and Emma are worth way more than ten from Yellow. They captured *sixteen* in the last Scouring alone. They both have the scars on their hands. Cipher's even got a new one on his foot. You can't just trade them away. And if you do, I'm going too!"

"No, I'm afraid you are not," Daniel says. "Trust the Provider, Hank. You know you have more to see here."

Hank looks to Seneca and sighs. "Yeah, alright. But I still say they're worth more than ten from Yellow."

"Ten will bring Green to one hundred forty-four," Daniel says. "And they will come with ten collars."

"How will we make the trade?" Emma asks.

"Quickly." Daniel stands and motions for us to do the same. "You will go straight to the Yellow team. They will give their ten, collared, in exchange for Cipher and Emma. Seneca and Jade, you will be given command of five each. Bring them back through our gate as soon as you can."

Daniel does not wait for further discussion. He leads us down through the tree, to the dark root with the doorway to the Scouring. As we go, he ignores most of my questions. He answers only about what we must do in the Scouring. It seems simple enough, as long as we can make the exchange before the other towers attack.

He taps his staff against the door, and vanishes. The door swings open, letting in the bright light from the Scouring.

Emma leads us out—each of us clasping hands to form a line after her. She hurries along the wall, to Yellow. We reach them before any other tower has approached.

Emma stops, standing stiffly.

A tall boy from the Yellow steps toward us. He wears a golden crown on his head and looks like he could be Emma's brother, with blonde hair and bright blue eyes. A girl stands beside him with a silver crown over straight, jet-black hair.

"Here are your ten." The boy's voice is rigid, like a king accustomed to obedience.

Everyone from Yellow—other than the boy and girl with crowns—steps forward in perfect unison. They wear identical pale yellow tunics. Their collars gleam brightly.

The Yellow leader fixes his eyes on me. "You, kneel."

I look to Emma, who nods assuringly. I start to kneel, but something doesn't feel right. Emma hasn't budged.

"What about you?" I ask her.

"My daughter comes freely," the tall boy says, and when I turn to him a blur of black streaks toward me.

The girl with the crown.

I react instantly, summoning the air, but can do nothing before a collar snaps around my neck.

*Be still*, the girl commands. *No power.*

She snatches my hands and stares down at the scars.

"He's the one?" the leader asks.

"He's the one," she says.

But I barely hear them. I'm still, as commanded, with desperate, pleading eyes on Emma.

"I'm sorry, Cipher," she says. "This was the only way."

J.B. SIMMONS is the bestselling author of the *Unbound* trilogy, *The Babel Tower*, and *Light in the Gloaming*. He lives and writes outside Washington, D.C. To learn more about J.B. and his books, visit **www.jbsimmons.com**.

Don't miss *The Yellow Tower*, the sequel to *The Green Tower* and the fourth book in The Five Towers Series, available on Amazon and more.

www.ingramcontent.com/pod-product-compliance
Lightning Source LLC
Chambersburg PA
CBHW051631180726
48284CB00006B/1683